W9-ATW-431

THE MARRIAGE BARGAIN

This Large Print Book carries the
Seal of Approval of N.A.V.H.

THE MARRIAGE BARGAIN

ANGEL MOORE

THORNDIKE PRESS

A part of Gale, Cengage Learning

GALE
CENGAGE Learning®

Farmington Hills, Mich • San Francisco • New York • Waterville, Maine
Meriden, Conn • Mason, Ohio • Chicago

GALE
CENGAGE Learning·

LIBRARY OF CONGRESS CATALOGING-IN-PUBLICATION DATA

Names: Moore, Angel, author.
Title: The marriage bargain / by Angel Moore.
Description: Large print edition. | Waterville, Maine : Thorndike Press, 2016. | © 2016 | Series: Thorndike Press large print gentle romance
Identifiers: LCCN 2016003246 | ISBN 9781410489357 (hardcover) | ISBN 1410489353 (hardcover)
Subjects: LCSH: Large type books. | GSAFD: Love stories.
Classification: LCC PS3613.O55395 M37 2016 | DDC 813/.6—dc23
LC record available at http://lccn.loc.gov/2016003246

Published in 2016 by arrangement with Harlequin Books S.A.

Printed in Mexico
1 2 3 4 5 6 7 20 19 18 17 16

Let nothing be done through strife
or vainglory;
but in lowliness of mind let each esteem
other better than themselves.
Look not every man on his own things,
but every man also on the things
of others.
— *Philippians* 2:3–4

To my editor, Emily Krupin.
Your encouragement makes
me work harder.

To my mother, Mary Ellen, for sharing
her love of reading. Thank you for
celebrating with me at every step
along the way and for teaching
me to be brave.

To Lisa, for the love only
true sisters know.

To Austin, my first editor and reader.
Your insight and knowledge
are priceless.

To Jason, for understanding when
Mama has to work.

To Bob, who taught me everything I
know about Happily-Ever-After.

And, as always, to God,
Who makes it all possible.

CHAPTER ONE

Pine Haven, Texas
January 1881

The sound of shattering glass snatched Lily Warren awake. She bolted upright in bed with a gasp, only to feel her lungs fill with acrid smoke. Coughing uncontrollably, she threw the quilt back and tugged on her dressing gown.

Unfamiliar with her surroundings, she fumbled about in the darkness, searching for the doorway to the stairs that led to her new shop.

Heavy footsteps pounded on the staircase outside her room. Lily turned toward the sound, desperate for fresh air. The coughing racked her chest, and she was getting dizzy.

She cried out between coughs. "Help!"

The door burst open, and the orange glow of flames gave her enough light to stumble toward her rescuer.

Her landlord, Edward Stone, came into

the room with an arm across his face in an apparent effort to keep from breathing in the smoke. "Do you have something to wrap up in? A blanket?" His voice was intense.

She reached for her mother's quilt on the bed, though the coughing hindered her movements.

He snatched it up and, before she knew what he was going to do, wrapped it around her shoulders and picked her up like a child.

She stiffened and argued, "I can walk."

"Try to keep your mouth closed until I get you outside." He kicked the doorway open wider and started down the stairs.

"What?" Pressed against his chest, she couldn't hear over the roar of the growing fire.

"Quiet! The smoke." He reached the bottom of the stairs and turned toward the back door.

She could see the flames licking up the side of the back wall and climbing across her workbench. All the beautiful hats she'd made for her shop were being consumed by the hungry fire.

Kicking and squirming against Edward, she screamed, "My stock!"

He tightened his hold on her and reversed his direction to take her out the front door. He turned back to face the building and lowered her to stand in front of him.

The church bell rang from the opposite end of the street.

She tried to move away from him, but her hair was tangled in the buckle on his suspenders. She cried out in pain as it pulled.

"Hold still." He spoke close to her ear. "I'll try not to hurt you, but I've got to put the fire out." He tugged at the knotted curls.

A voice barked behind them. "Stone! Is anyone still inside?" The sheriff came running up the street.

With a final and painful pull, Lily was free of him. She turned to see what must be most of the town's population coming from every direction.

Edward shot around her and hollered his answer to the sheriff as he went back through the front door of her shop. "No one else was here. I think it's contained in the workroom in the back. There's a rain barrel in the alley behind the back door." The sheriff ran toward the rear of the shop.

Lily stumbled on the ends of her mother's quilt when she started up the steps. A man she hadn't met in the two days since her arrival in Pine Haven restrained her. "You can't go in there, miss," he said.

"My stock is inside!" She turned to plead with him to let him go. He wasn't tall or

11

large, but was strong for his size, and she couldn't break free. "Everything I own is in there."

The lady from the general store came up beside them. "Miss Warren, you mustn't resist. The men need to put out the fire so it doesn't spread to the rest of town." Mrs. Croft put an arm around her shoulders. "Doc Willis, I've got her. Help them! Please!"

Smoke boiled through the open front door now. Lily could see Edward's shape through the haze as he swung his coat to beat back the flames. Every available man and woman scurried to form a line and pass buckets filled from the water troughs and barrels near the surrounding buildings.

Lily shrugged off Mrs. Croft's confining arm. "I've got to help at least." She let the quilt drop to the dirt and ran to fill a wide place in the line of townsfolk fighting to help their newest resident.

It had only been minutes, but seemed like hours, when Edward appeared in the front doorway with his charred coat lifted high in one hand. "It's out! We did it!"

Cheers went up from the crowd, and the line fell away. Everyone gathered near the steps of her shop.

Lily pushed her way through the people

and stopped at the open front door. Water covered the floors she'd polished on her first day. Mud tracked through to the workroom. She leaned against the jamb.

She turned to look at Edward. "How bad is it?" Water ran in tiny rivulets through the soot on his face.

"I'm afraid your stock is ruined. What didn't burn will be damaged by the smoke and water." He dragged an arm across his forehead and smeared the soot away from his eyes.

Mrs. Croft came through the crowd at the bottom of the steps. "Miss Warren, please." The woman held Lily's quilt up by the corners. She lowered her voice to a conspiratorial whisper, and her eyes darted toward the people gathered behind her. "You need to cover yourself."

Lily gasped and looked down at herself. The tie to her dressing gown had loosened while she passed one bucket of water after another. The lace of her nightgown peeked out where the robe gaped open. She snatched the quilt from Mrs. Croft and wrapped it around her shoulders, clenching it tight, high against her neck. The heat climbing up her throat let her know she was turning as pink as the nightgown everyone in town had just seen.

"Thank you, Mrs. Croft." The mortification she experienced at the woman's condemning stare almost dwarfed the loss of her belongings. Almost.

She turned back to Edward. "Thank you for saving me." She remembered the feel of his arms around her as he carried her from the building. Strong, determined, protecting.

"You don't owe me any thanks. I'm just sorry we couldn't save your merchandise." As her landlord, he'd want Lily's Millinery and Finery to be a success. How could it be now, with nothing to sell?

Mrs. Croft's tinny voice broke into their conversation. "How did you see the fire, Mr. Stone?" Her lips were pinched tight, and her eyes narrowed.

"I was on my porch and saw the glow through the shop windows." He seemed at ease explaining what happened, but Lily's stomach sank and pressure built behind her eyes when she looked at Mrs. Croft and knew the woman was making an accusation.

The busybody confirmed Lily's suspicions with her next words. "But your porch faces in the opposite direction." A hum of low conversations ran through the people who'd only just put out the fire. Now the woman from the general store was trying to start

14

another one. The kind that could destroy Lily's reputation. The potential damage could forever ruin her business before it opened.

Several of the people gathered looked over their shoulders in the direction of the blacksmith's shop and home. His porch faced a lane that ran perpendicular to Main Street. Lily held her breath.

Edward's tone was clipped. "I was leaning on the corner post and watching the night sky. The view of the moon is best from there."

"I see." Doubt hung on each syllable from Mrs. Croft. "It's just that when we came out to help, you were holding Miss Warren in your arms."

Mr. Croft interrupted. "Liza, he just pulled the woman from a burning building." He put a hand on his wife's shoulder. "Let's go home and get some rest. The whole town will be tired tomorrow after the excitement of tonight."

People murmured around them. Some were in agreement with Mr. Croft, but Lily knew in her soul that others were siding with Mrs. Croft. Only two days in her new town and something beyond her control had drawn her character into question. She couldn't let them all disperse without an attempt to protect herself.

"Mrs. Croft, I assure you nothing improper went on here tonight. Mr. Stone was merely rescuing me. If he hadn't come, I'd never have found my way out of my bedroom."

A light gasp escaped some of the ladies.

"I see." Mrs. Croft's eyes swept across Lily from top to bottom and then landed on Edward. "I guess it's okay where you come from to entertain gentlemen in your home after dark, but you'll soon learn that in Pine Haven we hold to a higher standard of propriety."

Edward took a step closer to the edge of the porch. "Miss Warren has told you there was no impropriety here." He looked at Mr. Croft and then the others standing in the street. "Thank you all for your help. By saving my building, you very likely saved many others from certain disaster."

Dr. Willis spoke up then. "And at least one life."

Lily let her gaze move over the crowd then. "Thank you all so much." She turned to Edward. "Especially you, Mr. Stone."

People began to walk away a few at a time, the rumble of voices fading into the night.

She pulled up the bottom of the quilt so she wouldn't stumble and stepped inside

16

the shop.

"Miss Warren, I don't think you should stay here tonight." Edward's voice was kind.

Lily stilled for a moment. "Is the building sound?"

"Yes. And tonight when I say my prayers, I will thank God that the fire didn't spread to your private rooms. But the smoke and water damage are serious." He gestured toward the floor and the workroom.

She stepped inside and took in the magnitude of the destruction. There was a trail of muddy water from the front door to the workroom where water had sloshed from the buckets as they were passed from the porch and through the shop to put out the fire in the back room. She picked her way slowly to keep from slipping and stood in the entry to the workroom. Water dripped from the workbench. The stench of the smoke hung thick in the air. And everywhere she looked, the remains of all her hard work lay soaked and covered in soot. Now she had to begin anew. Not from the beginning, but from a new beginning much further behind any point she'd imagined.

She squared her tired shoulders and spoke. "All the more reason for me to stay and get to work." She nodded in dismissal. "Thank you again for all you've done. I'm certain it would have been a lot worse if you hadn't seen the fire." She looked down at the quilt her mother had made. "I'm grateful you saved my mother's quilt. I don't have many of her things. This one is important to me." As much as she'd tried to keep her emotions in check, she couldn't stop the tears from spilling over her lashes now. With a sniff she stood straight and moved to the front door.

Edward followed her and stepped onto the porch. His hand came up to keep her from closing the door on him. "Cleanup can wait until morning. It's only a few hours."

She shook her head. "The water will damage the floors if I don't mop it up now."

"Then let me stay and help you."

She'd come to Pine Haven for independence. Her recent failed engagement had driven her to create a new life for herself. The first two days now seemed like a distant dream. Making hats and polishing the furniture her father had sent with her to use in her new shop had filled her hours. The memory of humming while she cleaned the floors and set up the private rooms to suit her needs faded behind a cloud of dense smoke.

This was a major setback, but she wouldn't become dependent on her landlord. Now. Or ever. "No. You best get home to your niece. I'll be fine." She'd met his young charge on the first day and knew the child would be home alone.

He chuckled a bit. "Ellen can sleep through anything. That child wouldn't hear the church bell or commotion unless it was in the room with her."

"It's good she has such peace. Sound sleep is often a sign of contentment."

Edward looked over his shoulder toward his house. "In all her seven years, I've never known her sleep to be disturbed. Not since she was a baby. For her, it's more about how she wears herself out when she's awake. The child has more worries than a body ought."

"All the more reason for you to go home now. In case she awakens and you aren't there." When Lily was five, her mother had died. Being young and frightened was something Lily had experienced firsthand.

He dipped his head in agreement. "Please get some rest. I'll be back in the morning so we can assess the damage and begin repairs."

Lily stood in the doorway to her workroom after he left. The hats she'd made yesterday were scorched and ruined. What wasn't blackened by fire was covered in ash or wilted from the water that had doused the flames. She thought about crying, until her bare feet reminded her of the floors and all the work she needed to do.

She shrugged off the quilt, bundled it into a ball and tossed it onto a crate in the corner of the front shop. Lighting a lantern, she went through the workroom into the alley behind her shop and retrieved the mop she'd used to clean the floors. Bucket in hand, she determined to prevent as much damage as possible. Repairing the building would take more skill than she possessed, but she could clean up the mess. Then Edward could get started as soon as he arrived in the morning.

Could she undo the damage done by Mrs. Croft's words in the aftermath of the fire? Why had the woman so blatantly accused her and Mr. Stone of poor behavior?

Losing a night's sleep did not compare to what she stood to lose if she didn't get her shop open before her father arrived in a few weeks' time. Now she not only needed to get Lily's Millinery and Finery open for business, she also had to repair the damage done to her reputation in front of the townsfolk by Mrs. Croft's words. Her own lapse in decorum when she was unaware of her appearance in her dressing gown in front of the entire town added to her problems.

The water on the floor was the least of her worries, but it was the only thing she could control at the moment.

Edward urged Ellen out of the front door the next morning.

"I want to see what happened." Ellen protested by dragging her feet.

"You can't go inside the building until I make sure it's safe for you to be there." He stooped to be eye level with her. "Promise me you won't try to sneak in."

Her reluctant nod came after a long pause. "What did she do to set Momma's shop on fire?" This was the reaction Edward had been afraid of. He knew his niece might blame Lily for the fire and use it as an excuse to spew the frustration and fear she was warring with against his tenant. "I said it was bad to let someone in Momma's shop." Her face turned into a pout.

"I'm not sure what caused the fire. That's one of the things I need to find out today." He pulled her into a quick hug. "Now you need to head off to school so I can get to work."

"I don't see why I got to hurry 'cause you got to work." He reminded himself to be patient. She was at the age where she often wanted an explanation for things. Knowing that was how she learned, he complied.

He put a hand on top of her head and pointed her in the direction of the school. "Because you are one of the reasons I work, ma'am."

Ellen went a few steps, swinging her lunch pail in one hand and holding her slate close to her chest in the other. Then she pivoted and looked at the shop across the street from their cabin. He watched her study the building, which showed no outward signs of the fire last night except for the film of smoke on the windows. She bolted back to wrap her arms around his middle. "I know you can fix it like new, Uncle Edward. You're the best uncle a girl could have."

"I'm going to do my best, Ellen." He kissed the top of her head. "You know you're my favorite niece."

She leaned back and scrunched her face at him. "I'm your only niece."

Edward peeled her arms from around him. "Just like I'm your only uncle." He chuckled and turned her toward the school again. "Now get to school, or I'll be the only uncle at school today being scolded by the teacher for letting you be late."

The school bell rang, announcing the

time, and she kicked up the dust around the hem of her skirt as she ran. "Bye, Uncle Edward," she hollered over her shoulder.

He laughed as she stumbled and caught herself. The child was fun and loving. He wished he could make her as happy as she deserved to be.

When he'd come back home after the fire, just as he expected, she was curled up in the middle of her bed. The quilt had slid to the floor, so he'd pulled it back over her. He'd marveled that the commotion in the street hadn't awakened her. Oh, to be so carefree.

Only she wasn't carefree. She waited every day with him for news from her mother. When his sister had insisted on leaving town with her husband to start a new business in Santa Fe, he'd begged her to reconsider. Ellen needed her mother. Jane and Wesley had wanted to get their business started and come back for Ellen in a few weeks. Edward wished they'd been contented with running the local hotel, but Wesley had lost interest in Pine Haven when he'd heard of the growing economy in Santa Fe. Edward had purchased the building he now leased to Lily in hopes that Jane could convince Wesley to stay and let her open a bakery to add to their business interests in Pine Haven.

In the end, nothing Edward said had changed their minds. And now the weeks had turned to months. No word from them for the past several weeks was causing him to worry. He tried to dampen the fear that pulled at his heart and caused him to wonder if something dreadful had happened. Ellen's future was his responsibility. He'd have to give her a proper home if his sister didn't return soon. He said another prayer for Jane and Wesley and went into his blacksmith shop to gather some tools.

He needed to start the cleanup and repairs on his building. Having Lily's father lease the shop from him had eased the strain to make the mortgage payments. But he couldn't in all good conscience take money from her while the building was damaged.

He'd stop in at the post office first and see if there was a letter from Jane.

"Quite a night we had, Stone," Jerry Winters, the postmaster, greeted him. "Glad you saw the flames. Hate to think what could have happened to my family, it being right next door and all."

Winston Ledford walked into the post office as Jerry was speaking. "It's a good thing for all of us that you had your eye on Miss Warren. I'll admit she's worthy of a second look." A smirk Edward didn't like crept across the saloon owner's face.

Edward's gut roiled. This was exactly the kind of gossip he worried about after Liza Croft made such a scene in front of most of the town. He refused to rise to Ledford's goading.

Instead, he nodded at Jerry Winters. "I think we were all blessed by God's mercy."

Mrs. Winters came from the private quarters behind the post office and joined her husband. "We all owe you a debt of gratitude, Mr. Stone."

"I doubt he'll be missing much of what goes on at the new hat shop, Mrs. Winters." Winston Ledford came to stand beside Edward at the counter. "Do you have any mail for me?"

The disapproval on Mrs. Winters's face almost made Edward chuckle. If it wasn't such a serious subject, he'd laugh at how soundly Ledford's comments were dismissed. She turned to search the cubbyholes behind her and handed several letters to the man.

Winston shuffled through the small stack, tipped his hat and said, "Good morning to you all." He opened the door to leave. "I think I'll stop by and see how our newest resident is this morning. Must have been quite a shock to her."

25

Edward's back tightened, and he drew a deep breath. "That won't be necessary, Ledford. I'm on my way there now to begin the repairs."

A cantankerous laugh burst from Winston. "As I suspected. You've already staked a claim on our new merchant." He stepped onto the sidewalk and turned to close the door. "Don't be surprised if you find yourself engaged in some friendly competition over the likes of Miss Warren." The door closed, and his grinning face filled the pane of glass before he turned in the direction of the building next door.

Edward followed him at a brisk pace.

"Stone, don't you want to know if you have any mail?" Mr. Winters called.

"I'll check back later." He was through the front door. "It's not fitting for Miss Warren to be subjected to the likes of Mr. Ledford without warning."

It was one thing for Mrs. Croft to make unfounded accusations, but for Winston Ledford to think that a fine, upstanding lady like Miss Lily Warren was open to his attentions was another matter. Edward wouldn't leave her unprotected from the saloon owner's lack of good manners.

Serving as an unsolicited chaperone was the only right thing to do. It was more about protecting Lily's reputation in the community, and thus his income from her rental, than anything else.

Edward opened the door to Lily's shop and found Winston Ledford leaning on the glass display case Lily had brought with her when she'd arrived only two days earlier. She caught sight of him over Ledford's shoulder. Was that relief in her gaze?

"Thank you for checking on me, Mr. Ledford, but I assure you it isn't necessary. I'm quite all right." She stepped from behind the case and walked toward Edward.

Once again he was struck by her beauty. When she'd first come to Pine Haven and stepped from the train, he couldn't help but notice her. Everyone noticed her. But within moments, her independence had become clear to him. She was lovely, but she wasn't the kind of woman who wanted to settle down and care for a home and family. Not the kind of woman he'd begun to think he might need for Ellen. After a childhood of being neglected and mistreated by his stepmother, he'd replaced any yearning for love with a mistrust of women years ago. If he did marry for Ellen's sake, he'd choose carefully.

"Good morning, Miss Warren." Edward set the wooden box he'd filled with tools on a crate near the front door and removed his hat. "I've come to get started on the repairs."

She lifted a handkerchief to her face and coughed. "That's very good of you."

Winston Ledford turned to face them. "If you're certain there's nothing I can do for you, Miss Warren, I'll leave you in the care of Mr. Stone." He sauntered toward the door. "He seems determined to watch over you." He tipped his hat at Lily and walked through the door Edward held open for him.

Edward closed the door with a snap. "I hope you aren't taken in by the likes of Mr. Ledford." He picked up his toolbox.

"I'm a big girl, Mr. Stone. You don't have to worry about me." Lily went back toward the workroom behind the shop. Perhaps the relief he'd seen in her face earlier was imagined. Nothing she'd done since he'd met her upon her arrival in town Monday had suggested she was anything other than a woman determined to make her own way in the world. Her single-minded focus might be the very thing that protected her from people like the saloon owner.

"That's good to know. Some women are swayed by fancy talk and refined appearances."

"I assure you, I appreciate fine things. I

28

also look for quality. In people and things."

She directed him toward the workroom. "Thank you for coming so early. I've done what I could about getting everything dry and removing the rubbish."

Her movements were swift and fluid, like a bird on air. She'd brushed her hair into a loose bun and changed her clothes, but the fatigue of her ordeal showed in eyes. Another coughing spell wrenched her breath.

"You didn't need to do all that by yourself, Miss Warren. I assured you I'd be here this morning."

She lifted a hand and waved it in dismissal of his words. "I couldn't sleep anyway. My schedule was tight before the fire. Now I'll need to work at a quicker pace than I'd planned."

He entered the workroom behind her. The back door stood open, and he could see the pile of rubble she'd created in the alley beyond. "You stayed up all night?"

"It's a matter of no consequence." She indicated the shelving on the left of the storeroom. "Do you think any of this can be salvaged?"

Obviously she'd moved beyond the fire and had set her mind on repairs. Most women would be wallowing in a pool of pity, bemoaning their misfortune. Her determination was admirable.

"First things first," he said. "I need to discover how the fire started, so we can make certain we don't have another incident." He turned to see her blush and lift a hand to her forehead. She rubbed her fingers across her brow in a smoothing motion.

"We won't have to worry about it again." A deep breath caused more coughing. "Please forgive me." She tucked the handkerchief back in the pocket of her apron.

"How are you feeling?"

"I'm fine. Just frustrated with the amount of work I've caused us both."

"You caused?"

Could Ellen be right? Had his tenant been the reason for the fire? The last thing he needed was for his niece to discover Lily had put the building in jeopardy. The child already resented her presence in the shop. Edward didn't have the energy to deal with more trouble in their lives — especially not from a woman he'd just met.

CHAPTER TWO

Edward prayed he'd misunderstood Lily. "What do you mean, 'you caused'?"

"It seems the fire was my fault." Lily pointed to the wall near the back door where the most damage appeared to be. "I was working late, trying to make a few extra hats. I had set a lantern on this workbench."

She didn't seem the irresponsible type. "Surely you didn't leave a lantern burning when you went to bed. You'd have noticed the light."

"No." She jerked her head to stare at him. "Of course not! I took the lantern with me."

She pointed to a small stack of charred kindling near the stove. It was considerably smaller than the amount he'd cut and placed there before her arrival. Normal circumstances wouldn't have caused her to use so much kindling.

"Right before I went upstairs, I swept up the trimmings from around the workbench.

31

Bits of ribbon and feathers. Things like that. I swept them into a pile near the door, intending to dispose of it this morning. Then I checked the stove. Some embers must have blown out and landed among the trash. It must have smoldered and caught when it got near the kindling. I don't know how else it could have started. I'm so sorry." Another cough stopped her from speaking. "I'll pay for the damages."

Edward stirred the kindling with the toe of his boot and studied the scorched wood and the wall in the corner of the room between the stove and the door.

"It's possible a gust of wind blew under the door and carried the embers back to the kindling." He turned to Lily, who was coughing again. "No one was hurt. That's the most important thing."

"Please forgive me. I never meant to start the fire." She covered her mouth again to cough.

"You took in a lot of smoke. Have you been to see the doc?"

"No. I'm fine. There's too much work to do to stop for a minor cough."

He knew how much smoke had been in her rooms. The stairwell had acted like a chimney and drawn the smoke upward. No doubt a draft around the windows had pulled the dangerous fumes under the door at the top of the landing.

"I'm taking you to see Doc Willis." He headed for the front of the shop. "Where's your coat?"

When she didn't follow, he turned and waited.

"You are not taking me —" a cough interrupted her words "— anywhere."

He raised his eyebrows. Would she be so stubborn as to refuse medical treatment? "Then I'll have to ask Doc Willis to come here." He opened the door and stepped onto the sidewalk. "We need to get this place ready for you to open your business. The sooner you get that cough taken care of, the sooner that will happen."

"Wait, please." She coughed again. "If it will set your mind at ease so we can get to work on the repairs, I'll go." She shrugged her arms into the sleeves of her coat and turned up the collar.

The January wind whipped around him, and he rubbed his arms against the cold. They walked briskly in the direction of the doctor's office. "I'll feel better knowing you aren't making yourself worse by not resting."

Lily turned to look at him. "You must be freezing."

"I'm fine." He dropped his hands to his sides.

"Your coat was ruined when you put out the fire."

"It was time for a new coat anyway. I'll go by the general store after lunch and get one." She walked beside him across the main intersection in town. He hoped she didn't notice the curious glances being sent their way. It was obvious to him that the events of the night before were on everyone's mind this morning.

"You must allow me to pay for it." She seemed too focused to notice the people who turned their heads to whisper when they passed. He wasn't sure that was a good thing. It might be better if she were more aware of what went on around her. If she were, they wouldn't be the object of town gossip. He knew it wasn't fair to blame her, but he didn't like the idea of anyone gossiping about him. Ellen would be harmed if he was cast in a poor light. And it wouldn't do Lily's new business any favors to open the shop in the midst of swirling lies smearing her name.

"I'll pay for my coat. And the repairs." He opened the door to the doctor's office.

She opened her mouth as she entered the building, most likely to argue the point with him, but quickly succumbed to another coughing spell.

Lily continued to cough while Edward called out, "Doc. I brought you a new patient."

Lily sank unceremoniously into a chair near the door. The smell of camphor and dust assaulted her senses. A curtain rustled and parted. The man who'd kept her from running back into her shop during the fire came into the room.

"Hello, Edward. Finally find yourself a wife?" The short man with spectacles looked from the blacksmith to Lily.

"A wife?" What was this man thinking?

"No, Doc. She's my new tenant. You probably saw her last night. I went by to start the repairs this morning." He pointed to Lily as she interrupted them with a cough. "This is how I found her. I think the smoke got to her. She's been hacking away."

"I saw her. Actually had to restrain her to keep her from following you into the burning building." The doctor motioned for her to have a seat on the table in the center of the room.

"I'm not injured, Dr. Willis." She moved to the table and sat stiff with her hands in her lap.

He seemed to ignore her. "Are you light-headed?" He peered into her eyes and checked the pulse at the base of her neck.

"I am not." She glared at Edward, who had retreated to stand near the door. "I told Mr. Stone this trip was unnecessary, but he insisted." She slid toward the edge of the table, but the doctor prevented her from getting up.

"Just the coughing?" He assembled his stethoscope and pressed the bell against her back. "Take a deep breath."

She drew in a breath, and the coughing began again.

He moved to the opposite side of her back. "Again." The results were the same.

"I don't think you've done any major damage to your lungs, but it's probably going to take a few days for you to recover from taking in so much smoke." He paused to look at her. "Your color is good. I think it's just a matter of getting some rest."

"I don't have time to rest. I've got a business to open." She coughed into her handkerchief again, hating that her body was betraying her so. She needed to work. There would be time for rest later.

"A hard worker, are you?" The doctor tilted his head to one side and studied her.

Lily straightened her shoulders. "I am. It's

how I was raised. We Warrens don't cotton to laziness or excuses."

He turned to Edward and nodded his head in Lily's direction. "She looks as good as any other lady around here. You oughta think about this one."

"I don't think so, Doc." Edward seemed to be laughing at her from his place in the corner of the room. First he'd insisted on bringing her here, and now he was a party to her ridicule. She wouldn't stand for it.

"I don't need a doctor." Anger gave her fresh strength, and she turned her eyes to the blacksmith. "Or a husband."

"As you wish." Dr. Willis backed away from the table. He turned toward the curtains where he'd made his entrance.

Another coughing spell overtook her. Between coughs Lily said, "Wait a minute, Doctor."

The doctor stopped with a hand on the curtain and raised an eyebrow. "Don't got all day, missy."

"I'm sorry. Can you give me something for the cough?" She hated to submit to the man but had no time for setbacks. Her father and sister would arrive in a few short weeks. She needed to have her shop open and bringing in business before then.

The doctor went to a glass cabinet against

the back wall. Lily caught Edward looking at her with a grin of satisfaction. He was enjoying having been right about insisting she see the doctor.

"I want you to use this flaxseed to make a tea." The doctor handed her a bottle. "You can do it several times a day. It will help with the cough and clearing your lungs."

She took the bottle reluctantly. "Thank you."

Dr. Willis nodded. "Sensible, too, Edward. You need to reconsider this one."

Lily might submit to his ministrations but not to his attitude. "Really, Doctor, I don't think it's appropriate for you to discuss me as if I'm a prize horse."

"I didn't say you were a prize. Just worth a second consideration." He looked at Edward standing with his back to the door. "But only if she's given to moments of quiet."

The blacksmith laughed then. "I haven't seen one yet, Doc."

Lily scowled. "If you'll tell me your fee, Doctor, we'll be on our way." She hoped this ordeal was drawing to an end. How was it possible for her to be at the mercy of not one, but two belligerent men?

Edward waited while Lily paid the doctor,

then held the door open for her to walk through before him.

"I'm coming back to the shop to get started on the repairs."

"Thank you for being so eager. I'm going to have to work harder than ever to get ready to open."

"Just don't try burning the candle at both ends."

"Very funny." She gave a tiny giggle. Then, in a fashion he could only imagine a cactus flower able to perform, her prickly expression transformed into beauty with a smile like none he'd ever seen. Golden hair framed her face. Vibrant blue eyes sought him out. His heart jolted. Nothing could lessen the power of her grace.

He shook his head. What was he thinking? She was beautiful all right. A rare beauty. But gentle and graceful? Not with the sharp tongue and feisty resistance he'd witnessed in the short time he'd known her.

Lily Warren might be named after a gentle spring flower, but her cactus-like thorns could prove dangerous, if not deadly, to a man not on his guard.

And Edward Stone was a man who would not let his guard down. Ever again.

"Possum run over your grave?"

"What?" He had to pay better attention.

"You're shaking your head and shivering."
Lily's expression teased him, but he
wouldn't tease back.

"No. Just a bad thought." He turned away
from her and continued down the sidewalk.
"Nothing to worry about." He'd make
certain of that.

Lily picked up her pace and left him to
follow. When they arrived at the shop, she
opened the door, and the bell announcing
their arrival clanged to the floor and
bounced.

She sighed. "Great. Something else to be
fixed."

"Be careful not to break anything else."

Her eyes widened in question. "Oh, so
that's my fault? I see. Looks like our relationship will be one of blame and accusation." The smile was there again, but Edward was determined to thwart its power.

"Our relationship will be landlord and
tenant." He stooped to retrieve the broken
bell from just inside the doorway. "And the
fault of this was mine, so I'll be responsible
for the repair."

"You think it can be fixed?" Her uncertain
gaze met his.

"Sure. It's a simple repair." He turned the
bell over in his hand. "I should have made
it stronger in the first place."

Blond brows lifted. "You made it?" Disbelief crossed her face.

"Don't look so surprised. I am a blacksmith."

"I'm sorry. The blacksmith in East River made horseshoes and wagon wheels. Not art."

Was she complimenting him? Did she realize it?

"I make horseshoes and wagon wheels, too. And iron gates, and farm tools . . ."

"I understand. Sort of a jack-of-all-trades, are you?"

"Are you suggesting I'm master of none?"

"Well, the bell did break . . ." Her smile was the only clue she was teasing him. Tormenting might be a better word, given the tightening of his gut when she looked at him.

"I wouldn't call myself an artisan. But I do enjoy creating unique things." He drifted into the past looking at the bell. It had been a gift for his sister, Jane. One she'd never taken the time to enjoy.

A swift movement had the bell in his pocket. Hidden with the memories it evoked.

When he raised his eyes, he found Lily staring with open curiosity.

"I best get to work, Miss Warren." He

41

stepped into the center of the room. The late-morning sun lit the street beyond the deep windows. Windows Jane had dreamed of filling with pastries and cakes.

Lily breezed through the opening, which led from the large front room into a work area, with a lightness he'd never seen in any woman. If he'd had to describe it, he'd say her steps floated across the floor.

He followed her, and together they came up with a plan for the repairs. He would tear out anything damaged beyond repair. She proved a strong helper by toting all the charred boards out to the alley behind the shop.

They stopped at midday, and he made a list of the supplies he'd need to get the shop back in good shape.

He prepared to leave. "I'll stop by the lumber mill and order what I need before I go to the general store. I'll get a quick bite of lunch and come back."

"What about your coat?" she asked.

"That's why I'm going to the general store."

"Let me come with you so I can pay for it. You wouldn't need a coat if there hadn't been a fire."

He shook his head. "No."

"I insist."

42

Edward turned to look her full in the face. "Miss Warren, what do you think Mrs. Croft would think of that? After all she insinuated last night?"

Lily's cheeks went pink.

He looked over his shoulder out the front window. "I'll bring my wagon when I come back. We can use it to haul away the debris."

"I can help with that." She was unlike any other woman of her type, and Edward was impressed by how determined she was to help. At first glance, she gave the appearance of a lady accustomed to fine things. But she hadn't shied away from any of the work brought on by the damage from the fire.

"No, ma'am." He still wouldn't let her help load the rubble piled in the alley.

Lily smiled. "You must be as strong as an ox." Shock covered her face almost before the words left her mouth.

"I can haul my share of a load." He couldn't resist teasing her. As hard as he tried, his reserve kept slipping. "Most people don't call me an ox."

"Maybe not to your face, Mr. Stone." At least she had the decency to blush when she said it.

Edward heard the rumble of laughter in his chest. It had been a long time since he'd laughed out loud. "I'll be back after lunch." He tipped his hat and escaped through the front door.

He sobered immediately on seeing Mrs. Croft exit the post office next door. Her scowl spoke louder than anything she could have said before she turned and walked in the direction of her store.

Dust stirred in the street as his boots beat a path away from Lily Warren and her shop. He'd only rented it to her father out of desperation. The mortgage on the shop needed to be paid, not to mention the cost of providing for Ellen. He couldn't afford to let the shop stand empty any longer. When Jane came back, they'd make new arrangements. Until — or unless — she did, he needed the money.

He had to protect Lily's reputation, because if her shop failed, he could lose the building to the bank. He turned the corner and headed to the general store. His hands were shoved deep into his pockets, but the cold of the day was biting at him. Or maybe it wasn't the cold of the day, but the cold realizations storming his thoughts.

Life was complicated now. More than he'd ever wanted it to be.

In the back of his mind was a growing dread crying out for his attention. As a single man, if something tragic had happened to his sister and her husband, he'd need to marry. A young girl shouldn't be raised by her lone uncle. Ellen would need a woman's hand. Someone who was strong and gentle at the same time.

Someone like Lily.

Lily opened the door and wrapped her older sister in a hug. Could it be eleven years since Daisy had married and moved away from East River, their childhood home? When they'd reunited on her arrival in Pine Haven, Lily understood why their father had come home after his recent visit to Daisy's family wanting to sell everything in East River and move here. When he and Jasmine arrived in the spring, he'd have all his daughters together again. They'd been apart too long.

One look at Daisy's face and Lily prepared herself to be scolded. Even at twenty-four years old, her sisters still treated her like the baby of the family.

"What happened?" Daisy shifted baby Rose onto her shoulder and looked around at the destruction left by the fire.

"It was an accident." Lily knew Daisy wouldn't be satisfied without some explanation.

"How did it happen?"

She pointed to the chair she'd set up in front of the hall tree so her customers could view their hat selections in the mirror. "Have a seat, and I'll explain." She pulled up a stool and told her sister all that had happened.

"So Edward Stone saved you?" Daisy pushed Rose's bonnet away from her face and handed the child to Lily. "Handsome, isn't he?"

Lily lifted the baby and took in the sight of her chubby face. "She's so like Momma. I'm glad you named her after her." She pulled Rose close and breathed in the sweet baby smell. Rose twined her fingers into Lily's hair and gave a firm yank.

"Ow . . . She's a strong one, too." Lily loosed the tiny hand and nestled the babe in the crook of her arm.

"That she is." Daisy's face shone with love for her daughter. "You didn't answer my question about Edward Stone."

"Did you ask a question?" She hoped to avoid this kind of question about any man, let alone one who was already being accused of paying her too much attention. She couldn't risk feeding those rumors. Not even to her sister, who obviously hadn't heard them yet.

She jostled the baby. "Where are the twins?"

"They're in school."

"I can't believe they're nine years old. Seems life has begun to move at such a rapid pace."

"It comes from growing older, I suppose." Daisy looked her square in the face. "Lily, what do you think of your landlord?"

Lily stilled and answered. "He's my landlord. Yes, he saved me, but he also saved his building. That's all there was to it."

Daisy turned first one way then another and surveyed the shop. "If you say so."

"I do." Lily swept her free arm toward the open space. "I wanted to have it in better shape, but I wasn't planning on a fire. What do you think?"

Daisy reached for Rose as the child started to whimper. "Don't worry. I'm sure Edward will have the repairs done in no time."

"I hope so. I've got to make this place work, or Papa will insist I live with him and Jasmine when they come." Lily fought back the fear of being isolated again. She'd spent too many years taking care of her sick father at home while all her friends had married and started families.

Daisy paced the floor, gently rocking the baby. "That wouldn't be so bad, would it?

47

You've always lived with Papa. Why is this shop so important to you now?"

"It just is. You wouldn't understand. You have your life. A family. A farm. I didn't have anything." Anxiety sent her voice up a notch. "Until now."

She put a hand on Daisy's arm and stopped her motion. "Daisy, you have to pray for me. Papa isn't convinced a woman my age should be on her own. But I've just got to do this. I can't live in the shadows anymore. I want my own life."

"You talk as if you've been locked away as a slave. I know that isn't true. I lived there, too, you remember."

"It's not that at all. It's just . . . well." Lily wasn't certain she could articulate her thoughts. "I love Papa, and I'm so pleased he's well now. We weren't sure for so long that he'd ever get better. I'd do it all again in a heartbeat." She willed Daisy to understand. "But I need this for me."

"Of course, I'll pray for you, sweetie. I'll even make sure all my friends come see you as soon as you open."

That was encouraging. She could almost see the unknown ladies milling around the shop, fingering the lace on a handkerchief or smiling at their reflection wearing a new hat. "Are the ladies of Pine Haven ready for

48

fancy hats and parasols?"

Daisy chuckled. "What ladies aren't?"

Lily was grateful for the support she saw in Daisy's expression. "Thank you. I promise I'll make you proud. Papa, too."

"The thought of having all of you here in Pine Haven is more than I ever dreamed. Your shop is like an extra blessing on top of that."

"I've got a lot of work to do to replace the things that were ruined. Thankfully, I hadn't opened all of the crates I brought." She indicated the crates stacked around the front of the shop. "These things are undamaged."

After lunch she'd gone over everything in her mind. Hopefully a couple of days would see the shop repaired. Maybe two more days after that and she'd be back on schedule for her new life.

She prayed the insinuations made by Mrs. Croft had been forgotten by those who heard them last night. That was the one detail she hadn't told her sister. If God answered as Lily wanted, she'd never hear of those accusations again.

She shook off the doubts that threatened from the recesses of her soul. A new life full of promise. She would do everything in her power to make it happen.

CHAPTER THREE

Edward pulled his wagon behind the building and loaded the debris. He came to the front of the shop to enter, so anyone watching from the nearby businesses would see him. He was determined to do his part to squelch the rumors. Going in the back way would only feed the gossipers.

Lily was kneeling in front of an open crate rummaging through its contents and didn't hear the door when he opened it.

"Think I'll have to stop by Doc Willis's office and let him know how you're taking it easy."

Startled, Lily jerked up straight. "I'm perfectly fine."

He watched her frustration as the coughing overtook her again. "As long as —" she coughed "— no one tries to scare the breath out of me."

He closed the door. "Have you rested at all?" Everywhere he turned he saw evidence that she'd been busy.

"I stopped working and visited with Daisy. She came by to check on me."

Did he dare bring up the subject that he'd heard being discussed everywhere he'd gone in the two hours since he'd left her? "I saw her when I was leaving the lumber mill."

"Were you able to get the lumber ordered?" She didn't seem the least bit curious about anything other than the progress of the repairs.

"I did. Will Thomas said he'll have the order ready for me after I haul off the debris behind the shop."

She stood and brushed her hands together. "Let me help you load it."

"It's done." Knowing she'd be stubborn, he hadn't let her know he had returned until after he loaded the rubble into the wagon.

"I told you I would help."

"Doc Willis said you need to rest. I only came inside to see if you have anything else that needs to go."

"No." She rubbed her hands down the front of her skirt to smooth it. "At least let me go with you to unload it." She stepped toward the workroom. "Where are you taking it?"

"I've got a small burn pit behind my shop. What can't be salvaged, I'll burn later."

51

She came back into the front of the shop tugging on work gloves. "Are you ready?"

"Miss Warren, you can't come with me."

"Why ever not? The sooner you unload, the sooner you can get the lumber order and start on the repairs."

He cast a glance out the front window. "Have you been anywhere today? Besides the doctor's office?"

Her brow furrowed. She was cute with her face scrunched in confusion. "No. There's been too much to do here to go visiting."

Was it possible she had no clue? "Did your sister go anywhere before she came to see you?"

"No. She stopped by on her way into town." She looked at him. "Why?"

He didn't know the best way to tell her, so he just said it straight out. "We seem to be the topic of conversation all over town today."

"We? You mean about the fire?"

"No," he said. Her face had relaxed, and he didn't think she understood what he was trying to tell her. "I mean you and me."

Her shoulders lifted, and she gave a small snort. "That's silly." With one hand she gestured between the two of them. "There is no 'we.' "

"I know that." He paused. "But . . ."

She rose up a bit taller now and drew in a slow breath. "But what?" She angled her head away from him as if it would prevent the full onslaught of something she didn't want to hear.

"It seems that Mrs. Croft's assumptions from last evening have captured the fancy of some of the townsfolk."

Her eyes closed, and she drew her pretty lips inward. He watched her sigh as the implications sank in.

"Everywhere I went, someone brought it up."

Lily dropped onto a crate and wrung her hands together. "Oh, my. I hoped it would be forgotten in the light of day. No one knows me here. Why would they think I'd be so bold as to entertain a man in my home — unchaperoned — late at night?" Her gaze snapped to his. "Unless . . . what kind of reputation do you have, Mr. Stone?"

How dare she imply that his name in town was without respect! "Me?"

"Yes, you! In East River no one would ever suspect me of any behavior other than that of a Christian lady."

"I had hoped because you're Daisy's sister these rumors would not take hold." He shrugged his shoulders. "But they have."

The front door opened, and Daisy entered

the shop. "Oh, Lily! I've just come from the general store." She put a hand on Lily's arm. "Why didn't you tell me what happened?"

Lily must not have expected it to be a problem, or surely she would have told her sister what had been said the night before.

Edward could see the panic filling her eyes when she answered. "Nothing happened! Except a fire!" She lowered her voice and asked, "What are they saying?"

Daisy hesitated. "I'm embarrassed to say." She glanced at Edward, then took Lily by the hand. "Mrs. Croft has given details about you being held in Mr. Stone's arms." She seemed to choose her words with great care. "In your dressing gown."

He needed Daisy to understand the truth. "I pulled her from a burning building. Her hair caught in my suspenders. There was no embrace. I carried her outside because she was overcome by the smoke."

Daisy shook her head. "That's not how Mrs. Croft portrayed it." She looked at Lily. "And because so many people were coming to see what was happening, they witnessed just enough to lend a hint of truth to her tale."

Lily stiffened her arms at her side and clinched her fists. "Truth? We'll tell them the truth! You tell them, Daisy. They'll believe you."

Daisy's husband, Tucker Barlow, came into the shop. Edward knew from his expression that this situation was not going to fade away.

Tucker removed his hat. "I see the news has made its way to all of you."

Lily almost begged for an answer from them. "What am I going to do?"

Edward didn't know what she was going to do. All he knew for sure was that his situation had become more desperate after he'd left Lily just before noon. He'd stopped in at the post office, and there was still no word from his sister, Jane.

He'd gone by the telegraph office and discovered the query he'd sent to the sheriff in Santa Fe had been answered. An outbreak of influenza had hit the community where Jane and Wesley lived, and they'd become gravely ill. The local doctor had sent them to a hospital in another community. No word on the name of the community or their condition.

If Jane and Wesley had passed, he was Ellen's only living relative. He'd do anything necessary to take care of her. He wouldn't risk losing this building. Talking of opening a bakery here would be one of the last things Ellen had shared with her mother. He'd keep the shop for Ellen to have when she was grown. A legacy in Jane's memory.

He cringed when the answer entered his mind, but he knew it was for the best. "What are *we* going to do?" He had to protect Ellen from the gossip that would surely swirl around the shop — and Lily if they didn't act quickly.

"We?" Lily countered.

They were standing in the workroom. The ravages of the fire all around them.

Edward pointed to a small frame Lily had hung on the wall over the workbench. "Are these the verses you live by?" The edges of the frame were scorched, but the intricate needlepoint was intact.

Lily followed his gaze. "Yes. Philippians is one of my favorite books in the Bible."

He read the words aloud. " 'Let nothing be done through strife or vainglory; but in lowliness of mind let each esteem other better than themselves. Look not every man on his own things, but every man also on the things of others.' " He looked at her, hoping she'd agree. "That's what we need to do now."

"What do you mean? I'm not at strife with anyone in Pine Haven. I'm not out for vanity. But I do need a good name to run a successful business. What man will want his wife to patronize my shop if he thinks poorly of my character?"

"I'm afraid that's already happened. People assumed the worst when they saw us together last night."

"But we weren't together."

He shook his head. "That's not what they saw. I don't think we'll be able to convince them otherwise."

Lily put her hands to her face and closed her eyes. After a moment she opened them and held her hands out, palms up. "I came here to be independent. How can I do that without the goodwill of the townsfolk? You've ruined everything!"

"Would you rather I'd let you die in the fire? I couldn't stand by and watch the building burn to the ground, knowing you were inside."

Her shoulders slumped. "You're right, of course. But what are we going to do?"

Daisy and Tucker stood quietly while he and Lily tried to sort out this conundrum.

What he had to say next was private. He didn't know Lily well, but he was most certain no lady would want witnesses for what he was about to say. "Will you excuse us, please?"

Daisy looked at Lily. Sisterly sympathy

emanated from her.

Tucker took his wife by the arm. "We'll go for a slice of pie at the hotel and come back after you've had time to talk."

When the door closed behind them, Edward turned to Lily. "You know you're going to have to marry me now."

Lily's jaw dropped. To his surprise, words seemed to fail her.

"There is more to consider here than just you and me. I received word today that it's very possible my sister and her husband may have died of influenza."

She closed her mouth. "I'm so sorry. Poor Ellen." She'd gone from incredulous when he spoke of marriage to compassion for his niece in an instant. He hoped it would help her understand why he was making this proposition.

"I won't allow gossip to cause an innocent little girl to lose the only family she may have left. If my name is smeared with yours, I could lose her. A judge could say I'm not fit to be a guardian as an unmarried man — especially if I'm purported to have committed unseemly behavior."

"But we're innocent."

"I know that, and you know that." He put a hand on her sleeve and turned her so she could see through the entry of the workroom to the windows in the front of the shop. Two women had stopped to peer in the glass. When they caught sight of Edward and Lily, they frowned and hurried away. "But we'll never convince them. Or the people who are like them."

"Did the doctor put this notion in your head?"

He shook his head. Never would he have imagined himself offering marriage to someone he'd just met. If it weren't for Ellen, he might not have offered.

Then he looked into those blue eyes, churning to violet with emotion, and knew he was doing this for Lily and himself, too. No one deserved to be destroyed by gossip and rumors. "Believe me, I was just as resistant as you. Until I spent part of the day trying to convince people that nothing happened. Now it looks like we don't have a choice."

He willed her to understand. "If you don't open your shop, I don't know how I can pay the mortgage. I can't lose this building. I need to be able to give it to Ellen when she's grown. Maybe it will help her remember her mother."

"But why would you want to marry me? I'm not your responsibility."

"It's not just about you." He drew in a

breath. "Ellen needs a mother. It's something I started pondering lately, and this must be God's way of answering."

"I can't mother her. My own mother passed when I was younger than Ellen. I won't know what to do."

"I think you will. You're strong. She'll need to be strong." He hesitated. This was not the way he ever imagined proposing to someone. For that matter, he hadn't really imagined proposing to anyone. His solitary life had suited him just fine before Jane left Ellen in his care. "But you're also gentle. She needs a woman's hand."

"How did this ever happen?" Lily's head sank into her hands.

"It seems that it was out of our control from the beginning."

She looked up at him. "Do you think we can do it? Raise Ellen and protect my reputation so the shop will be successful?"

"From what I've seen of you, I don't think the shop's success is in question, as long as we take care of your honor." He prayed he was doing the right thing. "As for Ellen, it looks like the good Lord left her in my care. I don't think He orchestrated your problems, but I'd say as His children, He's giving us a way to make the best of it."

"I can't think why you'd do this for me."

Lily bit her bottom lip.

"It's like the verse." He pointed to her needlework. "We're taking care of the needs of others. Ellen needs us both."

Lily's face turned pink, and she met his gaze. "What kind of relationship do you expect the two of us to have?"

He could tell it cost her a great deal to form the words. Then he felt the same heat rushing into his face. "Miss Warren, I'd expect for you to care for Ellen as a mother. This arrangement will be strictly for the sake of my niece."

Edward watched her as the breath she'd been holding seeped out of her to be replaced by relief.

"For the sake of Ellen?"

"Yes. And you."

"I didn't come to Pine Haven to find a husband. I'll never forget what you've done here today, Mr. Stone. You're giving up an awful lot to take on a wife you didn't want."

"I want Ellen to have a mother."

"In that case, I accept." She offered her hand for him to shake. Did she really see this as a business arrangement like the one he had with her father for the lease on his building?

It was a relief she seemed to accept his reasons so quickly, but the reality of how much his life was about to change threatened to overwhelm him at any moment.

"I do." Lily stood in front of Reverend Dismuke and repeated the marriage vows.

Daisy and Tucker had agreed with Edward, and it had only been a matter of hours before they'd arrived at the church. Long enough for Lily to change to her best dress. The lingering hint of smoke in its fibers reminded her of the reason she was doing this. When she'd prepared for bed the night before, she'd never have dreamed today would be her wedding day.

Edward took her hand and slid a small gold band onto her finger. She'd told him she didn't need a ring, but he'd insisted, saying it was another way to reinforce their union in the eyes of the community. He'd escorted her into the general store and asked her to choose from the tray of rings. She'd been relieved when he'd asked Mr. Croft to assist them, leaving Mrs. Croft sputtering and mumbling as she'd moved on to help another customer.

Lily looked at the delicate, plain ring. Edward didn't release her hand for the rest of the short ceremony. His hands were large but gentle. And strangely comforting, as if he was trying to reassure her they were doing the right thing.

"You may kiss the bride." Reverend Dismuke's words rang out in the nearly empty church. Only Daisy and Tucker, with their twin sons and baby daughter, sat on the bench opposite the reverend's wife, who kept an arm around the shoulders of Edward's niece. Lily wasn't sure if it was an effort on the woman's part to comfort Ellen or an attempt to keep the child from fleeing. The young girl had refused to attend until Edward told her she had no choice.

Edward took his other hand and turned Lily's chin to face him. A small smile played on his lips. He'd said they'd have an easier time overcoming the gossip if everyone was convinced their marriage was born of affection and not shame. But did he honestly intend to kiss her?

"Relax," he whispered. Then he grazed her cheek with the briefest of contact.

In an instant Lily found herself wrapped in her sister's hug while the preacher clapped Edward on the back and congratulated him.

Why was everyone so merry? They all knew she and Edward, given the choice, would never have married. Well, maybe the Dismukes didn't know that, but her family did.

Daisy held her hands and spoke, "We're taking Ellen home with us for the night." She gave a nod in the direction of the bench where Edward's niece still sat clinging to her handkerchief doll. Lily had never seen the child without that doll.

Lily watched as Edward accepted Tucker's welcome into their family. Lily hadn't thought about being alone with Edward. No, she needed Ellen to be at the cabin tonight. And every night.

"That's not necessary."

Daisy smiled and patted her hand. "We insist. I've already told her she can sleep in Rose's room."

"But . . ." Lily felt her life spinning like a toy top. She had to maintain some form of control.

Edward turned and met her gaze. He must have sensed her desperation, because he came to stand beside her. He was close enough for her to feel the warmth of him, but he didn't touch her. "Tucker just told me they've invited Ellen to their place."

"She can stay with us. There's no need." Better to face Ellen's reluctance than to face alone a husband she hadn't expected to have.

He leaned in to speak near her ear. His breath ran across her neck, leaving a chill

64

with each word. "We've got a lot of things to sort out. I'd like to do it without Ellen's eager ears close by."

What did he want to sort out? She straightened her shoulders. There were a myriad of things. How they would handle finances, daily chores, the rebuilding of the workroom in her shop, and how to protect Ellen.

She agreed.

"Thank you, Daisy. That's very kind of you." Lily smiled at her sister but knew the smile didn't reach her eyes. Numbness was the only sensation she experienced at the moment, and she feared it would fade into regret.

Ellen plodded over to Edward. "Do I gotta go to the Barlows' farm?" Her bottom lip protruded, and the doll hung from her crossed arms.

He lifted the little girl's chin with one knuckle. "You know you love to go visit the Barlows. You can play with baby Rose." He smiled at her and patted her shoulder. "You'll have a good time, I promise. You can come say hello in the morning on your way into town for school."

Daisy moved to stand behind Ellen and put a hand on her shoulder. "Why don't we go by your cabin and get some clothes?

Then we'll head out to the farm, and you can help John and James feed the animals."

Ellen's eyes aimed a dart of resentment at Lily before she agreed to Daisy's suggestion. "Bye, Uncle Edward."

"Goodbye, Ellen." As she started to tromp away, Edward called to her again. "Ellen, you forgot to tell your aunt Lily goodbye."

"Aunt Lily? I gotta call her 'aunt'?"

"You are permitted to call her Aunt Lily." He tilted his head to one side. "It's a privilege."

A long sigh came from her little body. "Bye, *Aunt* Lily."

"Goodbye, Ellen." She smiled at the girl, wondering how she must feel. Without warning, her home had changed today, and there was nothing she could do about it. In a way, Lily understood her childish frustration. She was almost tempted to cross her arms and pout, too.

Edward offered Lily his arm. She knew he was merely keeping up appearances. It was comforting and unsettling at the same time. Their marriage was the only way to remove themselves from the whirlwind of tortuous rumors they'd been caught up in for the past twenty-four hours.

Lily wanted to protect their good names. Individually. Hooking her hand on his arm and leaving the church felt as false as the lies Mrs. Croft had spread about them. Were they perpetrating one lie to negate the effects of another lie? Would God honor them for trying to save Ellen? She hoped so.

They rode in silence to her shop. Edward set the brake on the wagon.

"Do you need a few minutes to put your things together?" he asked.

Most of her clothes and personal belongings were still in trunks and crates. There would be little to pack.

She looked across the street to the cabin she would now share with Edward. Her husband.

Her husband? She had come here to escape a marriage to a man who only wanted a companion for his ailing mother. Now she sat in a wagon between the shop she was opening to start a new independent life and a cabin where her primary role would be to care for a young girl she'd only known a few days. A girl who'd made it plain that Lily was an intruder in her turbulent young life.

Lily had heard stories of people who disappeared in the night, leaving only a note for their loved ones, striking out on their own, hoping for a fresh start. She'd come here for that reason — with the blessing and help of her family. Had it only taken two days for her world to turn upside down?

Edward's touch on her sleeve drew her attention. "Are you all right?"

It was tempting to write a note and steal away in the night. But she could never leave her sisters and father like that. Not after all her father had done to give her a new life. Somehow she'd make this work. Edward had noble intentions, which was more than she could say for her former fiancé, Luther Aarens.

She shook off her thoughts and accepted her fate. "Fine, thank you."

Edward nodded toward her shop. "You'll want to get your clothes and such."

"Yes." She scooted to the edge of the wagon seat away from him and prepared to step down. "I'll need a little while to put some things back into the trunks."

"Wait a minute. I'll help you down." He climbed from the wagon and came around to assist her. With the briefest of contact, he lifted her and set her on the ground. "You go in and take care of that. I'll make space in the cabin for you."

She looked at him when he spoke, but his gaze went over her shoulder. When he did focus on her, she turned away. "I won't need much space." She twisted her hands together.

"I remember you had a couple of pieces of large furniture upstairs." He pointed to the window of her front room above the shop. "From when I helped carry it in."

Awkward held new meaning as they stood talking about her things. Things she hadn't thought she'd share with anyone. Things she'd brought to make her comfortable in her new home. Nothing was turning out as she'd planned.

She remembered a verse in Proverbs. "In all thy ways acknowledge Him, and He shall direct thy paths." Her faith in God would have to sustain her now. There was no course except to move forward as she'd agreed.

"We can move those things another day. If you don't mind, we can just get my clothes and personal items today. Perhaps Tucker can help with the furniture later."

Edward shuffled from one foot to another. He must be as nervous as she was. "That's good." He dipped his head and looked over his shoulder at the cabin. "I'll just be on my way, then."

He turned and took a step. Not knowing she was going to do it before it happened, Lily reached for his arm. He stilled and turned back to her.

"I know this isn't what either of us thought we'd be doing today." When he looked at her hand on his arm, she dropped it. "I hope we can make this work without everything being uncomfortable or awkward."

His thin lips curled into a half smile. He really was a giant of a man. Tall and broad with all the strength she imagined a black-smith would need to do his job. But the softness of the smile and the way his almost-black eyes twinkled was a pleasant surprise. "No promises about not feeling awkward for a while. I haven't shared my home with another living soul until Ellen came to live with me a few months ago. I'm not quite sure you and I will see eye to eye on every-thing. It's a big adjustment to get to know someone new. I'm guessing we complicated it more than a little bit by getting married before we could do that."

She felt herself smiling in return. "That's a wise observation, Mr. Stone. I'm sure you're right."

"That's what I mean."

The smile faded and she asked, "What?"

"Mr. Stone? Really? Is that how you intend to address me?"

She gave a small chuckle. "I see. No. I don't think that will do any longer." She drew back her shoulders and took hold of her future with all her strength. "Edward, I'll be about a half hour preparing my things to move into our home. If you'd be so good as to meet me in the shop after you've finished preparing a space for me, I'll be most grateful."

She gave a little giggle. "How was that?"

He laughed in a deep tone. "That's just fine." He nodded. "Just fine, indeed."

When he headed for the cabin, she entered the shop. As she climbed the stairs to the home she'd only spent two nights in, she marveled that it would be the only two nights of her life spent as an independent woman.

Her dream of a shop wasn't dead. She wouldn't let it die. But her independence was over. She prayed for God to help her as she packed away the things she'd so carefully placed in her new home. When she'd asked for a new life, she wasn't prepared for this twist. God would have to light her path, because it was one she'd never dreamed would be hers.

In one major event, she'd gone from Lily Warren, milliner and shop owner, to Lily Stone, milliner, shop owner, wife and mother.

CHAPTER FOUR

Edward tossed his dirty clothes into a pile by the bedroom door. His cabin wasn't grand, but it wasn't small. If he'd built it himself, it would not have had two bedrooms, but the house was part of the deal when he'd bought his blacksmith shop from the previous owner. As soon as he was old enough, he'd moved out on his own to escape the stepmother his father had brought home shortly after his dear mother had died. She'd given no affection to him or Jane. Time and again he'd wished his father had never married her. Finding work as an apprentice to the town blacksmith had given him a purpose and place in life.

Eventually he'd nurtured a vague hope of one day having a family of his own. But over the years, he'd found it safer to retreat alone at night into the sanctuary of his home. His mistrust of women in general was based on years of watching his father's wife take advantage of his father. Her sweet facade had quickly faded after she'd convinced his father to marry her. She'd never truly loved him and had been horrid to Edward and Jane. Nothing they did was ever good enough for her. She'd settled into their home as mistress and ordered them about in her aloof manner, as though she felt them beneath her care or attention. Jane had been too young when she married, but until Wesley had whisked her away to Santa Fe, Edward had thought it was for the best.

Edward stripped the linens from the bed and added them to the pile by the door. A small crate from the back porch would suffice for his personal items. He put his shaving cup and brush in and then tossed in the small mirror from the top of his chest of drawers. He pulled a rag from his back pocket and took a swipe at the dust on top of the furniture.

Backing up in the doorway, he took a last look around. Not what he'd have done in normal circumstances for bringing home a wife, but it was the best he could manage in the half hour she'd allotted him. He stowed the small crate in a corner near the stove and gathered up the laundry. He tossed it onto the workbench on the back porch and headed back into the front room.

A light rapping sounded on the door, and his breath caught. He was doing this for Ellen. She needed a mother. Life might be upside down, but that little girl would always have a home with him.

He lifted the latch on the door and pulled it open. Lily stood in the street at the bottom of the porch steps. She must have knocked and backed as far away as she could.

He dragged his palms down the sides of his pants. "Hi."

Pink color soaked into Lily's cheeks. She really was a beautiful lady. At this moment, she must be just as nervous as he was. "Hello."

Edward stepped through the doorway. "Did you get everything packed?"

"Everything I'll need until we can move the furniture." She didn't look at him.

He reached inside the cabin and took his hat from the peg by the door. "Okay. I'll go get everything, then." He pushed the hat onto his head and walked down the porch steps.

She hesitated. "Would you mind if I took a look inside first?"

"Inside the cabin?"

"Yes. I want to see how much space there is, so I can decide what to bring and what to leave behind."

"Oh." He took the hat off again. "That makes sense." He shrugged his shoulders and lifted an arm to invite her up the steps. He heard a thump and turned to see the door of the livery open. Jim Robbins stood in front of his place and made no effort to hide his interest in the goings-on at Edward's house. Edward turned and looked up the street. Mrs. Winters was sweeping the sidewalk in front of the post office. He pivoted and saw Will Thomas in the doorway of the lumber mill.

Edward put his hat back on and took Lily by the elbow. "It seems we're being watched."

She followed his gaze and saw the obvious interest their neighbors were showing. She giggled like a schoolgirl. It was a light sound, like water over rocks in a stream in summertime. "You'd think there was a fire or something."

He chuckled. "One would think so."

"What should we do? Wave? Or ignore them."

He drew in a breath. "Do you trust me?"

"I believe I've proved that already. After all, I did marry you less than an hour ago."

Mr. Croft walked by on the street and tipped his hat. He made a show of greeting

75

Mr. Robbins when he arrived at the livery.

Edward leaned in close. "What goes on here will affect us all. How well your business does, and how well our marriage is accepted. All of it could have consequences for us and for Ellen."

Lily looked over his shoulder and nodded. "I'd say this town is very interested in us at the moment. I hope it will fade in time. Quickly, would be my preference."

"Then I say we do our part to keep the busybodies from having anything to talk about."

"How do you propose to do that?"

"By living the part of a normal married couple."

Lily's eyes grew wide.

He gave her elbow a slight squeeze. "What I meant to say is if we give every indication of being a normal married couple, when we're outside the cabin, no one looking will have any reason to question our relationship. The best way for them to concentrate on someone else is for there to be nothing to see here."

"I think I see what you mean." Her face relaxed.

"Good. So we're agreed?"

She nodded.

"Here we go, then." Edward leaned close

and, with one hand behind her back and another behind her knees, he scooped her off her feet.

Caught unawares, she gave a tiny yelp and wrapped her arms around his neck. She whispered close to his ear. "What are you doing?"

"I'm carrying you across the threshold." He climbed the steps and walked into the cabin. He turned in the doorway and kicked the door closed with his foot.

Lily laughed. "I think I may have married a deranged man."

Edward laughed and set her on her feet. He put the distance of the room between them. "Not deranged." He closed the shutters across one of the front windows. "But never happy to be the center of attention." He closed the other shutters and dropped into a chair at the table.

Lily stepped to the cabinet next to the stove and looked out of the window that faced Main Street. "Then why did you make such a scene? Mr. Winters has joined his wife on the sidewalk, and they're talking to Mr. Croft. Mrs. Winters is smiling and looking in our direction."

"Close the shutters." Edward leaned back in the chair and stretched his legs out in front of him.

"It's the middle of the afternoon."

"I know. But if you don't want them walking by on this side of the street and trying to peek in the window, you'll close the shutters."

Lily swung the shutters closed. The dim interior of the room was lit only by the fire. He marveled again at how gracefully she moved.

He went to the stove and set the coffee to warm. "Why don't you sit by the fire? You've got to be bone tired."

A slight shrug of her shoulders was the only response.

"It's not the day either of us planned." He opened a tin of cookies Mrs. Dismuke had brought for Ellen. His niece might not want him to share her treats, but he'd deal with her later.

Lily sat on the edge of a chair facing the fire. "Nothing has gone like I planned for most of my life." He watched the back of her head as she shook it slowly back and forth. "I'd so hoped things would be different in Pine Haven."

Edward poured two cups of coffee. "Do you drink coffee?"

"Yes." She didn't turn away from the fire. Her shoulders slumped forward.

He brought a cup to her and set the tin of

cookies on the table by her chair. "This might help you." He retrieved his cup and sat on the bench in front of the fire facing her.

She sipped the brew, and her face twisted. "Oh, my."

"Not to your taste?"

"Is it to yours?" She looked up at him.

"Not really. But it's the best I've been able to do."

She sat up straight and set the cup on the table. "Did you bake the cookies?" A wary eye told him she was being cautious when it came to his efforts at cooking.

"No. The preacher's wife brought them for Ellen. They're quite good."

"Do you think Ellen will be upset with you for sharing them with me?"

He grinned. She'd only been in town a couple of days, but she'd already figured out Ellen's personality. "Probably. So consider it her wedding gift to you."

She took a cookie and nibbled at it. Then she took another bite and picked up a second cookie.

"Have you eaten today, Lily?"

"I don't remember. Everything has happened so fast." She stared into the fire again. "I think I had some lunch."

"Eat another cookie, then, and we'll get

some things figured out before we go get your trunks from the shop. I've got to take care of the wagon, too."

She put the half-eaten cookie down and stood. "I'm sorry. I forgot about the wagon."

"Relax." She was like a frightened colt, jumping at every noise. "We need to wait a bit before we go outside again. If it's all the same to you, I'd like to talk for a few minutes."

She paced to the fireplace and back to the chair. "What are we doing?"

Edward stood and set his coffee on the table. "We're making life better. For you. And for Ellen."

Blue eyes looked up then. "We are, aren't we?" She seemed to calm a bit.

"Yes." He'd have to guard against those eyes. They were the kind of blue that could pull a man in against his will. Like a gorgeous sky that demanded attention. He took a step back. "Would you like to look around? Ellen's room is through that door." He gestured to the door closest to the fireplace. "I've cleared some space for you in my room." He pointed to the other door on the back wall of the room.

Lily stiffened. He didn't see it, but as soon as he said the words he knew it happened.

"Your room?"

"What I meant to say is, you'll have the other room." He nodded toward the fire. "I'll be sleeping out here."

"But I couldn't take your room."

"If you don't mind, I'd like to keep my clothes and such in there, but I brought out my shaving things and stripped the bed. I thought you might have fresh linens you'd like to put on it."

"Really, we can bring the settee from my rooms at the shop. I can sleep there." She wrung her hands. "You'd never fit on it." She lifted one hand to indicate his height. "You're much too tall." She pointed to the center of the room. "We could move the chairs back and . . ."

She was talking so fast he had to break in. "That won't be necessary." He pointed to the floor. "This is where I slept when I came here as an apprentice. The former owner took me in."

"But now you're the owner, and a man ought to sleep in his own bed." Her voice became higher, and she was wringing her hands again.

He reached out and caught her hands in his. "Lily. Stop." He kept his tone calm. If she maintained this pace, she'd work herself into a frenzy. "It's going to be fine. I'll sleep out here. Ellen goes to bed early. She'll never know. You will take my bed. It's the best I could do with the time I had."

She withdrew her hands and put them to her cheeks. "It is all happening rather quickly, isn't it?" She lowered her hands and met his eye. "I'm sorry. I'm not usually the sort of person to panic."

"Anyone would be unsettled under the circumstances."

"You don't seem to be." She tilted her head to one side and drew her brows together. "Why is that?"

"I told you. I've been considering marriage for the sake of Ellen." He smiled at her. "Granted, I had thought to have more time for making the decision, but I was pondering it." He moved to the bedroom door and opened it. "If you'd like to take a look around, I'll see what I have that we could eat for supper."

"Thank you." She walked by him, and he went to see how much bread was left.

He had planned on making pancakes for Ellen and himself. It hardly seemed a fitting wedding supper. Even if they weren't in the throes of young love, they were married today. His bride deserved a fine meal.

Something banged on the floor in his bedroom.

Lily called out. "Sorry. I tripped on the

broom."

He walked over and stood in the doorway of the room. "I shouldn't have left it there. It's usually on the back porch." He'd never hesitated about going into his own room before. But it wasn't just his anymore.

"Thank you for doing such a nice job of preparing for me." She stood in the center of his room with her hands clasped in front of her. "It's very nice."

"I'm sure it's not what you're accustomed to." He backed away from the door.

"Really, it's fine." She stepped into the front room again. "Let's go get my things. I'd like to close up the shop. There's a lot to do this evening." She had walked to the front door while she talked. "Did you find anything to eat?"

Edward grabbed his hat from its peg. "Nothing fit for a wedding supper." He opened the door. "I think we've earned a treat. Let's get your things and go to the hotel for supper."

Lily laid her hairbrush between the comb and mirror in the satin-lined box her father had given her for her last birthday and closed the lid. She ran her hand across the wooden box and marveled at its uniqueness. The beauty of the ornate dresser set made her smile every time she used it. It reminded her of her father's love.

Every woman deserved to feel special. She'd come to Pine Haven to bring beautiful things to the ladies in town. It was one thing she could do well. She knew what ladies liked and how the smallest treasure could brighten even the most menial life.

Now, three days into her new adventure and she was preparing for bed in a home she shared with a husband she just met.

Dinner had been delicious. The thick slices of ham served with the fluffiest potatoes were as fine as any she'd eaten. They'd dined at the hotel her father was buying and would run with her sister Jasmine, when he arrived in a few weeks' time. If it hadn't been her wedding supper, she knew she'd have been able to enjoy it more. Never had she dreamed her wedding would be a hasty affair orchestrated to prevent the demise of her good name in a town of strangers.

Lord, I don't know why all this happened. Help me to handle it in a way that pleases You. Please bless and protect Edward and Ellen.

She lowered the wick, and the lamp went out. Lying in bed and staring at the moonlight that shone around the shutters brought no calm to her rattled soul.

A rap at the door startled her. "Lily? Are you awake?"

Lily sat up in bed and pulled her mother's quilt under her chin. "Yes." Her voice was so low she wasn't sure Edward could hear her.

"I hate to disturb you, but I left my Bible by the bed."

"Just a minute." She climbed out of the bed and slid into her dressing gown. This time she cinched it securely. A loose robe would never happen to her again. Of course, the only time it mattered had already passed.

She barely opened the door. "Do you have a lamp? I put mine out and don't know where the matches are."

"Yes." Edward retrieved a lamp from the table by his chair near the fireplace and handed it to her. "I'm sorry to bother you. I'm having a bit of trouble getting to sleep. I usually read the Bible at night."

"I understand." She turned into the room and found the well-worn book. "I was just saying my prayers."

A smile lit his eyes. "I hope you said one for me."

Glad for the relative darkness, she passed the lamp back to him as her cheeks flamed warm. "I did. And for Ellen, too." She handed him the Bible and backed away from the door.

"Thank you."

"You're welcome." She looked over her shoulder into the room. "I guess I'll turn in now."

He nodded. "Well, good night, then. I'll see you in the morning. We've got a lot of work to do."

"Yes. I'll be ready." She closed the door and leaned against it. How would she ever get to sleep tonight? An exciting adventure into independence had turned into the journey that would last her lifetime. She prayed God would give her the strength to make it.

When she awoke the next morning, the cabin was quiet. She dressed without delay, grateful she'd thought to bring her pitcher and bowl with her. The privacy of Edward's bedroom shielded her from having to face her new life before she was alert. She opened the shutters over the window to be greeted by a sun much higher in the sky than she'd expected. How had she slept so late?

Opening the door into the front room, she braced for her first encounter with her husband. Her husband.

God, give me strength.

86

This was quickly becoming her constant prayer. God must be showing His sense of humor today, because Edward was nowhere to be seen. She took a peek into Ellen's room. Everything was just as it had been the night before.

Sunlight streamed through the windows in the front room. No time for breakfast now. She went back to her room and snatched up her hat and coat. This was no way to begin her new life. What would Edward think of her shirking her responsibilities on their first day of working to repair the shop?

Lily walked across the street without seeing anyone. She found the shop empty, too. Where was Edward? She hung her hat and coat on the hall tree and got to work. A full hour later the front door opened. Edward came in carrying a package wrapped in brown paper. He propped it in the window-sill and shrugged out of his coat.

"Oh, good. You're here." He hung his coat next to hers. "Did you sleep well?"

"Where were you?" Lily's stomach growled in hunger.

"Excuse me?" Edward went to the front door and started to remove the wooden trim from around the window he'd broken so he could get into the shop on the night of the fire.

"I've been here for over an hour. I thought we were going to work together this morning." Why didn't he look at her? Was he as uncomfortable as she was?

"I've been working for several hours, Lily." He dropped the trim pieces into a pile at his feet and scrubbed the end of the hammer along the edge of the frame to remove the remaining bits of broken glass.

"I wish you'd awakened me." Lily had established a comfortable working relationship with Edward as her landlord. But today he was also her husband. She didn't know how to behave toward him.

"I knocked on the door."

"I didn't hear you. You could have made certain I was awake."

He dropped the hammer into the small box of tools near his feet and turned to her. "Really?"

"Of course." She backed up a step from him. "I wanted to be here early. I don't know when I've slept so late."

"How was I supposed to respect your privacy and wake you without coming into the room?"

Lily looked at her feet. "Oh. I see." She walked to the glass display case and picked

88

up the rag she'd been using to wipe the soot from the furniture. Edward must be as off balance by their situation as she was.

She heard him tearing the paper from the package he'd brought with him.

"Will you hold this glass steady while I nail the trim work back into place?"

She dropped the rag and brushed her hands together. "Certainly."

Edward set the pane on the lip of the frame and held it steady. "Put your hands here and here."

Lily followed his instructions. He stooped to pick up the first piece of trim and slid it between her and the door. She stretched as far as possible to one side, so he could hammer without hitting her. He worked with several small nails between his lips. Each time he hammered one into place he retrieved another.

Talking around the nails, he admitted, "I knew you hadn't slept the night before. You needed the rest."

"I'm sorry." She shifted so he could put the next piece of trim on the opposite side of her, all while holding the pane of glass. "I wanted to help you."

"There was nothing you could do this morning. I was picking up the supplies we need." He tapped the last piece into place, and she backed away. It was difficult to be so close to him working, knowing neither of them had intended to be working together at all, much less as husband and wife.

"Well, all the same, I'd have been here if I were awake." Her stomach rumbled again.

"Let me guess." He picked up the box of tools and headed for the workroom. "You didn't eat breakfast."

She followed to retrieve the broom and dustpan. She might not have gone with him to buy the supplies, but she would clean up the mess. "No. I wasn't sure where you were. I was late enough as it was."

He dropped the box onto the workbench. "Lily, we need to establish some kind of expectations for our relationship and act accordingly."

She stilled, broom in hand, and leaned against the doorway between the shop and the workroom.

Edward exhaled as if he were gathering his nerve. "We were able to work together in a friendly manner before the fire. I'd like for us to continue to do that. We've both been on pins and needles since we decided to get married. We both did it for noble reasons. Do you think you can relax? I declare, the more nervous you are around me, the more nervous it makes me." He

90

stopped and drew in a deep breath.

A rumbling laugh bubbled up in her throat. She tried to swallow it but couldn't. "You're so right. We're no different than we were two days ago."

His eyebrows shot up. "Maybe a little different."

She did laugh then. "Yes, but we're the same people. With the same goals."

"Some of the goals are different, too." He scrunched up his face a bit.

"You know what I mean." She stepped forward and put a hand on his arm. "I agree with you. Let's continue as the friends we were becoming before the fire."

"Good." He looked at her and then at her hand on his arm.

She dropped her hand. "I'm glad we got that settled." She turned to go back into the shop and sweep up the glass.

Edward followed her. "Would you like some lunch?"

"Yes, I would. As soon as I sweep up this mess, I'll go upstairs and put something together for us. All my food stores are still here."

"All right." He nodded toward the workroom. "Then I'll get to work in here."

"Okay, then." She swept up the glass, wondering what her life would be like now.

Everything she'd envisioned was like the glass at her feet. Shattered. Beyond repair. Replaced by something new. The new glass served the same purpose, but the old glass would soon be forgotten. Could she forget her dreams of independence? Would her new life afford her the same fulfillment? Establishing her shop would make her financially independent. That would be a comfort to her as she watched the rest of her dreams disappear. Tonight Ellen would return, and Lily's new role as mother to the young girl would begin.

Lily knew opening a new business would be a great challenge. She was certain winning Ellen's trust would be greater.

CHAPTER FIVE

Edward stepped into the front of the shop and heard Lily cry, "Oh, no!"

She let out a yelp, and he was at the workroom door as she stumbled backward. The highest shelf in the storeroom was just beyond reach from her stool. She'd climbed onto the workbench, overreaching to push the extra hatboxes out of the way.

Seeing her arms flailing, he crossed the shop floor as she lost her struggle to right herself. The breath whooshed out of her as she landed against his chest.

"Wonderful." Edward set her to her feet. "I see you're still following Doc's orders."

Disapproval, not surprise, covered her face.

"I was just trying to make room to work." She brushed her hands together to remove the dust. "I'm perfectly fine."

"Just how fine would you be if I hadn't come along?"

"How do you know I wasn't startled by you coming into the shop unannounced?"

"Because I heard your screech while I was outside."

"Never you mind. I'm not hurt, and I've more work to do." Lily twirled and marched to the front of the shop.

"You're welcome." He followed her.

Lily hung her head but smirked. "Thank you so much for helping me catch my balance."

"Catch your balance? You'd be lying on the floor broken if I hadn't come in here when I did! You might want to be more careful if you intend to open your shop next week. Or at all."

"You're right. I have a tendency to lessen the intensity of things after the fact." She smiled. "Thank you for saving my life."

"Catching your balance? Saving your life?" Edward laughed. "Is there no middle ground with you, Lily?"

Her eyebrows shot up when he spoke her name. Would she be able to relax and accept a modicum of familiarity from him?

He grimaced and indicated the bell he'd dropped on the table when he'd rushed to help her. "I came to mount this."

She reached for the bell. "It's lovely." She studied his handiwork. It hadn't taken long to repair, but it was intricate work. He was glad she approved.

"I brought a new bracket to make sure it doesn't fall again." Their fingers brushed when she handed the bell to him. A tingling sensation caught him off guard. He didn't know if he was more surprised by how the touch of her fingers stirred his skin or how her words of kindness and approval brushed against his wary heart.

"Thank you. I've work to do in the back room. I'll leave you to it." Her quick steps confirmed her hurry to escape his presence. "If you need me, just give a shout." She darted a glance over her shoulder.

"It's a bit more likely you'll be calling out for help from me," Edward muttered as he turned to work on the bell.

"I heard that." She laughed. "You're probably right, but allow me the opportunity to think I might be safe on my own."

He'd replaced the burned shelves in the workroom by midafternoon, then left her to get her supplies set up as she pleased. That had given him time to go across the street to his shop and repair the bell. He hoped it was the last thing she'd need. After two days away from his shop, he was behind on his work.

Edward dropped the bell, and it clanged

95

on the wooden floor.

"Are you all right out there, or do you need my help?" Lily's sarcasm danced into the room on her words.

"Got it." He inspected the bell for damage. "Thankfully, my foot broke its fall."

"Good thing it didn't hit you in the head. You'd have to make a new one." Lily snickered from the opening to the workroom.

He stood with his hands holding the bell above the door and angled his face to see her. Just as he suspected. A wide grin.

"Very funny." He chuckled before turning back to his work. He gave the nail one final rap and released the bell and bracket.

"Good as new." He started gathering his tools and putting them back in the box.

"Great."

He picked up his toolbox. "Is that everything?" He watched as she looked around the shop.

"I think so. The rest will be up to me. I've got to make new stock. I'm hoping it will only take a few days."

"Provided you don't sleep the mornings away?" He dipped his hat and stepped out the door. "I'll see you at home in a little while."

Edward heard her stamp her small foot on the floorboards as he closed the door, and a grin tugged at his mouth.

Standing on the steps of the building — his building — he marveled at the life one small creature could bring to a place. Not since his sister left town had he sparred with a woman. He found it invigorating.

A shudder ran up his back, and he tromped off the porch. That was not a healthy path to travel. Following the excitement of conversation with a young woman was not where he was headed in life. Not at all.

Their marriage was about Ellen. He'd serve himself well to remember that.

Edward opened the door to Ellen's room. "Come to the table, young lady. Aunt Lily called you several minutes ago."

His niece sat in the middle of the bed with her arms folded around the doll his sister had made for her. "I don't like carrots." Her bottom lip protruded.

He sat on the side of the bed. "You're saying you'd rather have pancakes again?" He tousled her hair, hoping to improve her disposition.

"I'm saying I don't like carrots." She kept her arms crossed, but lifted them and flopped them back down across her chest. "I don't know why you married her, anyway.

First she took Momma's shop. Now she's taking you."

"She's not taking anything. She's cooked us a fine supper, and we are going to eat it with the gratitude she deserves."

"I don't like her."

Edward stood. "I don't like your attitude. Lily is here because I asked her to be. You will be kind to her." He moved to the door. "You've got two minutes to be at the table with a respectful attitude."

He closed the door and turned to see Lily standing at the table watching him.

"You heard?"

She nodded.

"She'll adjust."

Lily turned back to the stove and put food on a plate. She placed it on the table with two others. She took her seat at the foot of the table and folded her hands in her lap.

The clock on the mantel chimed seven times.

Edward sat at the head of the table.

Lily looked to Ellen's door. Nothing.

Edward bowed his head and said grace over the food. When he opened his eyes, Ellen was standing at his elbow.

"Take your seat and apologize to Aunt Lily for delaying the meal."

Ellen shuffled her feet and plopped into

her chair. "Sorry."

"Ellen." He would not let her win what he was certain would be the first of many battles of wills.

The child narrowed her eyes at him and turned to Lily. The sugary sweetness of her words belied her true feelings. "I'm so sorry, Aunt Lily, for delaying this meal. I know it can't taste better if it gets cold."

He watched Lily draw in her bottom lip and chew it. How had he managed to find himself at the table with not one, but two reluctant females? Both would rather be anywhere than here with him.

Lord, I think I'm gonna need the wisdom of Solomon to bring these two together.

"You may find a cooling supper preferable to a chunk of bread and a cup of milk in your room before bed."

Edward wasn't sure who was more surprised by Lily's words. Ellen or him.

"You can't do that!" Ellen jumped up. "Uncle Edward won't let you!"

Lily looked at him. He had no doubt this moment would define how his new family would be from this night on.

"Sit down and be silent, Ellen. You may stay at the table only if you eat quietly. If you show any disrespect, you will do as your aunt has said."

Ellen opened her mouth, and he raised a finger in caution. She closed her mouth and looked at Lily and then him.

"Would anyone like a biscuit?" Lily passed the bowl of bread to Ellen, who took one and handed the bowl to him.

Ellen's attitude had degenerated to rudeness in the previous weeks, while they'd waited for word from her parents. He'd overlooked it because he was sorry for her. Watching Lily require good behavior or promise consequences confirmed he'd made the right choice for Ellen by marrying her.

He took a bite of the fluffy biscuit and closed his eyes. It was delicious.

"Well?" He opened his eyes at Lily's question.

"It's wonderful. I had no idea you were such a fine cook."

Lily spoke to Ellen. "Do you like it?"

Ellen looked to Edward for permission to speak. At his nod, she said, "Yes, ma'am."

Lily gave the child a small smile. "I'm glad. Now try your carrots. I think you'll find the brown sugar makes them taste a bit like candy."

By the end of the meal, Edward wondered if Lily was not just the right choice for Ellen but for him, as well.

Something was missing. On Friday after lunch, Lily stood in the middle of her shop and spun in a circle, taking in everything she'd arranged with such care. One hand came to her mouth, and she tapped a finger against her lips as she contemplated what it needed.

The clanging bell drew her attention. Edward's mouth lifted for a split second before settling into a bland expression. "I was passing by and saw you through the glass. How's everything coming along?"

She turned to the display case and back to the front windows.

"If you must know, something isn't right."

Edward took in the shop and shrugged his broad shoulders. "It all looks fine."

Lily drew her brows together. "Of course, it looks fine to you. You're a man."

His blank response caught her eye.

"That's not an insult, just an observation."

She spun again to the windows. "If I could just put my finger on what it is." She tapped one finger against her lips again.

"Not sure I can help you, but . . ."

"Aha! Oh, yes, you can! Wait right here." She dashed into the workroom and plundered through the crates she'd emptied. A lid fell to the floor, revealing what she searched for. "Eureka!"

She rushed back to the front room with a fashion magazine she'd received from Paris. Flipping through the pages, she found the picture she needed.

"Can you make this?" She pointed to a drawing of hat stands advertised for sale. They were different heights with a metal base anchoring a post that was capped with a metal cup inverted to hold a hat. They would be perfect in the front windows. She could order stands, but they wouldn't arrive before she opened.

"Of course, you can make these! You're an artist. The bell proves that." She was becoming overexcited, but this would set her apart from the other shops in town. The only other place that carried hats was the general store. Their hats were stored in boxes on a high shelf, and the owner had to open every one for any customer who showed an interest.

Edward studied the drawing. "Seems simple enough. How many do you want?"

"At least a dozen, in different heights and sizes." She pointed to the windows. "This was the best I could do, but stands will be so much better." She'd arranged small crates upside down and draped them with a length of fabric before placing the hats at various angles. Gloves hung over the edges of the boxes, and an open parasol was propped in the corner of one window.

"A dozen? Sure you need so many?"

"Yes. At least. I'll put some in the windows, a couple on the sideboard, and some on this table." She indicated the center of the room. "The hall tree has hooks, so I won't need any on that side of the room."

Lily smiled at the thought of the finished displays. "Can you have them by Monday?"

Edward chuckled. "Monday? You do realize this is Friday?"

"Yes. I'll pay for them. I really need them before I open." She looked out the front window into the street beyond. "As a matter of fact, I'm going to keep the shades down so the display will be a complete surprise when I open on Monday."

She pushed the magazine into his grip and started to dismantle the window display.

"I won't be able to finish by then." Edward came to stand close behind her.

Lily straightened to her full height. "Why ever not? They seem simple enough to me." She went back to her task, the matter settled in her mind.

"May I suggest you stick to making hats

—" he waved a hand at the various displays "— and whatever else it is you do? Let me handle the blacksmith work."

She stopped her work as quickly as she'd started. "Hmm . . . I'm much too busy to argue with you today. And it would only serve to slow you down. Not a risk I'm willing to take." She pursed her mouth in a small show of triumph.

"I doubt you'd ever pass on an opportunity for a good argument, Lily."

She refused to give him the satisfaction of a retort. "Do as many as you can. I'll put them in the window and make do inside the shop until you finish the rest. I think six will be a good start."

At his lifted brow, she added, "You can have six for me, can't you?"

He stood without a word and watched her face. She didn't know what it was, but something made him decide to help her. In an instant his eyes shone with determination.

"I can do six, but I won't promise more."

Lily put a hand on his. "Thank you so much."

"They won't be ready until Monday morning. I'll bring them over first thing. You may have to delay the opening for a little while that morning to do your setup, but I can't do anything faster than that."

"Perfect." A new excitement filled her. She was going to make this work. Her days of toiling away in the background of her father's life were over. A bright future was in reach. And reach for it, she would.

Edward pulled his hand from hers.

"Oh, my. I did get a bit carried away. Sorry." She put a hand to her hair and pushed the blond curls behind her ears. Keeping the unruly tresses in a bun was a never-ending struggle.

"I'll be on my way, then." He slapped the magazine against the palm of his hand. "I just got a large order from a new customer. Mustn't keep her waiting." He gave a nod and slipped out the door. "But I won't accept payment for them."

"Why ever not?"

"You're my wife now. My responsibility is to provide for you."

Lily stiffened. "If you refuse payment, I'll rescind the order."

"Why? It's proper for a husband to provide for his wife."

"We both know this is not an ordinary marriage. You've done me a great favor by protecting my good name. The least I can do is make the most of this shop to help provide for our family and save this property."

She watched his eyes as he processed it all. "You may pay me for the materials. Nothing more."

"But your time. If you're making these, you won't be doing other projects that will pay for your time and materials."

Edward put up a hand. "I'll work in the evenings. That's my final word on the matter."

Lily knew pushing him further would insult his dignity as a man. She followed him onto the sidewalk. "Thank you, Edward."

"Uncle Edward? What are you doing?" Ellen sidled up next to Edward's far side. She tucked herself behind his leg and peered up at Lily. Her hair was mussed and her dress dirty.

He put a hand on the girl's shoulder. "I was checking on Aunt Lily."

"Hello," Lily said to Ellen.

"Uncle Edward told me you wouldn't take up his time."

"Ellen. Be kind." His cheeks flamed. Was that guilt in his eyes?

"Did he, now? Well, I'll let him get back to his work, then."

"You best. He's got lots of work to do and

don't got time to waste on you."

Lily took a half step back. This was a strong-minded child. At only seven, she possessed the directness of someone much older without the wisdom to hold her tongue.

"Ellen, apologize this minute." Edward looked into the child's upturned face. She seemed to hold her own against her uncle. He dwarfed her in size but not spirit.

"Didn't say nothin' wrong."

"Ellen, say you're sorry."

A small foot scuffed the boards on the sidewalk. Ellen looked at Lily and then back at Edward in what appeared to be an effort to discern his seriousness.

"Sorry." Ellen's hands had been behind her back, but now she pulled the tattered and dirty handkerchief doll into the circle of the arms she folded across her chest.

"For?" Edward prompted his niece.

"For speaking when I should be quiet."

"I accept your apology."

"Can I go home now?" Ellen's words were quiet but resolute.

"Run on back to the shop. I'll be there in a bit." Edward gave Ellen a nudge and turned to Lily.

"I'm sorry. She can be difficult sometimes, but I'm doing the best I can."

107

God, forgive me for judging him so narrowly. Of course, there's more to this man than what I've seen in just a few days.

"I'm sure it's been hard for her since her parents left."

"No girl should be without her momma," Edward said.

Lily knew the pain of growing up without a mother. When hers passed away, she had been five years old. It was the hardest part of childhood. Her father had tried to fill the void of maternal nurturing in their home with a housekeeper. Beverly Norton had done her best. Lily and her sisters loved Beverly, but there was still something missing.

Lily had taken to mothering others in an effort to fill the hole in her young heart. First her doll, then her favorite dog and, finally, her father during his long illness. She'd been swallowed up in her efforts to replace her mother. Lily's Millinery and Finery was her attempt at finding herself again.

"I've been praying for them to return." It sounded feeble, but what else could she say?

He nodded his head with no outward sign of hope. "That's what we pray for. Every night. Can't say my hope isn't all but gone."

"Ellen is quite a handful."

He met her frank statement with a cold stare. "That's why I need your help."

"I didn't mean anything by that, Edward."

"Yes, you did, Lily. You might wish you didn't, but you did." He stepped off the sidewalk.

"Please, I wasn't trying to say you aren't doing a fine job with her."

Edward turned for a brief moment. "I'm doing my best. That's all my sister asked." He nodded his head in dismissal of further argument. "I'll be home late. Don't wait supper for me."

And he was gone, his shoulders not quite as square as before but still very much a man in charge of his world.

Would she ever learn to hold her tongue? There she stood moments ago thinking the child didn't know when to be silent, and she'd committed the same sin.

Lord, help me to be swift to hear and slow to speak. It's such a challenge for me.

"Duck." Edward stepped onto the porch of the general store with Ellen on his back. Tiny arms encircled his neck. She was getting so big he thought she might bump her head when he entered.

Giggles filled his ear when she leaned in close. "Can I have candy?" She asked the same question every Saturday morning.

He slid the child to stand on her feet. "Two pieces. Go pick out what you want, but wait until Mrs. Croft isn't busy to ask for it. I've got to get a few supplies." Little feet tapped a happy rhythm as they left him near the doorway.

Edward picked up a box of matches and went in search of shaving soap. He reached for the bar he usually bought and caught sight of Lily as she came through the front door. Moving behind a barrel of brooms, he was able to study her unnoticed. Her hat was set at an angle, her hair swept low over her forehead.

Lily looked in the opposite direction from where he stood. Her coat was buttoned against the gray morning, and she wore fine gloves. The hat was fancier than any he'd seen in Pine Haven. She was like a wave of beauty and all things fine coming into their midst.

Before he'd left the house, she'd told him she was going to change clothes and run errands. Then she planned to work in her shop afterward.

He still hadn't adjusted to having her in his life. The pancakes she'd made for breakfast had surpassed his meager cooking skills. Everything about her had improved his life.

She pivoted on the heel of a small boot and caught a glimpse of him. He feigned interest in a broom before acknowledging her with a tip of his hat. She came toward him with a purpose that pinned him to the spot.

"I didn't realize you'd be here." Her smile lit the dark corner of the store.

"Just needed a few things." He held up the box of matches.

Lily raised a delicate hand to touch her hair. "I need to replace some things that were damaged in the fire."

"I was about to speak to Mr. Croft about adding you to my account. You can charge your purchases."

Lily shook her head. "I told you I'm prepared to care for all of my needs. It was never my intent to be a burden on you."

Did she know how her words cut him? Or how he wished he could say he didn't need her money? How he hated the loan on the shop. If he'd never borrowed the money, he'd never have been in a position to need to have a tenant.

But then he might not have had reason to spend time with Lily. And she wouldn't have agreed to care for Ellen. Even with the good he saw in knowing her, he despised being beholden to her financially. One day he'd

111

pay for everything she needed. He'd pay off the mortgage and free himself of that burden as quickly as possible. Then he'd be able to take care of his wife without the shame of needing her money.

She changed the subject. "How is my order coming along?" Directness was definitely one of her character traits. Not common in a young lady, but nice to see for a change.

"I'm making progress."

"Oh, I hoped seeing you out on the town meant you'd finished." Her pert response almost made him laugh. Until he realized she wasn't teasing.

"I have things to tend to. Your order will be ready as, and when, promised." He tipped his hat to her and went to gather Ellen.

"Did you pick your candy?" His niece waited at the counter with her chin resting on fingers that clutched the edge of the glass case.

"Mrs. Croft made me wait while she helps another lady. Said I could wait till you were ready." The little face went from longing for the anticipated treat to scrunched with disapproval over being pushed aside.

Edward placed his items on the counter and gave her a wink. "Mr. Croft can help us." He lifted a hand to signal the owner. Mr. Croft added Lily to his account and tallied his purchases.

He couldn't help but notice Lily out of the corner of his eye as he paid. She held a blue fabric to the light in the front window. Without turning, he knew it matched her eyes perfectly — something he scolded himself for knowing. Mrs. Croft busied herself trying to convince Lily to make a purchase.

"Can we go to Mrs. Milly's today? I wanna play with Reilly." Ellen yanked on the end of his coat. "I hadn't got to go nowhere after school in too many days. All you do is work. I ain't havin' no fun."

"Lick that sugar off your lips, little missy." He watched the valiant effort to catch every speck of her weekly treat with her tongue. "You should know better than to complain when your mouth is full of candy."

A tiny hand went against her forehead. "I forgot. Thanks for the candy. Can I go play with Reilly now? He gots a new marble, and I wanna see it."

Edward put a hand on her shoulder and directed her to the door. "I don't see why not, since you asked so nice and all."

"Thanks for coming in, Mr. Stone," Liza Croft called to him as he opened the door.

Her next words were addressed to Lily but followed him for the rest of the day. "I'm surprised you and your husband aren't shopping together."

Lily's sharp intake of breath brought him to a stop in the open doorway.

"My husband is a very busy man. I don't think a woman should drain the life out of her husband by demanding his constant attention."

Edward walked out and let the door close behind him. A smile crossed his face at the thought of Lily's words of rebuke searing Mrs. Croft's nosy ears. In the time since he and Lily met, he'd learned she could stand her ground. They might not exactly be friends, but in this situation he knew they were allies.

CHAPTER SIX

Sunday morning dawned clear and cool. After breakfast Lily dressed in her favorite blue dress, added a wool coat and walked the short distance to the church with Edward. Ellen had gone ahead to attend a children's class taught by Mrs. Winters before the service.

She cast a glance at Edward, who was stretching his neck to one side. "Did you sleep well?"

He straightened and said, "Yes."

"Really? And your neck isn't bothering you?"

"Just a little stiff."

"I'd feel better if you let me sleep on the settee and you took the bed. We could ask Tucker to come tomorrow and help you move my furniture from the rooms above the shop to your home." She paused, wondering what he would think of her next suggestion. "We could set up my bed in Ellen's

115

room. There's ample space there. I could share with her."

Edward stopped, forcing her to wait on him. "We talked about this. Ellen needs things to be as normal as possible. That doesn't mean for her aunt to sleep in one room, while her uncle sleeps in another."

Lily tilted her head to one side and met his gaze. "That's exactly what we are doing."

"But Ellen doesn't know it." He started to walk again.

"Not yet, but the way you snore, it's only a matter of time."

"The way I snore?" He turned toward her. "I don't snore."

"Loud enough to wake me in the middle of the night." She laughed. "I thought a wild animal had gone under the house to keep warm and found itself caught."

"That can't be true."

"Oh, yes. Like wild dogs growling a warning to anyone who dares to come near."

"Well, if Ellen asks, I'll tell her I was disturbing you and moved to the front room so you could rest."

Lily's laughter ended. It wasn't right for him to work hard all day and sleep on the floor at night. There had to be a better solution. She'd think of something.

The muted sounds of singing reached her as they approached the church door. She closed her eyes in silent prayer.

Lord, please give me friends here. Help me make a good impression on the people of Pine Haven.

No sooner had she settled on the bench next to Edward than the door creaked open again and clanged to a close. Ellen clomped up the middle aisle to her uncle's side. Lily glimpsed his disapproval in the glance he shot the little girl. Ellen shrugged her shoulders and began to sing with utter joy.

Lily shook her head and smiled at the girl's oblivion to the distraction her entrance caused. The wet bodice of Ellen's dress suggested she'd been to the well for a drink of water. The braids Lily had carefully fashioned after much disagreement that morning were loose. She looked as though she'd been playing tag instead of attending a Bible lesson.

Lily spotted her sister, Daisy, a few rows in front of her. Daisy held baby Rose in her lap and sat between her sons. Tucker sat on the end of the bench. She wasn't jealous of Daisy. Not really. Lily had a family now. She'd chosen to marry Edward. But the fact that he didn't love her was clear from the start. She stuffed the dreams of having

117

children of her own back into her heart and forced her attention on the service.

At least, that was her intention. Every time she shifted in the seat, she brushed against Edward's arm. She felt like a restless child trying, without success, to sit through the service without moving. The third time she bumped his shoulder, he looked down and captured her gaze with his. And there in that moment she stilled. The calm in his eyes poured peace into hers. At his discreet smile, she focused toward the front of the church and sedately took in the rest of the minister's sermon.

When the service ended, Lily and Edward were among the first of the congregation to make their way to the door. Reverend Dismuke shook her hand and welcomed her. His wife, Peggy, invited Lily to visit when she had time. Lily thanked them, complimented the minister on his message and descended the steps to stand in the churchyard while Edward excused himself to speak to someone about a job he was working on.

As the people came out of the small church, she looked down Main Street, taking in the sights of the new town that was now her home. Preparing the shop to open had kept her too busy to explore Pine Haven. During her first week, she'd only visited the doctor's office, the bank and the general store.

Of course, she'd been to the church and the hotel on her wedding day. Pleasure at the memory surprised her. Why would she smile at the thought of how her life had changed that day? Now her plans were gone. Replaced with their plans. Plans so vague they were yet to be made clear.

The vision of a handsome man in a leather apron manifested before her eyes. Only, instead of an apron, he wore his Sunday best.

Lily had been so lost in thought, she didn't notice Edward's approach. Even at midday the man cast a shadow over her small frame.

He tipped his hat. "Having pleasant thoughts?"

Her smile had betrayed her. "Just enjoying the day and surveying the town." Lily grabbed for any excuse to keep from letting him know her thoughts were of him. He couldn't know that. "It was a lovely service."

He smiled in agreement. This handsome churchgoer wasn't the same man who had carried her across the threshold. In midair, with strong arms. Against a broad chest. The man she'd seen this week was as strong as his stature. This Edward had a softness in his eyes.

Ellen stood beside him, holding his hand and frowning up at Lily.

"What did you learn in class today, Ellen?" Lily twisted the cords of her reticule around the fingers of her gloves as she spoke.

"Stuff about God."

Edward gave Ellen a telling look.

Lily tried again. "What exactly did you learn? About God's love? Or a particular Bible story?"

The girl pointed at Lily's reticule. "You tied your hands in a knot."

"Oh, my." Lily pulled the cords in vain. The knots grew tighter as she tugged.

"May I?" Edward reached a tentative hand toward her.

"No, thank you. I'll get it." She continued to struggle with the cords.

Ellen blurted out, "I want to go play."

"Do not interrupt, Ellen." Edward reached for Lily's hands. "Please."

She relented and held out her hands. The cords had tied her gloves together. "I do seem to be making it worse."

Dust flew up and scattered on Lily's shoes and skirt as Ellen kicked the ground at her feet.

"Ellen, be still. You'll soil Aunt Lily's

dress." Edward didn't look up as he worked with the mass of tangles. His large hands made the heavy cords of the reticule seem tiny.

"There you go." He released the last of the knots and backed away, slipping his hands into the pockets of his trousers. He stared over her shoulder and asked, "Tell me. Did you get everything set up so you can open tomorrow?"

Was he as uncomfortable as she? When they worked together, they kept busy. This was the first occasion for them to be together as a family in the community. Their first day of rest and worship.

Ellen was clearly not enjoying herself. She stood close to Edward, arms folded, pouting while she waited for permission to leave them.

"I'm almost ready. There are a couple of things to do before you bring the hat stands in the morning." Lily studied Edward's profile. Today he was clean shaven. His brown hair curled behind his ears a bit. His shirt was not new, but it was clean. The brim of his well-worn hat shaded his face.

Daisy and Tucker approached them with their growing family. The twins asked to go run and play with the other children while the adults talked.

"Okay, boys, but don't go far. Your momma's got lunch ready for us at home." Tucker waved the boys away.

"We'll stay close!" James, the older twin, answered for both boys and tugged on his brother's arm. "Come on, John. They won't think we're coming if you don't hurry up." John took long, awkward strides to stay upright as James dragged him away.

"Can I go?" Ellen pulled on Edward's elbow.

"Just for a few minutes."

"Thanks!" She pivoted on one heel and lifted the other leg to run.

"Not so fast, young lady." Edward put a hand on her shoulder and turned her to face Lily. "You haven't answered the question about your Bible lesson."

"It was about family." Ellen jerked to look at him.

"What about family?" Edward's voice was deep and even.

Ellen twisted her face to Lily and drew in a deep sigh.

"Answer the question or go to the wagon without playing," Edward prodded.

"Okay, okay. Just let me think a minute." Ellen chewed her bottom lip and her eyebrows twisted toward one another. Lily could almost see the wheels of her mind turning.

In an instant Ellen's eyes opened wide, and she held up one finger to touch the corner of her mouth. "It was about honoring your momma and papa. And since I don't get to see mine, I didn't want to hear it. I went outside and played by the water till it was time for church." A curt nod of her head, and Ellen flew away so fast Edward couldn't catch her.

Lily met Edward's unhappy gaze. "She's really hurting." She watched Ellen catch up to the boys.

"This is what I was afraid would happen. She's lashing out in pain because she doesn't know how to handle not knowing where her folks are."

"We'll get her through it." Lily put her left hand on his sleeve. Then she saw Daisy slip a thoughtful glance at Tucker. Oddly, Edward hadn't seemed to mind. He actually turned toward her when she put her hand on his sleeve. She jerked it away and held the offending reticule with both hands.

A smile turned up one corner of his thin lips. His dark eyes danced. She could see her embarrassment reflecting in their depths. He was enjoying her discomfort. Too much.

Daisy chimed in then. "Edward, will you

and Ellen join us for the afternoon? Lily promised when she arrived on Monday that she'd spend her first Sunday with us at the farm. We'd love to have you."

"Thank you for the invite, but I think Ellen needs my attention today. It's been a busy week. That will probably explain part of her poor behavior earlier." He nodded at the group. "Y'all have a nice afternoon."

"Well, you and Ellen are welcome anytime. We'd love to have you out real soon." Daisy handed baby Rose to Tucker.

Tucker smiled at his daughter. "I'll bring Lily back to town this evening, Edward." He put an arm around his wife, and they walked toward their wagon.

Lily had looked forward to spending time with Daisy and her family, but it didn't seem right to leave Edward to deal with Ellen alone. Not when that was their agreement.

"Are you certain? I can stay."

"You go. I'm going to try to help her come around to understanding our new arrangement. A little resistance at first was to be expected." He looked across the church yard to where the children played. "It's time for her to accept things now."

"Are you going to talk to her about her parents?" Lily knew it would be difficult.

Edward shook his head. "I won't tell her anything unless I know for certain it's true." He looked into her eyes. "Thank you for offering to stay with us. You go enjoy your family. Maybe Ellen will be in a better mood by the time you return."

"I'll pray for you. She's a strong-willed soul. It won't be easy for her to accept me as long as she's holding out hope for her parents to return."

"She'll adjust. It'll take time, but she will."

Lily watched him walk away with a heart heavy with thoughts of his sister. She wished she could do something to mend the pain he and Ellen shared. Braiding hair and cooking meals wasn't enough to make up for the loss the two of them were bearing. She prayed that somehow his sister and brother-in-law would return.

If they did, would Edward still want her to be his wife?

Edward sat on his porch and whittled. Ellen played with her handkerchief doll in the cabin behind him. Through the barely open window, he could hear her cooing and pretending to coax the doll to sleep. She hummed the song her mother had sung to her as a babe.

The afternoon sun had settled low on the

horizon when he saw Tucker's wagon coming up the road. At a distance he recognized Lily by the hat she'd worn to church.

He was glad she had family in the area. He couldn't fathom why her father had sent her to Pine Haven alone. Lily's reputation wouldn't have been compromised if her father had been here. But would he have been able to convince her to marry him and care for Ellen if she hadn't been concerned about what people thought of her?

Tucker slowed his wagon as he neared Edward's cabin. It was built to face a lane that ran beside his shop. The back of the cabin butted up close to the side of his shop, leaving just enough space to prevent the cabin from catching fire if there was ever an accident with the forge. The porch lined the front of the cabin and sat perpendicular to the main road. He enjoyed sitting outside in the evening after being closed in all day with the fire and metal of his work. It wasn't always possible in the winter, but sunshine had warmed the mild day.

"Evening, Tucker. Lily." Edward stood and dropped the small horse he was whittling onto the table by his chair. He stepped off the porch to help Lily from the wagon.

"Good evening to you." Tucker pulled the brake as the wagon came to a stop. "Not as cold as I thought it'd be. I need to get Mack shoed if you've got time this week."

"Be glad to. Just let me know when." Edward answered Tucker, but his gaze went beyond his friend to rest on Lily. She sat with her back straight. Her coat was buttoned all the way up, and she tugged at the wide ribbon of her hat. He smiled at how the color matched her eyes. He was certain it was intentional.

Tucker spoke and drew his attention. "I'm coming to town late tomorrow morning with Daisy. She wants to visit the shop on Lily's first day. Can I bring him by on the way in and leave him with you?"

"That'll be good." Edward watched as Lily continued to avoid looking at him. Was she uncomfortable with all men, or just him?

"First thing in the morning I've got some business to handle for Lily." He offered his hand to her as she moved to the edge of the wagon seat.

"Thank you." Lily gave him little more than a glance as she spoke. "I trust you were able to complete my order." Her eyes challenged him.

"Remember I promised you six stands tomorrow. The rest will be done by the end of the week." He released her hand, and they backed away from the wagon.

"Please don't be late. The windows will have to be dressed before I can open."

"I won't be. You just make sure you're ready. In my experience, it's not usually a woman waiting on a man, but rather the exact opposite." He tried not to grin at her, but the temptation to taunt her was irresistible. Her cheeks brightened at his words. He could almost see the wheels turning in her mind for something to say. No doubt, she'd thought of several things but was weighing the right choice.

"Perhaps your experiences have been with the wrong sort of woman."

Yes, she'd chosen well. Not the nicest statement, but the one that brought the most reaction. Probably her first thought.

"I'm not in the habit of associating with the wrong sort of woman."

"So you do admit you are in the habit of associating with women." She was smirking now. How had she gotten the upper hand in a conversation about when he would deliver an order?

"Uncle Edward? Can you come inside? I need you." Ellen's voice broke into the conversation through the window.

"In a minute, honey," he said over his shoulder without looking back.

Ellen tugged the window until it opened

128

wide. "It's important. I can't do it by myself." There was no real emergency, but a childish urgency in her words. He watched her stare at Lily. Did Lily threaten his niece's peace of mind? He'd hoped his talk with her after lunch would ease the tension between Ellen and Lily, but it seemed to have had the opposite effect.

"I'm coming, Ellen. Just as soon as I finish my business with Mr. Barlow."

The distant sound of hammering came from the direction of the main intersection in town.

Tucker indicated the noise with a nod of his head. "Have they been at that all afternoon?"

"Pretty much." Edward's distaste for working on Sunday was surpassed only by his disappointment that the town council was permitting a saloon to be built in the center of the growing town. "I wish they weren't building the place at all, much less working on the Lord's Day."

"Everything that comes to town because of the railroad isn't good for us." Tucker shook his head. "We'll have to pray for God to keep our community safe."

"That, and make sure Sheriff Collins stays on top of any riffraff who try to settle here," Edward agreed.

"Surely, the good people of Pine Haven will outnumber any new folks who try to change the community." Lily's pinched expression showed her reluctance to believe evil could find a home in her new town.

"We do now. But it'll take prayer and courage to keep the sort of evil that comes with a saloon from pollutin' the town." Edward wished he could be as naive as Lily. Life had taught him hard lessons. Sadly, they were lessons she, too, would learn in time.

"Uncle Edward? Are you coming?" Ellen's voice rang through the open window, her tone impatient.

"I'll see you in the morning, Edward." Tucker released the brake.

"If I'm not here, just leave Mack. I'll get right on it when I get back."

"Good night, Edward. Good night, Lily. Ellen." Tucker tipped his hat at the ladies.

"Bye, Mr. Barlow." Ellen stood framed in the open window, her hands on the sill. She sent a look to Lily that Edward was sure she hadn't intended for him to see.

Tucker steered the horses forward and pulled the wagon away from Edward's porch. Edward didn't move to go inside until Lily and the pretty hat disappeared through the front door. The last thing Ellen needed was to feel that he'd overlooked her by allowing himself to be distracted by Lily.

Lord, help me not to focus on what's not good for me. You know I get in more trouble than I can handle that way.

He pulled the front door open to find Ellen back at play with her doll, whatever assistance she'd needed earlier forgotten. Something about Lily didn't sit right with his niece. Over the past few months, he'd determined that nothing — and no one — would put Ellen at risk. She was his responsibility until her parents returned. No amount of curiosity or intrigue surrounding a petite blonde lady would move him to violate the promises he'd made to his sister and himself — not even if that lady was his wife.

Lily came into the front room, her hat and coat gone. "Have you two eaten supper?"

Ellen pretended she didn't hear the question, but Edward saw her cut her eyes at Lily. He put a hand on the girl's head and ruffled her hair. "No. We had a big lunch today. I was just about to see what I could round up for a light supper."

Lily was already tying on an apron. "How about some scrambled eggs and toast?"

"Sounds good to me." He turned to Ellen. "How about you, Ellen?"

She didn't look up. "I don't care." Her voice was rife with tension.

"Okay, then." Lily turned her back to them and put the cast iron skillet on the stove. "Eggs and toast for Edward, bread and milk in her room for Ellen." She pulled a bowl off the shelf and began to crack eggs into it.

Ellen's mouth dropped open. She looked at him and then at Lily. "But . . ."

"No buts." Lily didn't look away from her task. "We warned you that your manners would be polite or you would eat bread and milk in your room." She pulled the bread to her and began to slice thick pieces of toast.

"Uncle Edward." Ellen came to tug on his sleeve. "Don't make me go to my room. It's too early. I want to play some more."

He could feel Lily's gaze on him when she retrieved the butter from the table. He couldn't risk siding with Ellen and under-mining Lily's new authority. Parenting was hard. Being fair and wise wasn't easy. There weren't always absolute answers. He would do the best he could. "It's your choice, Ellen. You know the rules. If you are disrespectful, you choose to go to your room."

The little girl stood, palms up, eyes wide. "I can't believe this."

Lily turned then. "If you do not change

your tone, you will have water with your bread. Disrespect for your elders will not be tolerated in our home."

Ellen stamped her foot. "It's not your home! It's my home!" She turned, ran into her room and slammed the door.

"Ellen, come back here." Edward called after her, but there was no response.

"I think we best give her time to calm down." Lily stood, wiping her hands on the apron. "Did something happen today that I'm unaware of?"

"I had a talk with her. I hoped it would make things better. She feels threatened by you." He shook his head. "I'm not sure what to think of it."

"Did she ask about her parents?" Lily's voice was barely more than a whisper.

"Yes. I tried to be vague, but she kept pressing."

The butter in the skillet started to crackle on the stove. Lily whipped the eggs with a fork and poured them into the pan. "How did you handle that?"

He came close to keep Ellen from overhearing their conversation. "I told her we have to pray for them, that they were sick and had been to the doctor. I didn't have the heart to tell her no one knows what happened after that."

"Poor child." She stirred the eggs. "If I'd known, I wouldn't have been so firm."

"You had no way to know. And, even so, she must be respectful."

"Yes, but we've got to show mercy in her situation. She'll never listen to me if she thinks I'm unkind."

"You were not unkind. You were trying to teach her."

"There's a time and place for everything. And when you're worried about your parents being far away and sick, it's not a time to go to bed with bread and water." Lily scooped the eggs out of the pan and onto a plate of toast.

"You go comfort her." Lily cracked more eggs and dropped them into the bowl. "I'll fix her something to eat. Tell her you'll read to her after supper. That always calmed me when I was a girl missing my mother."

He left her at the stove and went into Ellen's room, marveling that Lily would dismiss the poor treatment his niece had thrust on her and then cook a meal and offer comfort. Even so, he'd see that Ellen apologized before the meal.

Lily was exactly what Ellen needed. If only he could convince Ellen to let Lily care for her.

CHAPTER SEVEN

Lily admired the row of newly made hats lined up on her workbench. This might be Texas, a land known for hard work and strength, but Lily didn't believe there was a woman alive who didn't want to be feminine and look pretty. Even her sister Jasmine, who loved to ride the range and tend cattle, liked a fancy hat now and again. Lily would soon see if the women of Pine Haven would appreciate her offerings.

Concern for how to reach Ellen had combined with excitement over opening her shop and kept her from sleeping the night before. She'd awakened early and left breakfast for Edward and Ellen. She had to get everything just as she wanted in the shop. In her best dress she watched the hands of the clock creep slowly toward the hour of opening. Except for the windows — their shades pulled low waiting for Edward's arrival — she was ready.

No one coming today would see any evidence of last week's fire. Edward had worked quickly on the structure, and she'd worked long hours to make new stock.

Hoping the normalcy of the activity would calm her nerves, Lily decided to busy herself by creating another hat. She pinned two long feathers above the brim. Turning it from side to side, she decided to follow her first instincts and add a small tuft of silk net organza. She reached for her scissors just as the front bell announced a visitor.

"I'm coming." She set the hat on her workbench and brushed bits of thread and ribbon from her skirt. They floated to the floor to join the kaleidoscope of colors she'd used to make her inventory.

Lily stepped through the doorway into the front of the shop. "I thought you'd never get here." She stopped behind the glass case. With the windows covered, the dim room cast the face of her giant visitor in shadow.

"Hello to you, too." Edward approached her. He carried a display stand in one hand. He set it on the case and watched her face. "I finished."

Lily's mouth dropped open. She lifted a hand and traced the base of the delicate stand with her fingers. It was fashioned into a leaf. From the center of the leaf rose a stem. On each side of the stem, at different heights, additional leaves arched outward. Lily's hand followed the stem to touch the top of the stand. Thin metal curled to form a calla lily. The pistil in the center, perfectly shaped, completed the work of art.

"I can't believe it." The words came out like a soft breeze. "This is nothing like the picture I showed you."

"If you don't like it, you don't have to use them." Edward's response snapped Lily from her bewilderment.

"It's amazing! I've never seen anything so beautiful."

"Are you sure you like it?" Doubt played in his eyes.

"I'm positive. I just don't know what to say." Lily put up a hand to her cheek and felt the warmth of her blush. She was moved almost to tears by the beauty of his work. "I never imagined this. I don't know how to thank you." She moved her fingers to cover her lips and shook her head slowly back and forth. After several moments she tore her gaze from the beautiful display and lowered her hand.

"I was worried you wouldn't be able to finish."

"I had a slow couple of days." Edward

backed up and nodded his head in the direction of the door. "Do you want to see the others?"

Lily eyed the stand again. "Of course." She crossed the boarded floor and went through the door he held open for her. They approached the back of his wagon, and he threw back the edge of a heavy canvas to reveal more of the beautiful stands, each nestled in the bed of straw. Varied heights and length of leaves, balanced on unique bases.

"I thought you might want the stands to reflect the concept of Lily's Millinery and Finery, even when you removed a hat to show a customer." Edward spoke from beside her as Lily took in the sight of his craftsmanship. "You can hang gloves or hankies on the leaves. I thought you might get more use of your shop space that way."

"What a wonderful idea." She was touched by his thoughtfulness. He may have been overworked and stressed to the limit by raising his niece alone, but his creativity wasn't diminished.

A sudden movement and high-pitched sneeze drew their attention to the far edge of the canvas near the seat of the wagon. The sound of metal snapping accompanied the sneeze.

"Ellen?" Edward spoke the child's name slowly and deliberately. His eyes narrowed in on the exact spot that now stirred beneath the canvas.

A whisper was his only answer. "Yes, Uncle Edward?"

He pulled the canvas from the wagon and exposed Ellen's hiding place behind his seat. "Get up, child."

"I'd rather not, if it's all the same to you." Ellen met his gaze without cowering. Lily could see the bravery to stand her ground was a show of spirit and not outright defiance.

"It's not the same to me." Edward lowered his chin and pinned her with his stare.

Lily watched the struggle between the two strong-minded people. Even though she'd only met them days before, she had seen firsthand the contest of wills that took place daily in their home. She was certain her marriage to Edward was the source of much of their recent conflict.

Ellen stood without moving from her spot. The hem of her calico dress almost hid the broken display stand at her feet. The edge of a leaf stuck through the hay that lined the wagon and hung on the lace of her small boot. She frowned at the offending leaf.

"It wouldn'a broke if you'd let me come

with you in the first place." Her already full lower lip protruded farther.

"I didn't want you to come because I didn't want anything to get broken." Edward stepped around the lowered gate on the back of the wagon and retrieved the broken stand. He pulled the leaf free from her laces. "Tell Aunt Lily you're sorry."

Ellen jerked her head in Lily's direction. The pouting mouth became a snarl. "It ain't hers yet. She ain't paid for it. I'll tell *you* I'm sorry, but it ain't got nothin' to do with *her.*"

Lily almost expected the child to spit as a way to punctuate her distaste at the idea.

"Ellen. Apologize this minute." Edward's voice brooked no argument, but Lily saw a challenge fly through Ellen's eyes before she turned back to Lily.

"I am so very sorry to have broken my uncle Edward's work." Ellen twisted up her mouth and cocked her head to one side. The saccharine in her voice spoke of bitterness Lily understood now. Having lost her own mother at the age of five, she had known the importance of her father's attention and the mounting jealousy from even a hint that someone would take it away. She imagined Ellen must feel the same way about her treasured uncle.

140

"I'm sure he can repair it, Ellen." Lily watched the girl's pride swell at Lily's words.

"You bet he can. He's the best blacksmith in Texas. Probably in the whole United States." Ellen gave a curt nod to emphasize her opinion. "I ain't never seen him turn down a job 'cause it was hard. He can make or fix anything."

"I imagine you're right." Lily smiled at the little girl standing like a statue in the back of the wagon. "These stands are beautiful and much fancier than what I ordered." Lily was beginning to realize Ellen's gruffness came from a place of deep pain. A pain Lily understood. "Would you like to come inside and have a look around?"

The little girl's brown eyes looked to Edward. "What do you think? Do you need help toting all this in?" There was an apparent reluctance to respond to Lily, but a child's curiosity about what was happening inside the shop must have prompted Ellen to stow away in the wagon in the first place.

"That depends on you, Ellen. Will you be careful?" Edward's tone warned that she would be held accountable for her actions.

"Yes, sir." Ellen's confidence and determination didn't waver. She stepped toward the edge of the wagon closest to Edward.

"You will help me repair this after school

today." He held the pieces of the broken stand for Ellen to see, then put them under the seat to protect them from further damage.

"That'll be easy." Ellen grinned and wrapped her arms around his neck. "Now help me down, so I can see what she's done to Momma's shop."

Edward hoisted Ellen to the ground. "It's Aunt Lily's shop now."

"She's gonna have a hat store here, but it's still Momma's shop." A frown clouded her dark eyes. Ellen spoke to Edward but turned her head to Lily. "In my heart it always will be."

Recognizing the challenge, Lily said, "Your mother picked a wonderful building for a business. Come inside and see what I've done so far."

Edward called Ellen out of her reverie as she stood, hands on her hips, eyes drawn together, watching Lily's back disappear inside the shop.

"Take a stand with you. If you're going to help, you can start by helping me unload the wagon." He handed her one of the smaller stands and turned to pick up two of the largest ones. "And mind your manners. Lily has worked hard here, and we need to

142

respect her efforts."

"She better not mess up Momma's shop. One day, Momma's coming back, and we're gonna open a bakery here." Ellen stepped onto the porch. "That's all I got to say about it."

"That's all you better say about it, or you'll be having a long conversation with me later. Now go inside and be nice." Edward winked at her to soften his words. He took a deep breath and braced himself before they entered the shop together.

He had no idea what had just transpired at the wagon, but he had a feeling Ellen may have met her match with Lily. He was training Ellen to be strong. He wanted her to stand up for what she believed in. He didn't want her to be weak in any way. But, given her attitude toward Lily, he needed to work on finding a balance to include teaching her to be kind.

Edward and Ellen stopped just inside the door and took in everything. Lily had arranged her wares with care. A large round table stood in the center of the room. The wood was polished down to the ornately carved pedestal. Against one side wall stood a hall tree with a large mirror. Lily had placed a chair in front of it. He assumed she'd seat her guests there while they tried on her hats. A long chest stood against the opposite wall.

Ellen broke the silence. "Where do you want me to put this? It's kinda heavy."

"You can put them all on the floor by the windows. I'll arrange them in a few minutes." Lily spread her arms wide. "What do you think, Ellen?"

Ellen set the small stand down with a thud and went to look in the mirror.

"Remember to be careful, Ellen." Edward set his load near the opposite window.

"I didn't break nothin'." Ellen turned to Lily. "Why you got such a big mirror? Don't you know what you look like?"

"Ellen." Edward sent her a warning glare.

"It's for my customers." Lily approached the mirror and met Ellen's gaze in the reflection. "Seeing how a new hat looks on you is important before you buy it. Sometimes a lady wants to see how the color looks with her eyes. Or she may want it to match her hair or dress."

"Can't see why you don't just put on something to keep your head warm in the winter and be done with it." Ellen stared at herself and tugged on the ribbons of her worn bonnet.

Lily seemed to hesitate a moment at Ellen's logic. Edward could see both of their faces in the mirror as he walked to the door to bring in more of the stands.

"You are right about a hat helping to keep you warm. But isn't it nice to have something to make you feel pretty, too?" Lily rested her hand on Ellen's shoulder.

"What good is pretty? Momma had lots of pretty hats, and she's gone."

"Ellen, let's not talk about that right now." Shocked by her outburst, Edward tried to silence her.

But Ellen's tirade wasn't finished. "If she hadn't been so worried about being pretty and having fancy things, maybe her and Pa could have stayed here and not left me." The girl dashed out of the door.

Lily stood with her hand over her mouth. She slowly turned to Edward. "I'm so sorry. I didn't mean to upset her." She lowered her hand to the base of her throat.

Edward silently scolded himself for noticing the delicate hand and the silkiness of golden hair draped across her shoulders. His niece had just run from the room after lashing out at Lily because she felt wounded anew by a reminder of the mother she felt had abandoned her.

Could he take away the hurt Ellen put in Lily's pain-filled eyes? That was a question he wasn't sure he wanted answered.

"I'm the one who should be apologizing. I'm sorry for Ellen's behavior." He looked through the window and watched as Ellen sat on the seat of the wagon and scrubbed tears from her cheeks with the back of her hand. He knew she hated to cry, especially in front of others.

He hoped he could explain. "You couldn't have known about my sister's dreams. When she was younger, all she wanted was to open a bakery. Cooking and serving others seemed to fulfill her. Then she married Wesley. Ellen was born the next year. Jane was so excited. She lived for Wesley and Ellen."

"She sounds like a lovely person."

"She was."

"I hope you aren't giving up on them." Lily's tone was almost pleading.

"I don't want to. I wish they'd never left."

"Why did they?"

Edward smirked a little at the memory. "Wesley wasn't the type to be content. Always wanted more. Got all dressed up in fancy clothes trying to impress people. At first, Jane didn't change. Then he had a small success with the hotel here in town. He convinced her they could make a real go of it in Santa Fe."

"Oh, my." Lily's voice was a faint whisper. "Poor Ellen." Pity filled her eyes.

146

He cleared his throat. As hard as he tried not to, he still choked up at the possibility that Jane might never come home. "I best get the rest of the stands off the wagon and get Ellen to school."

Lily gave him a sad smile, one that said she understood.

It took several trips to the wagon as he dug the stands out of the straw and brought them inside. Edward heard Lily moving around in the stockroom while he unloaded the wagon. He set the last stand on the floor and called out a goodbye. Because she'd insisted, he placed a bill on the glass case. Her soft voice caused him to stop as he reached the door.

Lily looked everywhere in the room but at him. "Please explain to Ellen that I didn't mean to bring up bad memories for her."

"I will. She'll be fine. She's learning to be tough. Life deals you a lot of hard things. It's best to learn that when you're young. Keeps you from being disappointed later in life."

"Not always, Edward. Not always." A depth of sadness seemed to rise from her heart and fill the rich blue eyes. Lily picked up his bill. "If you'll give me a moment, I'll pay you." She disappeared into the store-room again.

When Lily returned, Edward took the bills she offered and stuffed them into his pocket without counting them as she backed away from him.

"I guess I'll see you at supper." He hated the distance he sensed between them. They both wanted the best for Ellen, yet at every turn the child tried her hardest to rebuff Lily's efforts.

"I may be late. It depends on how busy I am today."

"I'll try to have the rest of the stands by the end of the week."

"That'll be fine." She was already moving toward the windows to arrange the hats in preparation for opening the shop.

He lifted his hat and opened the door. "And again, I'm sorry for Ellen's words. She was unkind."

"I understand." Lily stood still as he closed the door behind him.

Edward climbed into the wagon beside a silent Ellen. Lifting the reins, he released the brake and sent the horse forward.

Sad blue eyes threatened to haunt him for the rest of the day. As he and Ellen repaired the broken stand that afternoon, he saw visions of the gentle creature working in a shop, building a dream to succeed.

When Lily came home late that evening,

Ellen was ready for bed. She had done her homework and chores and was playing quietly in her room.

"How was your day?" he asked when she closed the door.

"Long." He watched as she pulled off her gloves.

"Did you have a lot of trade?" He went to the stove and uncovered the bowl of soup he'd kept for her. He put it on a tray and added a cup of coffee.

"If you don't mind, I'm very tired. I'd like to go straight to bed." She looked toward Ellen's room. "Is there anything I can do to help with Ellen before I do?"

He wondered what had happened. This was not the response he expected after the excitement she'd shown over opening. "Ellen is ready for bed. Everything she needs is done."

She unbuttoned her coat, and he saw the slump of her shoulders.

"What about you, Lily? Is there anything I can do for you?" He indicated the tray. "I made some soup."

A tired smile did nothing to lift her face. "Thank you."

"You must be exhausted. Would you like me to carry the tray into the bedroom for you? I can put it on the table by the chair.

149

You can relax and eat at your leisure."

"That would be perfect."

She stood in the center of the room while he took the tray to her room. When he came out again, he stopped in front of her. "You know you can tell me anything."

Lily put a hand on his arm. Its lightness reminded him that though she was a strong woman, she was also a delicate creature. "I just need to rest right now."

"I'll say good night, then." He backed away so she could walk into her room. "Ellen, come say good-night to Aunt Lily."

The little girl came to the doorway of her bedroom. "Good night."

Lily's smile was genuine this time. "Good night, Ellen. I pray you will sleep well tonight."

Ellen stared after her as Lily went into the room and closed the door. "What's wrong with her? She looks sad."

"She does, doesn't she?" Edward watched the door, wondering what happened today to bring this normally cheerful — if not fiery — woman to such a melancholy state. "Let's get you tucked into bed. You can say a prayer for her tonight, too."

He led Ellen to her room, promising himself that he'd spend extra time in prayer for both of them. He'd put wings on those prayers tomorrow and try to find out what had gone wrong today. Maybe it would be something he could remedy.

CHAPTER EIGHT

No customers yesterday didn't mean today wouldn't be good. Last night she'd felt guilty going to bed without telling Edward about the day, but she didn't have the heart to expose her failure to anyone, especially him. After all he'd done to assure her success, it didn't seem right to tell him no one had entered the shop except for her sister. Daisy had dropped in for a brief visit and promised to come again later in the week.

Lily heard the bell and slid off her stool in the storeroom. She was determined to be hopeful.

Lord, please let this be a customer. I can't make a success of this business without Your help.

"It's me." Ellen stood just inside the front door, holding the display stand she'd broken.

"Oh. Hello, Ellen." Lily came around the display case.

"Uncle Edward made me bring you this." She held out the smallest of the stands Edward had made. "He said you prob'ly need it."

Lily reached out to receive the stand. "Thank you. It looks wonderful. You can't even tell it was ever broken." Lily placed the stand in the center of one of the front windows. She had hoped to have the stand today but had set one of the hats and a pair of gloves in the spot just in case it wasn't finished until the other stands were ready. She picked up the hat and set it on the stand, tying the ribbon in a loose bow.

"What do you think?" Lily asked Ellen, who still stood by the door. The little girl's eyes missed nothing as she took in the shop. Like her uncle, she was observant.

"Not too bad," she finally answered, "if you like all this frilly stuff." Ellen's answer may have been meant as a rebuff, but Lily caught a glimpse of wonder in her face.

"Most ladies do like pretty things." Lily held the gloves she wanted to display with the hat. "Would you like to hang these on the leaf? Your uncle's idea to make these stands hold more than one item was wonderful."

"No, thanks." Ellen gave a cursory perusal of the shop and turned on her heel. "Uncle

153

Edward sent me over as soon as I finished my chores. I've got to get to school."

"I'll be sure to thank him when I get home." Lily moved to the doorway as Ellen walked out.

"He's just doing his job. That's how he makes money to take care of me."

"I know you must be proud of him. He's a good uncle." Lily tried again to speak to Ellen without the tension that seeped into their conversations.

"The best. He only has time for me. Nobody else." A stubborn tilt to her head made Ellen cuter than she knew. The fierce protection was precious but unnecessary. Lily had no interest in taking Edward's time from her. Luther Aarens had made certain that Lily had no interest in a man. Their failed engagement, the way he'd treated her, was the reason she was determined to keep her heart as her own.

Perhaps there was a way to put the child at ease.

"I'm sure you're right. I felt the same way about my father after my mother died when I was a little girl."

"Your momma died?" The anger seemed to drain out of Ellen. She wilted before Lily's eyes.

In a soft voice, Lily answered. "She did. I

was just a little younger than you are. I still miss her."

"You do?" Ellen whispered when she looked up at Lily.

Time stood still as a little girl and a grown woman shared the pain only someone in their situations could understand, each remembering a love made more dear by its loss. Death had stolen one mother. A lust for life had taken the other.

Lily nodded her head softly. "I do." She bent at the waist so she could be face-to-face with Ellen. "The love of your momma stays with you forever. It's the part of her that lives in your heart. I think it's a way God lets us keep them close."

"I do feel it." Ellen's eyes were filled with tears now. A smile pulled at one corner of her mouth. "Especially when I'm playing with the doll she made me." She reached into the pocket of her pinafore and pulled out the worn doll Lily had seen so many times. "Momma said if I practiced with my doll, then I'd learn how to be a good momma, too. She said her momma made her a doll like this, and that's how she knew how to take care of me." Sobs broke from the child, and Lily wrapped her in tender arms.

She murmured softly. "What a wonderful

gift she gave you. She taught you how to love."

Ellen sniffed and backed away. "But she left me. I must not be the kind of girl a momma can love. I don't think I know how to love nobody now. Except Uncle Edward." She wiped her sleeve across her face to dry her eyes.

"I've seen how you protect your doll." Lily pushed Ellen's hair away from her face and cradled the small cheeks in her palms. "Protection is one way to show love."

"It is?" Scrunched eyebrows formed a disbelieving frown.

"It is. I'm sure your mother trusts your uncle Edward to protect you. She showed how much she loves you when she picked him to take care of you. His protection is the way he shows you he loves you. It's the way you love your doll." Lily gave her a smile and winked. "It's also how you love him. That's why you've been trying to protect him from me."

"How'd you know?" Ellen backed up, surprised.

"Because I did it to my papa when I was a little girl. If ever a lady got close to my papa, I'd get between them and make sure she knew my papa was busy taking care of me and my sisters. That he didn't want

156

another lady because there was no lady like my momma."

"Did you get in trouble like I do?" Ellen's childlike honesty spoke without reservation.

"I did." Lily stood to her full height again but kept a comforting hand on Ellen's shoulder.

"Did another woman get your papa?" Wide eyes seemed to fear the answer to this question.

"No, Ellen. No other woman did."

"So you protected him from all of them?"

"After a while I learned Papa didn't need me to protect him. He's a big strong man who would never do anything to harm me or my sisters. He loved us so much that he would protect us."

"Uncle Edward is strong. He's big and strong." Pride burst from her young face.

"That he is. So don't you worry about protecting him, especially from me. I'm not going to try to take him from you. I understand how you feel. And I've learned enough about your uncle Edward to know he'll always protect you. You don't have to worry."

"But you married him. People get married 'cause they're in love. Uncle Edward must love you a lot more than me. He didn't even know you good, and he married you."

Did she dare to share the secret of her marriage with this child? "Your uncle did marry me for love. One of the reasons he married me was because he loves you."

The little face twisted in confusion. "I don't get it."

"He thought if he married me, you and I could be friends." She prayed she was helping by telling Ellen these things. "I was alone, and you have been missing your momma. He thought we could have each other while we wait to hear from your momma."

Lord, please bring Jane home. Don't let this be false hope I'm pouring into this little girl.

Ellen looked at the doll she clung to. Then she looked up at Lily. "I'm glad we talked."

"Me, too." Lily smiled.

"You're too pretty for me to stay mad at all the time. I was gettin' tired of having to say mean things to you."

"Thank you. I'm glad we got everything straight. Now we can be nice to each other." Lily stroked Ellen's hair, and her fingers caught in the knots that tangled the mass of brown waves. "You're very pretty, too, Ellen."

Pink tinted the girl's cheeks. "No, I'm not." She turned her face into one shoulder.

Lily reached under her chin and urged the

child's small face to the front. "Yes. You are." The words were kind and soft-spoken. "I'm sure you're as pretty as your momma. You go home and ask your uncle." With another smile, Lily chucked Ellen under the chin and urged her on her way.

"Make sure and tell Uncle Edward thank you, if you see him before I do." She waved as Ellen bounced off the porch onto the dirt below.

"I will." She returned the wave and called over her shoulder. "See you later, Aunt Lily."

Aunt Lily? Without being prompted? Hmm. Lily smiled at the sound of that. Perhaps she and Ellen could be friends, after all. It was nice to think there would be no more incidents of taunting from the girl.

If only Ellen's uncle didn't set her nerves on edge. Maybe that would come in time.

Not that it mattered. Making a success of her shop before her father and Jasmine arrived demanded all of her attention. After the shop was established, she'd be so busy she wouldn't have time to remember Ellen's words. *Uncle Edward must love you a lot.* Ellen was too young to understand why Lily and Edward had married.

So why did the thought gnaw at her spirit? Did part of her still long to be truly loved? Her determination not to disappear into the

159

background and be taken for granted had become a way to keep herself, and her heart, locked away from life.

Finding herself plunged into the middle of a new family had tilted her world on its axis. She had to be cautious to maintain her emotional equilibrium.

Edward nestled a small wooden horse in the straw-filled crate. He hadn't imagined his whittling would be an added source of income until Mrs. Croft had noticed one of the horses he'd carved for Ellen. Selling the toys to the general store kept him from feeling as though he was wasting the time he spent on his front porch. Time he used to think. The Lord knew he'd been doing a lot of that in recent days.

"Good morning, Stone." Edward turned to see Donald Croft in the open doorway.

"I was just on my way to see you." He put the last horse in the crate. "I got these done as quickly as I could. Thanks for letting me know you were running low."

Mr. Croft stepped into the blacksmith shop and picked up one of the horses. "Can't imagine how you do it. These are fast sellers. The kids love 'em." He moved the straw aside to survey the array of toys in the crate. "This oughta cover your tab and anything you may be needing for this week."

Liza Croft's shrill voice carried from the street outside. "Donald, where are you?"

"In here, Liza." The general store owner stepped nearer to the door and waved her inside.

"I declare, all I did was go into the bank for two minutes, and you disappeared." She came to stand beside her husband. "Well, aren't those the prettiest ones yet?" She picked up the smallest horse. "I'm going to put this one up for my niece. She'll love it."

With a swish of her ample skirt, she turned and went through the door into the street. She called over her shoulder. "Don't take too long, we're already late opening up today."

Mr. Croft shook his head. "It's a wonder I make a living at all. Some days she buys things faster than I can sell 'em."

Edward knew better than to comment. Mr. Croft might complain about his wife, but everyone in town knew it was a callous front to cover for the deep love he had for her.

Pulling the crate toward him, Mr. Croft spoke again. "I see your wife opened up shop yesterday."

Edward turned to look out the door at his building across the street. "I hope she's been busy."

Mr. Croft's face twisted into a frown. "I don't see how she can make a go of it with such a small selection. It's not like Milly Ledford's dress shop. Everybody wins in her case. I sell the fabric, and she makes the dresses. Hats and gloves don't seem to me to be a way to make a living." He looked out the doorway as a lady paused and looked at the hats in Lily's window before continuing on her way down the street. "See what I mean. I just don't think there's enough hat business in town to keep her open."

Edward straightened and took a step toward the door. "I hope she's successful. It's a help to me to have the place rented. And the town is growing."

Mr. Croft picked up Edward's crate. "Maybe. You never know. She'll need to offer a fine product is all I've got to say."

Edward grimaced inwardly. "Thanks for buying the horses."

"You're mighty welcome. Go ahead and work on some more carvings if you get the time. What about some kittens or puppies? The little girls might like those."

Edward nodded in agreement. "I'll see what I can do."

He walked to the front of the shop when

Mr. Croft left and saw Mrs. Dismuke, the reverend's wife, look in the window of Lily's shop. He caught a glimpse of Lily watching hopefully through the window.

When Mrs. Dismuke walked away, Lily dropped her head and stepped to the rear of the store. She looked back and saw him watching her just before she went into the storeroom. A shadow of disappointment crossed her face. Edward was not pleased at the way it made him feel. Her business was her responsibility, not his.

But her success would benefit him. At least that's what he told himself as he headed across the street.

The bell on the front door rang when he entered the shop.

"I'm coming," Lily called out as she stepped from the storeroom into the shop. "Welcome to Lily's Millinery and . . ."

The greeting died on her lips when she saw him in the doorway. He closed the door against the chill of the day and turned toward her, hat in hand.

"Oh, it's you." Disappointment rang in her voice.

"Good morning to you, too." Edward smiled to tease her.

"I'm sorry. I didn't mean to be rude." She looked past him through the windows. "I thought you were a customer."

"No need to apologize." His gaze took in her efforts. "You've done a fine job in preparing your shop." He nodded toward the hats in the window. "Quite a variety of colors and styles you've got there."

"Thank you." She adjusted the ribbon on the hat taking center stage on the tallest stand he'd made. "The display stands are wonderful. I'm certain they'll be a big boost to the reputation my shop will build as people discover I'm open for business." She shifted the gloves on the leaf below the hat. "They are sure to be a topic of discussion."

"I'm glad you're pleased." He pulled at his collar and shifted his weight from one foot to the other. "So the customers like them, too?"

"No one has said anything yet." She looked to the street again.

"Oh." He moved to the glass case in the back of the store. "Have you had any customers yet?" Her answer could explain her sullen mood from the night before.

"Not yet, but it's early. I've seen several ladies looking in the windows." Lily talked faster than usual. "Ladies take a while to make decisions. They like to look and ponder before they decide if they're interested. I'm sure they'll be coming in soon."

"Have you placed an advertisement? Most folks in town read the paper. It comes out once a week."

"I have a notice coming out in tomorrow's edition." The small snort that followed the statement surprised him. What had he said to get her dander up so?

"Well, you don't have to get all snippy. I was only trying to help."

"I'm not snippy." Lily forced a delicate cough. "There's been so much dust to clean up. I still have a little tickle in my throat." Was she stretching the truth by trying to cover the fact that she'd snorted at him?

He reached a hand out to a small hat, then withdrew it before he touched the yellow ribbon.

"Do you like it?" Lily walked behind the counter and picked up the straw creation. "I made it to match this one." She gestured to the coordinating larger hat. "I thought a mother and daughter might enjoy the pair." What was she thinking? Why would she speak to him about a mother and daughter wearing matching hats, when she knew he hadn't heard from his sister? He didn't need to be reminded of all that Ellen was missing.

Edward took a step back. "You're probably right."

"I'm sorry, Edward. I didn't mean to bring up a painful subject." Lily laid a hand on his arm.

"It's not a problem. I'm sure some little girl and her mother will love them." Another step back and her hand fell away from him. It just wouldn't be Jane and Ellen unless God brought his sister home safely.

He glanced over his shoulder to the street. "Well, I've got to get back to work."

"Please forgive me. I often speak without thinking. It's my worst trait. I really do try to control it." In all fairness, he knew she hadn't intended the words to hurt.

Edward held up a hand and interrupted her. "There's nothing to forgive, Lily. You're offering your wares to ladies who like this sort of thing." He moved toward the door and put his hat on, jamming it down a little farther than necessary. He wouldn't let himself react to Lily. He needed to bury his frustration over the disappearance of his sister.

Lily placed a hand on his arm again. He stared at her hand for a moment and then turned his face to hers.

He saw remorse in her eyes. "I really am sorry. I don't know why I always manage to say something that makes you uncomfortable."

He smiled a little then. "We'll get it sorted out." Over time they would resolve all the uncomfortable feelings. She'd grow accustomed to his ways, and he'd learn to understand her. What then? Eventually Ellen would grow up and start a life of her own. Would they be two friends sharing a home?

The sunlight coming through the windows dimmed, and he looked over his shoulder to see Mrs. Dismuke reaching for the door. Milly Ledford, the local dressmaker, stood behind her. Lily dropped her hand from Edward's arm and backed away.

Was she embarrassed to be seen close to him? Perhaps concerned they might misinterpret her hand on his arm as affection? Her face turned the slightest shade of pink.

Her next words to him confirmed his thoughts. "Thanks for stopping in." It was as though she were dealing with a customer or tradesman.

Edward chuckled and tipped his hat to the prospective customers. "Ladies." He turned back to Lily. "Lily." Unable to stop himself, he reached up and ran a finger down her warm cheek. "I'll see you at home later."

Lily lifted a hand to cover the trail of his

finger on her face. What on earth had possessed him to do that? And why was she so pleased that he had?

She had no time to ponder his amusement. Her first customers had arrived. Lily ushered the ladies into the shop. The glances the two ladies exchanged were obvious. It seemed the topic of their sudden marriage had not been forgotten. She set her mind not to care what anyone thought, as long as they bought hats.

"Good morning, Mrs. Dismuke. Mrs. Ledford." She lifted an arm to indicate the interior of the fresh space. "Please take a moment to look around."

"Call me Milly." The dressmaker smiled a warm greeting. "I've been dying to get in here and see what you have."

"Me, too. And call me Peggy. Your sister and I are dear friends." The reverend's wife held up a package. "I looked in the window earlier, but wanted to pick up this dress Milly made for me first. Do you think you might have a hat to match the color?"

"Let's open it up and see." As she untied the string holding the brown paper together, the bell jangled on the front door. Two more ladies entered the shop. "Welcome to Lily's Millinery and Finery. If you'd like to take a look around, I'll be with you as soon as I can."

Lily's heart skipped a beat. In just a few short minutes, she'd gone from wondering if anyone would come to having more customers than she could help at one time. She glanced through the front window and caught sight of Edward as he tied on his apron. His eyes might be smiling, but the distance made it difficult to be sure.

"Oh, look, Milly. I think this one will be perfect." Peggy Dismuke's delighted voice brought Lily back to the moment.

Bustling through the rest of her busy day gave Lily no time to think about the handsome blacksmith. But when she flipped the sign to close the shop and pulled down the shade, his image seemed to float in the room behind her.

She turned to survey the space. The floors needed to be swept, and many of the items needed to be straightened. The sight of several empty display stands made her heart smile. With energy she hadn't known she possessed, Lily set to work pulling stock from the back room and arranging more of her original creations in the shop.

Lily forced herself to stop before she was finished. The shop would have to wait while she fulfilled her obligations to Edward and

Ellen. There was supper to prepare and chores to do at home. She walked across the street, bundled against the brisk January evening.

"You're late." Edward sat at the table helping Ellen with her sums.

Not exactly a warm greeting. Lily shrugged out of her coat. "It was a busy afternoon. I've still got loads more work to do, but supper can't wait any longer."

Ellen dropped her pencil. "All done." She pushed her school things together in a stack and stood. "What's for supper?"

"I'm going to fry some slices of ham and boil some potatoes." Lily wrapped an apron around her skirt. "Would you like to help?"

"Sure!" Ellen carried her things to her room. "I'll be right back."

Edward watched Ellen leave. "What just happened?"

His surprise at Ellen's response almost made Lily laugh. "She's decided we can be friends."

"Oh, she did?" He added wood to the stove. "You'll have to tell me all about it."

Lily put a pot of water on to boil. "Not much to tell. We talked. Now she knows I understand her."

Ellen bounced back into the room. "What can I do? Fry the ham? Peel the potatoes?"

Lily chuckled at Ellen's eagerness. "Let's start with the basics and work up to knives and the stove on a night when I'm not in such a rush." Lily was peeling the potatoes. "You can set the table, and I'll let you pour the drinks. You can help me mix up the corn bread batter. I'll fry some small cakes on the stove."

The evening meal went without incident. It was refreshing to eat without wondering what might send Ellen into one of her moods. Lily admitted it was an added pleasure to watch Edward's disbelief at the change in the relationship between his niece and her.

"When we finish, I'll wash the dishes while you get ready for bed, Ellen." Lily needed to go back to the store for at least a couple of hours.

Edward pushed his chair away from the table. "That was a wonderful meal. Thank you, Lily." He tousled Ellen's hair. "And thank you, too, Ellen."

Ellen glowed under his praise. "I'm gonna learn real quick. I wanna be a good cook, so when Momma and Papa come to get me I can show them what a big girl I am now."

Edward stilled. The pain on his face showed how much he wanted Ellen to be able to do just that. "We'll keep praying, Ellen." He turned to Lily.

"I need to do a bit more work tonight." He picked up his hat.

"Um, I need to work tonight." She hadn't thought he wouldn't be around to get Ellen to bed.

"Why? You've been there all day. Can't it wait until morning?" He put the hat on and reached for his coat. He was talking to her, but he was preparing to walk out the door.

"What about me?" Ellen came out of her room in her nightgown. She still wore her braids and socks.

"Aunt Lily will be here with you." Edward shrugged his shoulders. "I'm sorry, Lily, but I didn't know you'd need the time, and I already promised a delivery first thing in the morning. I've got to finish."

Lily looked at him. "It's time for bed, Ellen." She opened the door. "I'll be in to read with you in a minute."

She stepped onto the porch, and Edward followed. "You promised that marrying you wouldn't keep me from running my shop." She folded her arms across her chest, not sure if it was because of the chill in the air or the stress between the two of them.

Edward was calm. He towered over her but didn't move to intimidate her. "And you promised to do all the things a mother would do for Ellen."

"I am." She swung her arms wide now. "I came to cook supper when I had more work to do."

"I'm sorry I didn't realize the kind of time you'd need in the evenings." He looked remorseful. "I need to get this order ready." He scuffed his boot against the boards of the porch. "If you'll watch her tonight, I'll make breakfast tomorrow, and you can go to the shop early."

She had a lot of work to do to be ready to open again tomorrow, but it wasn't wise to leave the child alone.

Ellen called from her room. "I'm ready to read now."

Edward waited for Lily's response.

"Oh, all right. I'll go in early tomorrow." She put a hand on the door. "But we need to iron out some details of how we're both supposed to get all our work done and take care of Ellen."

The child's voice rang out again. "Are you coming, Aunt Lily? I've got a storybook that Momma gave me."

"Thank you." Edward stepped off the porch. "Don't wait up. Just make sure the door isn't bolted, so I won't have to wake you."

He walked into the darkness without looking back. Lily wondered how hard the fight would be to maintain her independence. The promises were falling apart, and they'd only been married a week.

She'd take care of Ellen. But she'd take care of her business, too.

CHAPTER NINE

Edward stood in the bank at the teller's window on Wednesday morning. He sensed Lily's arrival before he turned away, cash in hand. He saw her before she saw him. A becoming touch of pink lit her cheeks. But he refused to concentrate on her beauty.

"I didn't expect to see you here this morning, Lily. I thought you'd be busy preparing for another busy day."

"I finished getting everything ready and had a couple of errands to run."

"Well, I'm glad you were able to take care of everything this morning." He'd been sorry to keep her from working the night before, but he'd had no choice.

Her small hand shot out and grasped his arm. The white glove was trimmed with tiny pearl buttons. He silently scolded himself for noticing the minute details.

"I was wondering if you could come by the shop later today." Lily's face was fresh and open as she waited for his reply.

"What is it you need?" Edward took a step back, and her hand fell. He folded his money and stuffed it into his shirt pocket.

"I have an idea for a sign for the shop." The feather on her hat danced near her eyes. It swooped forward from its perch and swept across the edge of her forehead. As soft as the feather looked, he knew her hair would be softer. If he kept being distracted like this, she'd visit him in his dreams tonight. What was the matter with him?

"I'm very busy today." His voice sounded gruff, but he didn't want everyone listening to their conversation. He could see the bank owner, Lester Bennett, watching from his desk behind the half wall separating the lobby from the rest of the bank.

Both gloves wrung the reticule she held. "Okay." Her voice was small compared to the exuberance it had held a moment earlier. "At your convenience." She looked toward the teller window. "I'll just be off, then. I've got to deposit the receipts from yesterday. I still have another errand before I open today." She reached into the reticule and pulled out a handful of bills.

"Lily, you shouldn't keep that kind of cash on hand overnight." Worried someone might realize she was alone in the shop and try to rob her, he felt it important to caution her.

The now-familiar stiffness of her posture returned. "I seem to remember it was your suggestion that I take care of the hat business and you would take care of the blacksmithing." With a slight lift of her chin she added, "I am willing to abide by your original suggestion. I'm quite capable of taking care of my business." With a sharp turn, her tiny feet tapped across the wooden floor to the teller window.

Edward lifted his eyebrows and pushed his hat farther down on his brow. What a stubborn woman. She frustrated and intrigued him at the same time. Her lips set together in determination were beautiful.

He spun around and headed outside. He stepped off the boards and onto the dust of the street and lifted a silent prayer.

Lord, she's a mite stubborn, but it'd be a shame for her to be hurt over it. If she won't listen to me, I hope You send someone she will listen to.

He walked across to his shop and swung the big front doors wide. When he turned to go inside, he saw Lily step out of the bank into the morning sunshine. She tugged her glove on and fastened the pearl button at her wrist. Pivoting toward the post office, she stumbled and almost lost her balance.

He was on the point of going to her aid when Winston Ledford came out of the bank and caught her by the elbow.

Seeing that man with his hand on Lily's arm sent a flash of anger through Edward's chest. He'd give him one second to let go.

Then Lily turned to Ledford and started a conversation. Edward wasn't close enough to hear their words. He stood speechless when she grasped the man's arm and nodded. She lifted the hem of her skirt with her other hand. Ledford took her hand from his arm and placed it on his shoulder before squatting at her feet. He reached toward her foot and paused.

What was she thinking? How dare she stand in the street with the saloon owner! And lift her skirt like that. She leaned on Ledford's shoulder for what seemed like an eternity, and then she backed away from him.

A smug look crossed the man's face as he stood and brushed his hands together. More words were exchanged, and Ledford dipped his head at Lily. Edward caught the moment Ledford saw him watching the scene.

Mr. Ledford eyed her, and the two continued talking.

Lily put up a gloved hand and touched the feather at her brow. Was she flirting with a saloon owner? What good could he do as her husband trying to guard her reputation if she insisted on this sort of behavior?

He heard Ledford laugh. A slight movement and Lily turned her attention across to the blacksmith shop. Edward couldn't prevent the scowl that crossed his face. She turned back to her conversation. He was fuming. Enough was enough. Just as he moved to step across the street, Ledford nodded his head at her and walked away.

Edward ignored the hand the man lifted in greeting to him. He slapped his work gloves against his thigh and turned to march into his shop. He wasn't sure what had just happened. But he was certain he'd speak to her about it, so it wouldn't happen again.

Just as soon as he calmed down enough to be civil.

After lunch, Lily sat in the workroom making yet another hat suitable for a lovely spring dress. Yellow daisies circled the ribbon she'd woven through the straw at the base of the hat just above the brim. She reached for a length of white ribbon with one hand as she turned the hat first one way and then another. The front bell rang.

"Coming," Lily called out and slid from her stool. Two young ladies waited inside the front door. She took in their dresses, such as they were — bare shoulders, and necklines plunged to places no lady would consider proper. The fabrics were sheer in places, and bows pulled up the fabric at intervals to make the short skirts even shorter, revealing a hint of colorful petticoats. The dresses weren't identical but were so much alike Lily knew they'd come from the same place. They hadn't been purchased locally.

She quickly recovered her composure. "How may I help you, ladies?"

Her customers looked at each other and grinned. The younger of the two spoke first. "Winston sent us to see you. Said you might have some things we'd be interested in." While she spoke, the lady's eyes perused the hats on the hall tree against the side wall. Lily didn't think she could be more than twenty years old. Her painted cheeks and lips made it hard to be sure.

The other lady looked toward the back of the store and the glass display case where Lily kept her most expensive offerings. The materials were too delicate to risk putting them out where customers and their children could handle them.

"I think I see just the thing for my new yellow dress." This lady was a little older than the first, perhaps closer to thirty. Her makeup creased in the lines around her eyes. Lily decided life must have treated the woman unkindly.

"Winston?" Lily asked.

"Winston Ledford." The young lady spoke again. "Said he met you outside the bank this morning." She picked up a black parasol from the stand in the hall tree and opened it. With a slight spin of her wrist, the parasol twirled in the afternoon sunlight coming through the front windows.

Lily looked outside just in time to see Liza Croft turn from her display window and march across the street in the direction of the general store. She looked like a woman on a mission.

"Oh, Mr. Ledford." The rather distasteful encounter with the man came back to her. "He assisted me when my shoe became wedged in the sidewalk." Lily remembered him saying he'd send his girls by her shop.

He must have thought she wouldn't know how to handle these ladies. The smirk she'd seen in his eyes had been a challenge.

Lily walked behind the glass case and asked the older lady which hat she'd like to see.

"That one." She pointed to a hat Lily had made before her shop opened. It had turned

181

out better than she'd imagined in the beginning. It was some of her best work, and she'd priced it accordingly. She pulled the white felt creation with organza and tiny roses from its place in the case. Several ladies had admired it, but no one had been willing to pay its price.

"Here you are." Lily smiled at the woman as she handed her the hat. "My name is Lily."

After a slight hesitation and a lifting of a brow, the lady responded. "I'm Virginia Jones. Most folks call me Ginger."

Lily adjusted a gilded mirror stand so Ginger could see her reflection. "Would you like to try it on?"

Ginger paused and leveled a frank stare at her. "You really want me to? Or are you just saying that because you're afraid to tell us to leave?"

Lily met the challenge from Ginger head-on. "Miss Jones, I'm in business to sell hats."

The young lady put down the parasol and laughed. "She's got you there, Ginger. I mean Miss Jones." She bowed in a mock curtsy.

"Be quiet, Lovey," Ginger snapped at her young companion. Then she turned back to Lily. "I think I would like to try this hat on, then." She reached up and removed the wisp of a hat she wore and set it on the case.

"If she's going to call you Miss Jones, I can be Lavinia Aiken, instead of Lovey. No sense in you being the only one treated like a lady." Lovey twisted her mouth in a smirk at Ginger.

"Of course, Miss Aiken. My goal is for all my customers to be treated well." Lily smiled at the younger woman before coming around the counter to help Ginger set the white hat on the crown of her head. "I have a splendid hat pin that would be perfect."

Ginger turned her head back and forth in front of the small mirror while holding the hat in place. "May as well do it up proper. Winston's buying today." She gave Lily a wink and spoke to Lovey. "You need to pick out something nice, too. No sense leaving empty-handed when we're being treated so well for a change."

Lily brought a cushion holding an array of hat pins from inside the case. She pulled one with a pearl-encrusted handle and laid it across her open palm to show Ginger. "What do you think?"

"It's right pretty. Is it expensive?" A smile crept into the dark eyes that had softened from cynicism to fun after Lily had made known her intention of selling her a hat.

Lily smiled back, enjoying the thought of Winston Ledford having to pay for his attempt at embarrassing her. "As a matter of fact, Miss Jones, it's one of my most expensive pieces."

"Then I think I'll just have to take it." Ginger accepted the pin and secured the hat to her head. She walked to the hall tree and took in her reflection from different angles. "What about you, Lovey? What has captured your fancy?"

Lily helped the two ladies choose several items. She followed them onto the sidewalk and thanked them for their patronage. "Please tell Mr. Ledford how much I appreciate him sending you by today." Ginger and Lovey laughed as they walked away, sharing the joke that, while Winston had attempted to intimidate Lily, all three ladies had benefited at his expense. The fancy hatboxes they carried were evidence of their success.

Turning to go back into her shop, Lily caught sight of Edward in the reflection of the display window. Liza Croft stood beside him wearing a deep frown. If Lily thought Edward looked unhappy this morning outside his shop, the expression he wore now would be considered thunderous. She stepped inside and closed the door, saying a prayer.

Lord, I don't know why some things happen, but thank You for the business. Please help Ginger and Lovey to know Your love and turn from the lives Mr. Ledford has made for them.

Lily set about straightening the merchandise that had been set in disarray by the two ladies. When the front bell rang, she put on a smile and turned to greet whoever was at the door.

Edward closed the door with unnecessary force and rounded to face her. "Just what do you think you're doing?"

Startled by his outburst, Lily didn't answer.

His brows came together in a deep crease that drew her into the depths of his brown eyes. It was like swimming in dark coffee. Hot and strong coffee. With a bite!

Edward pointed in the direction of the saloon without taking his eyes from her shocked face. "What are you doing entertaining those women?"

"Entertaining?" Lily fisted her hands and planted one on each hip. "Is that what you think I was doing?"

"I saw you laughing with them."

"We were laughing, but you have no idea

185

what amused us, not that it's any of your business." Lily moved closer to him. She had to look up to see into his face. A storm lit her eyes. "I didn't come to Pine Haven to be bossed around by a man. If I'd wanted that, I could have stayed in East River and married Luther Aarens. At least he had better manners than to raise his voice to me."

"I heard you sending Mr. Ledford your thanks. That was quite a display you put on in front of the bank this morning, after my warning you to be careful. This town won't take kindly if you associate with the likes of the people from the saloon."

"Don't you come in here and tell me who I can and cannot associate with." Lily lifted a finger to poke his chest. He backed away as she stalked forward. "I opened this store to sell hats." Again she drove her finger into his chest. "I'll have you know those women spent enough money this afternoon to pay my rent to you for the next month." She took another step forward, and he was backed against the door. "And the laughter you heard was from three women who got the best of a man who tried to intimidate me."

"Intimidate you? How?" Edward couldn't move back, but she continued to move forward. She was straining her neck to look

186

up at him now.

"Mr. Ledford told me this morning he'd send his girls around to my shop. Oh, he thought that was a fine joke. He had the nerve to laugh in my face. Sending them here was his way of provoking me."

"Why didn't you tell him no or send them on their way?" Edward reached up and captured her hand in his.

"Because I opened this shop to sell merchandise. They had money. His money. What better way to get back at him than to sell them my most expensive items?" She tried to tug her hand free, but he held it snugly. So she poked him again with the tip of her finger. "And what you saw this morning was me with my shoe stuck in the boards of the sidewalk. Mr. Ledford came out of the bank just in time to keep me from falling. He pulled my shoe loose from the planks. Nothing more." She suddenly deflated. Her head dropped, and her hand went limp in his.

Edward watched the color drain from her delicate face.

"Oh, no," she whispered. "If you think what you think . . ." Her voice trailed off to nothing. She raised her head to look at him. "What must everyone else think?"

Her eyes had turned violet with her temper. Now they swam in a blue sea of sorrow.

"I'm afraid they think what I thought." Edward released her hand. He didn't want to hurt her, but he couldn't send her a false message of support, either. This brave lady had come to town in a flourish of flowers and lace, but if she wasn't careful, her dream of success would die.

"I can't refuse to serve a customer because I don't agree with them. Those ladies were sent here to embarrass me. I thought I was being a good Christian to treat them with respect. If they don't see the value in themselves, shouldn't I show it to them by loving them? Jesus was always associating with people no one else would talk to."

"If you keep talking like that, Reverend Dismuke will want you to give a testimony in church come Sunday." He smiled at her and chuckled.

She giggled. "Do you think I should finish with the Scripture in Proverbs about the wealth of the sinner being laid up for the just, or do you think that would be too much?"

He laughed with her. "You might want to save that one for your second sermon."

Lily stopped and confessed, "I was pleased to take the wretched man's money."

He tried to ease her anxiety. "My concern is for your reputation. I know you're a good woman. Your father is a fine Christian man. But people in a small town can be unforgiving when they get the wrong impression."

"I couldn't help getting stuck in the sidewalk." Her back straightened, and her face regained some of its color.

Edward held up both hands in an attempt to prevent another stampede. He thought he might have a bruise from where she'd poked his chest. "I know that. But people only see bits and pieces. They don't know you."

"I've certainly done a fine job so far — parading through town in my nightclothes. Now I've been seen cavorting with the saloon owner and selling hats to his saloon girls. I'll be lucky to have a business at all by the end of the month." An exasperated, gushing sigh punctuated her words.

"It seems to me that none of it was your fault." Edward thought about each statement. It painted a bleak picture when she strung it all together like that. " 'Cavorting' is too strong a word. I'd say something like, 'consorting.' " He tilted his head to one side, hoping she'd appreciate his attempt at humor.

She shook her head and gave a slight

groan. "You're right. That sounds so much better." Her shoulders lifted as she took in a deep breath and lowered as she let it out. "There's not much I can do about it now."

"I'll try to help. I can make sure Reverend Dismuke knows why you welcomed those ladies into your shop. He can probably pass the word along to his wife, who can help by calming the fires of gossip started by Mrs. Croft."

Lily's eyes grew wide. "So that's where all this is coming from?"

Edward watched her, wondering what was in her mind. The emotions Lily had displayed in the past few minutes ranged from rage to sorrow to shame and back.

Resolve brought calm to her features. "Thank you for bringing these things to my attention. I assure you, I'll do everything in my power to make certain you are not embarrassed to have me as your wife."

"Lily, that's not what I meant." A new level of friendship had opened between them. Sharing spiritual truths and unpleasant facts, in an effort to come to a positive solution, was a difficult process for the best of friends. He thought they'd made progress by handling the events of the day. They'd ended the conversation with good humor, but in an instant she was all business again.

"But I saw you with Mrs. Croft before you came in here."

"Be reasonable, Lily." Edward captured her hand and turned it over in his. Today was the first day he'd noticed her hands without gloves. Calluses from the broom and pricks from her sewing needles and the tools of a milliner were scattered across her palm and fingers. He knew the other hand would be the same. This delicate-looking creature had an inner strength he hadn't seen until today. There was more to Lily Stone than the feminine surface she showed to the world. "Do you think I'd stand and talk to her without defending your honor?"

Her eyes were violet again, but he could see her fighting to believe him. She finally shook her head. "I guess not."

He dropped her hand and tipped his hat to her. "If you'll excuse me, Mrs. Stone, I have business with the reverend." He smiled at her, and the light that danced into her eyes ensured him of her gratitude.

"Thank you, Mr. Stone." She followed him outside. "Remember to come back when you have a few minutes so we can discuss the sign I want you to make."

The image foremost in his mind as he walked away was of her ashen face as she realized the situation she was in.

She was his wife now. It was his responsibility to protect her. He just hadn't known when he'd married her how often he'd have to protect her from herself.

CHAPTER TEN

Saturday dawned clear and cool. Lily dressed for the day with forced excitement for the first Saturday her business would be open. Surely she'd meet new people and have new customers today. Thursday and Friday had passed without a single sale. Oh, she'd seen several ladies on the sidewalk cast a look her way. In the end, they'd all gone away without stopping. Some had dared to come close enough to look in the window. She'd even heard one mother tell her young daughter they'd try to order her a hat from the general store because it wouldn't be right to shop at Lily's after what they'd heard.

Lily checked her reflection in the long mirror her father had given her on her sixteenth birthday. Edward had moved it over from her rooms a few days after their wedding.

She ran her hands down the front of her

skirt to smooth the fabric. She wore blue again to match her eyes. The rich color always made her feel more feminine. After all, she was trying to sell stylish accessories to women who lived hard lives in the open country. Soft ruffles swooped up the side of the skirt and met in a large bow at the back of her dress. The bodice had small buttons and a lace collar. She knew just the hat she'd wear if she decided to venture out today. It was small with a tuft of blue organza nestled beneath a nosegay of tiny berries. She pulled it from its box and put it on the bed.

First, she had to prepare breakfast. A few minutes later, Ellen came from her room rubbing her eyes and moaning about being tired.

"It's Saturday. You should be excited about a day with no school." Lily put a plate of scrambled eggs in front of the child. "You can play and even come visit me at the shop later if you'd like."

Edward opened the door and came in from the outside. A cool wind whirled into the room before he could close the door. "It's a bit chilly this morning, ladies." He tousled Ellen's sleepy head and sat at the table.

"Here you go." Lily handed him a plate

and joined them at the table.

Lily bowed her head while Edward gave thanks for their food. She prayed she'd have sales today that she could thank God for tonight.

Ellen perked up after a few bites of food. "Aunt Lily says I can go to the store today."

"She did?" Edward looked at Lily. "You can do that if you'd like." He grinned at Ellen. "Unless you want to help me with a special project."

"What?" Ellen was so excited she almost knocked over her milk when she waved her arms.

"Easy." He chuckled and moved the cup away from the edge of the table. "You'll have to choose without knowing." Lily watched the interaction between uncle and niece. The way he made little things fun for Ellen was sweet. He'd be a wonderful father.

Father? As his wife, if he had children, it would be with her. Lily choked on her biscuit. Edward thumped her on the back until she waved him off.

"Are you okay?" he asked.

"Fine." She sputtered again and took a drink of her coffee. "Thank you."

"What will it be, Ellen? A day in the hat shop or an adventure with me?"

"Hey!" Lily laughed. "Well, Ellen, do you

195

want to try your hand at making a beautiful hat or work in a hot, smelly room and end up covered in soot?"

They all laughed then.

"I want to get dirty and smelly!" Ellen gave a strong nod of her head and speared another bite of eggs.

Edward smiled at Lily. "Nice try. But you just don't have my special touch for wooing her."

Lily stood and started to gather the dishes. "Next time I'll see about adding in a live toad or maybe a day of cleaning the stoves." Wrinkling her nose and scrunching her lips, she pulled a face at both of them. She still hadn't adjusted to sharing a house with the two of them. But on days like today, it didn't seem as difficult as she'd first thought it would be.

Everyone left the house in good spirits a few minutes later. Lily had just settled in to work on a new hat when the bell chimed. She bolted from the stool and stepped into the shop. "Good morning. Welcome to Lily's Millinery and Finery."

Daisy bustled into the shop. "Oh, Lily, how are you?" She hugged Lily.

Lily pulled away from her older sister without meeting her eyes. "I'm fine. Thank you." She looked out the window toward the street. "Did you come to town alone?"

"No. The boys are with Tucker at the livery. Then they're coming around to pick up the supplies I got from the general store. I dropped by Peggy's earlier, and she wanted me to leave the baby with her while we shopped." Daisy made her way to the hall tree against the side wall. "This is lovely." She pulled the spring hat with yellow daisies Lily had made earlier in the week. "I must try this on."

"Sit down and let me help you." Lily removed Daisy's modest bonnet and straightened her hair. She reached for the hat. "This will be just right for you, I think. It's perfect for spring."

Daisy eyed her reflection in the large mirror. "I love it. I just bought a length of yellow gingham to make a new dress. This is exactly what I need for the spring picnic at church." She rubbed her abdomen and met Lily's gaze in the mirror. "I'll be needing some new clothes with more room around the middle by then." A smile creased her face.

"Daisy! How wonderful!" Lily hugged her sister. Daisy's face was aglow with joy for the life that grew inside her.

"Isn't it? Tucker's happy. The boys are beside themselves. They love Rose, but I think they want a brother this time."

"What about you?"

"I'll be thrilled with whatever God decides to bless us with. A healthy child is my only prayer." Daisy loosened the ribbon from the hat and pulled it from her head. "I'll take this, ma'am. Will you please wrap it up for me?" Her sober voice made Lily laugh.

"Yes, Mrs. Barlow. Is there anything else I can get for you today? Gloves, perhaps, or a parasol?" Lily wrapped the hat in tissue paper and put it in a hatbox.

"What do I owe you?"

Lily pushed the box across the glass case to her sister. "Not a thing. You and Tucker have been more help than I knew I would need. It's my gift to you."

Daisy frowned. "I can't accept it, Lily. I know what's going on." Her face grew serious.

"Whatever do you mean?"

"Peggy told me when I stopped at her house. What a horrid week it must have been for you." Daisy opened her reticule and pulled out some money.

"I won't take your money, Daisy. I did very well at the beginning of the week. Business will pick up. People just need to realize my shop is open." Lily nipped into the back room for a few seconds and returned with

198

another hat. She went to the hall tree and put it in the spot that had held the hat Daisy had chosen.

"It's more than that, Lily." She came to stand near the hall tree. "Peggy said it didn't go well when she tried to talk to Mrs. Croft. She wasn't receptive to Peggy's explanations about your actions." At Lily's downcast look, she added, "I'm sorry. Because she's in the middle of town and most people do business at their store, she's developed a lot of influence. Which is sad, because most people know better than to hang on her every word."

Lily shrugged off her sister's sympathy. "Don't worry about it. People will see the truth. It may take time, but I came here to bring beauty to the ladies of this community. That's exactly what I'm going to do." She walked to the front display and watched two ladies come out of the post office next door. They looked in her window but scurried away when they saw her standing inside.

She turned back to Daisy. "When you and Peggy show up at church wearing my hats, ladies are going to want to come here, too. You're the prettiest way I know to drum up interest in my shop. So hurry up and make that pretty dress."

"I'm praying for you." Daisy hugged her tightly and retrieved her package.

"Thank you. I need it."

"How are you and Edward doing?"

"It's awkward, I guess." She pulled at the edge of her sleeve. "Ellen has decided to accept my presence. That's made things easier."

"But?"

"Daisy, you must know something of how I feel. You didn't expect to be married to Tucker when it happened."

"No, I didn't." Her sister put a hand on her arm. "It's not quite the same thing. I knew Tucker. We'd been dear friends."

Lily heaved a sigh. "Well, Edward wants to tell me what to do and how to run my business."

"Really? What has he said?"

She shrugged. "He thinks I should put my money in the bank every day when I close." It didn't sound horrible when she said it out loud. "He says I need to be careful who I choose to associate with."

Daisy made a small sound. "Hmm . . . that sounds like a husband trying to protect his wife." She gave Lily a serious look. "Try not to turn him away with your need for independence. God must have thought you two needed each other."

Lily shook her head. "I think God wanted Ellen to be safe." She opened the door for Daisy and found Edward on the porch.

"Edward." Lily put her hand at the base of her throat. "You startled me." Her hand went up to touch the hair at the base of her neck.

"I'm sorry." He took off his hat and held it in both hands. "I came to check with you about making a sign."

Daisy cleared her throat behind Lily. "How do you do, Edward?"

"Daisy." Edward dipped his head in a greeting. "I'm fine, thank you. Just saw your husband coming out of the livery. He said he's on his way to pick you up at the general store, if you're finished with your shopping."

Lily backed up to allow Daisy to pass through the door.

"Thank you." Daisy went onto the porch and turned back to Lily. "Tucker and I want you all to come to lunch tomorrow."

Lily started to refuse, but Edward accepted. "We'd like that. It'll be good for Ellen. Thank you."

"Come right after church," Daisy said.

She stepped outside and waved as Daisy left. "I'm looking forward to it. An afternoon in the countryside will do us all some good."

Daisy made her way across the street, and

Lily turned to Edward.

"If you'll give me a moment, I've made a rough drawing of what I have in mind. I'll get it and show you where I'd like the sign to be mounted." Lily wrung her hands together as she spoke.

They stepped inside. "Has it been any better today?" His gaze dared her to deny she knew what he meant.

"No." She motioned for him to follow her into the workroom. "Peggy Dismuke came in and bought some handkerchiefs to send to her sister."

"It'll get better."

She opened her mouth to contradict him, but he held up a finger and tilted his head to one side. "I promise. Something else will happen. To someone else. And everyone will forget why you and I got married." He put the finger down and put his hat back on. "Now get your drawing, and let's see what you have in mind for a sign. Hopefully something to draw some positive attention in your direction." He smiled and leaned against the opening between the shop and the workroom.

A small smile caressed her lips and made its way to her eyes. Try as she might, she didn't understand how this man was such a comfort to her. He'd turned her life upside down.

She was grateful he was staying close by to help with the consequences of the upheaval.

On Sunday afternoon Edward entered Tucker and Daisy's cabin. Lily sat in the front room visiting with her sister. He and Tucker had been in the barn while the kids played outside after lunch.

"We need to load up and head back to town, Lily." He didn't like the looks of the sky.

"Surely you don't need to leave so soon?" Daisy put Rose back in her cradle and reached a hand to Tucker, who joined them.

Tucker put an arm around his wife and lifted a hand to point through the open door. "It seems there's a storm heading our way."

"Oh, my." Daisy went to the door and called to the kids to come quickly.

"How bad is it?" Lily moved to stand and Edward put a hand under her elbow to assist her from the chair. A trickle of heat trailed up the length of his arm. He saw she was not unaffected when she turned to him. He tried to focus on Ellen approaching with the twins.

"We better hurry, Uncle Edward. That looks like a mighty bad storm. I wanna get home now." Ellen's voice presented a brave front, but a slight tremble revealed her true anxiety.

Tucker closed the door against the growing wind. "You best hurry on."

"I want to be safe at home before the full force of this storm hits." Edward was concerned for his family. He wasn't accustomed to having a family to look after, but he wanted to do his best.

Lily turned back to him. "I hope the storm passes quickly so it won't hinder me from opening my shop tomorrow."

The quiet that met her words chilled more than the storm ever could. It was obvious no one here thought she'd have any customers tomorrow. He was doing everything he could think of to support her, but the fact was that people were avoiding her place.

"Oh, please, don't look at me like that." Lily implored Daisy to understand. "I simply must open. I can't let the gossip change me. Opening the store every day is the only way I know to combat the lies that have been spread about me."

"I don't think you'll have to worry about opening tomorrow." He didn't want to give her false hope.

"Why would you say that?" Lily grabbed her coat and rammed her arms into the sleeves. Try as he might, Edward couldn't match her speed. She was fastening the buttons before he could grasp the woolen collar to pull it straight. "How can I build a good name in Pine Haven if my own family and friends don't have faith in me?"

Daisy spoke up. "Lily, we have faith in you. I know your store will be a success. I heard more than one lady admire Peggy's new hat today. Rest assured she was singing your praises when they did."

Lily spun to look at him. "Why don't you think I need to worry about opening tomorrow, then?"

Edward put a hand on her shoulder. "It doesn't look to me like anyone will be going anywhere to shop tomorrow. This storm shows all the signs of keeping us tucked into our homes for several days."

Lily looked from one face to another. She lowered her head and reached for her reticule.

"Well, I need to be at home just in case." She peered through the window at the brooding gray sky. "Who knows? It may blow over without a whimper."

"Right. If you don't mind, I'd like to head on back just in case your optimism doesn't materialize." Edward shoved his hat down over his brow. "Ready, Ellen?"

"Yes, sir." The little girl tied her bonnet tight and pushed her hands deep into her pockets. "Bye, everybody!" Out the door she flew and clambered onto the wagon seat.

Edward offered his hand to Lily to help her into the wagon. In the rush to leave, she hadn't put on her ever-present gloves. When she put her hand in his, he felt the calluses on her palms he'd noticed once before. This woman he'd heard talking about frills and pampering wasn't taking the time to pamper herself. She appeared soft from a distance, but closer inspection showed the depth of strength and determination she possessed.

He walked around the front of the horses and checked the harnesses before he stepped up to join them. He passed a heavy blanket for Ellen and Lily to tuck around their legs.

"Ellen, move over and give Lily more room on the seat." Edward shifted to the far edge of the seat to allow Ellen to slide closer to him. He'd have to drive the team hard to get home before the storm broke. The last thing he needed was for Lily to bounce right off the wagon. "We'll be going home in a hurry. It's gonna be a bumpy ride." He released the brake and signaled his team to head for home.

"Do you think we'll get home before it storms?" Ellen had to raise her voice to be heard above the sounds of the horses and wagon. Each bump sent the three passengers jostling against each other.

"I'm trying my best." Edward held the reins firm and drove the team as hard as he dared on the rough terrain.

They hit a deep rut in the road, and Ellen's small frame lifted off the seat. Edward and Lily reached for her at the same time.

"You handle the team, and I'll hold her." Lily pulled Ellen close and wrapped her tightly with both arms.

The trip to town dragged on for what seemed like ages. Edward thought they just might make it home before the storm hit. No sooner had town come into view than sheets of sleet began to pelt the trio as they huddled together on the seat. He looked over at Lily's flimsy hat and knew it was already ruined. Ellen's bonnet would dry by the fire, but the feathers and ribbon Lily preferred were beyond repair. Another reminder that such things might please the eye but the troubles of life could wreak havoc on them without warning.

"Push Ellen under the seat and slide next

to me." Edward was shouting now over the fierce wind.

"I don't want to!" Ellen clung to him.

"Now, child." Edward's voice brooked no argument. Lily helped her slide under the seat and moved next to him.

"Pull the blanket over our heads. I'm afraid this will get worse before it gets better."

Lily fought the wind and worsening sleet, but managed to pull the blanket around him and then tuck herself close with the blanket over their heads.

Her small frame fit against him, invoking a strong desire to protect her. He began to wonder if they would have been better off staying at Daisy's cabin. It was too late to turn back now. They'd have to press on for home.

Ellen was directly beneath them. Edward felt her small arms wrap around one boot. She hated storms. The week her parents left her with him, they'd had terrible rain for days. The continuous thunder and lightning had buried fright deep in the child's soul. Why hadn't he seen this one coming earlier? He should have had her safe at home. It was his duty to protect Lily as much as Ellen, even if Lily insisted she could take care of herself.

Blinding snow fell with the frozen rain, stinging his hands and arms. His hat protected his head, but he knew Lily would be getting the worst of it. Ellen was safe under the bench. There was no refuge between them and town. They had no choice but to struggle on through the storm.

He shouted at Lily. "Put your head down!"

"I can't! If I do, I won't be able to hold the blanket over your head."

"I've got the blanket. Come here!" He lifted his arm and tucked her in close to his chest. He held the reins with one hand, snagged the far edge of the blanket with the other and pushed it into her hand. "Hang on to this!"

A streak of lightning lit the sky, and the team startled. It took all his strength to keep them from bolting. Ellen shrieked beneath the seat and tightened her hold on his boot. The echoing thunder rumbled low beneath the howling wind.

Edward narrowed his eyes, searching for the road that threatened to fade from view in the intensity of the storm. He pushed the horses as hard as he dared. "God, help us to get home safe."

"Amen!" Lily shouted from her cocoon beneath the edge of his elbow.

Edward didn't realize he'd prayed out

loud. But right now they needed all the help they could get. He maneuvered the team around the last bend in the road before the edge of town and pulled on the reins. "Whoa, boys!"

He pulled the wagon to a stop under the roof that extended off the front of the livery. Icicles hung from the wagon. White puffs from the horses' nostrils floated up to be carried off by the wind.

"Make a run for the front porch." The sleet still pelted down. He had to raise his voice for Lily and Ellen to hear him. "I'm going to get the team inside the livery. Start the fire and get Ellen out of those wet clothes."

CHAPTER ELEVEN

"Let's go inside." Lily put a hand on Ellen's shoulder and urged her toward the front door of the cabin. The wind buffeted them on the porch.

"Don't!" The scream tore from Ellen. Her chin quivered, and she began to tremble. Melting snow dripped from her dress and coat. Black shoes pranced like a nervous horse in the middle of the frozen drift forming at her feet. Something just before terror emanated from the child's eyes.

Lily knelt before her and put a hand on each shoulder. "We're safe now, Ellen."

"Where's Uncle Edward? I want my uncle Edward!" The frightened voice rose to a fever pitch.

"He's putting the horses in the livery so they'll be safe, too." Lily spoke loud enough to be heard over the wind, but gently in an effort to calm the child.

"I want Uncle Edward." Sobs wrenched

through Ellen. Lily pulled her close and pressed the child's wet face to her shoulder.

"He's coming, precious. Don't you worry. He's safe. He'll be right here." Lily swayed from side to side, rocking Ellen in her arms. "We're all safe." Lightning flashed and thunder followed before the light faded. The clap was deafening. Ellen and Lily both jumped and clutched each other more tightly. The child's scream was muffled by Lily's coat.

Edward ducked under the eave of the porch and knelt behind Ellen. "It's okay, baby girl. I'm here." He turned her to face him and wrapped his arms around her.

Lily immediately felt the chill of separation as Ellen's warmth pulled away from her. Snow blew onto the small porch with relentless force.

"I'll start the fire." She stood and skirted around the two as they clung to each other in the cold.

Lily searched in the dim cabin for matches near the hearth. Thankful he had laid the fire, she struck the match against the bricks and lit the kindling near the iron grate. She blew on the small flame, and the fire caught in earnest. She filled the kettle with water from a pitcher near the stove. Setting it to boil, she opened the front door again.

"Can you carry her in? The fire's going." Lily hoped Edward could hear her. The storm raged and blew its fury onto the porch, but the strength of it paled in comparison to the emotions she saw in the two shadowed figures. Ellen was curled against Edward, her tiny arms snaked around his neck. He held her close and spoke near her ear. Lily felt like an intruder in the scene. What tragedy racked their hearts and caused them to remain in a dangerous storm? Did the elements of nature dim in view of the heartache they nursed?

Edward rose at her words, lifting Ellen with him. He scooped her legs up and carried her like a baby in his arms. Lily backed into the room, holding the door wide for them to enter. He had to turn sideways to get through the doorway with Ellen.

Lily spread a blanket on the bench near the hearth, and Edward laid Ellen on it.

"Please get her some dry clothes and a towel."

She scurried to get the things he asked for, returning to find Ellen had stopped crying. Ellen sat on the bench facing the fire. Edward tugged at her coat and dropped it near his feet, in a wet heap with her shoes.

Lily pulled the shoes from the pile. "Edward, loosen the laces and put these on the

213

hearth while I change her clothes." The kettle whistled. "Will you make tea?"

"Yes." He put the shoes down and went to the stove.

Minutes later Lily pulled a nightgown over Ellen's head and started to work on the long, thick hair with a towel.

Lily wrapped Ellen in a blanket and was pulling on her last sock when Edward handed Ellen the warm drink. "Be careful. It's very hot."

Lily smiled at the child, whose brown eyes reflected the flames.

"Thank you, Aunt Lily." Ellen's voice was a ragged whisper, her throat raw from crying in the storm.

Lily cupped her cheek in one hand. The fire had started to warm the tiny girl. "You're welcome, Ellen. Now let's see if I can find you something to eat."

"I'll take care of supper." Edward shrugged out of his coat. Water hit the floor, and rivulets traced the grain of the wood toward the fireplace. He hung the heavy garment on a hook near the fire's edge.

A smile teased Lily's face. "I'll do it."

"What about something simple and filling?" He sat on the hearth and tugged off his boots. Water spilled onto the floor at his feet. He rolled thick socks down his calves.

"You are making a mess." Lily picked up a bucket from the corner of the kitchen and rushed to put it in front of him. It was unusual to be this close to him. The awkwardness of the past weeks faded in the urgency of the moment.

He wrung the water from his socks into the bucket and laid them across the edge of the hearth near Ellen's. "I'd say it's a bit late to worry about how much melting snow and ice is in here." He pointed to direct her attention to the floor beneath her feet.

Lily looked down to see a growing puddle. Water ran from the front edge of her coat. Her dress swished with moisture, and her shoes were worse than Ellen's had been. Warmth filled her face when she looked back to Edward, and she giggled.

"I see your point." She removed her coat, hoping the rest of the water would be contained in one area. She hung it next to his on another iron hook. "These hooks are handy here."

"Jane insisted on them." He picked up Ellen's dress and wrung the water from it into the bucket at his feet. "She didn't want me soaking the floor when it rained."

"Momma doesn't like a mess." Ellen's fingers laced around her tea. The color was returning to her face. "You'd be in trouble today, Uncle Edward."

With an endearing gentleness, he ruffled Ellen's damp hair, his hand so large it dwarfed the child's head. "You are right."

Lily sensed she was an interloper in their world. She wanted to be at ease with Edward like she was now with Ellen.

Or did she?

"Sit here." Edward stood and indicated his place on the bench next to Ellen. "You need to get out of those wet shoes."

In the glow of the firelight, the cabin closed in on her. "I'm fine. Thanks." She would have backed away, but he caught her by the elbow and tugged her toward the seat.

"Don't be silly. You'll catch your death if you don't get out of those wet things."

Lily dropped onto the bench beside Ellen.

"Can you help me unlace my shoes, Ellen? My feet are a bit damp." She smiled at the girl and winked. "But don't you worry. I never get sick."

"Never?" Ellen slid off the bench and squatted at Lily's feet.

"Absolutely never." Lily shook her head in slow, exaggerated seriousness. "Why, once I had to walk all the way home from town in the pouring rain. It's about five miles from East River to my papa's ranch. I didn't even sneeze once."

Edward attempted to follow her lead. "So, five miles? That's a long walk for a lady. You must be pretty tough." He had moved to the kitchen.

Lily smiled at Edward and spoke to Ellen. "I'm tough all right. Just not real pretty."

"That's not true. You're pretty as can be." Ellen pulled the first wet shoe from Lily with a swoosh of effort. She landed on her seat on the hearth, and everyone laughed.

"Thank you, Ellen, but you're too kind. I'm tough because I was always taking care of whoever was sick at my house. Kinda made me strong." The second shoe came off without resistance. "Don't you worry about me catching anything. I'm much too slow at running," Lily teased Ellen, and gave her a quick embrace.

"Thank you, child." She set the shoes on the hearth to dry. "My toes are already starting to thaw." She moved near the bucket and looked at Edward. "If you'll turn the other way, sir, I'll take care of getting rid of some of the water in my skirt."

He stared for a moment as if he was lost. His eyes were on her stocking feet, watching her toes wiggle in their new freedom.

"Edward," Lily prompted. "Please." With one finger and a twist of her wrist, she made a swirling pattern.

"Oh. Of course." He walked behind the screen in the back corner.

"I think a quick twist will work wonders on this old skirt." Lily talked to Ellen as she wrung the water from her clothes into the bucket at her feet. She heard Edward washing his hands in the basin. "What do you think you want for supper?"

"Can I come out now?"

"Just a minute." She squeezed the last of the water her strength could wrench from the heavy skirt. "Now is fine." Lily dropped the hem to hang limp at her feet. The fabric might be ruined. She'd try her best to clean and restore the shape of the garment later.

He came out wiping his hands on a small towel. "I'll help. What about scrambled eggs? Maybe we could fry a few potatoes." He flipped the towel over one shoulder and moved to the stove. In quick fashion he had lit the burner and started cutting the potatoes.

"I'll make coffee." Lily poked at the pins holding her hair. "I'm about to dry out here."

"Ellen, you can slice the bread." Edward dropped the potatoes into the hot grease in the cast iron skillet. Then he pulled out a bowl and began to crack open eggs to scramble.

"You surprise me. You know, before, I never would have pictured you as an efficient cook." Lily filled the coffeepot with water from the pitcher and set it on the back burner.

"Oh, he ain't much of a cook. Pancakes and eggs is about all we ever ate before you came." Ellen tore the bread in her haste to slice it.

"Don't talk bad about my cooking, or you'll have to do it." Edward pointed a fork at Ellen as he teased her.

Lily put a hand over the child's and guided her as she sliced the next piece. "Saw it slowly and gently. Back and forth. Then you'll have a nice piece to cover with butter." She released Ellen's hand and watched her cut the next piece. "Very nice.

"Do you want to learn more about how to cook, Ellen?" Lily thought it might be another way for her to bond with the child.

Ellen shrugged one shoulder and slid the plate of bread to the middle of the table. "Mrs. Dismuke tried to give me some lessons. She said I'm too young."

"I was your age when Mrs. Beverly started letting me help in the kitchen." Lily watched curiosity cross Ellen's face.

"Who's Mrs. Beverly?"

219

"She's my papa's housekeeper. She took care of us after my momma passed on."

"And she let you cook when you were seven?"

"Not by myself. She let me watch her at first. I could help stir and mix things together. I had to learn how to be careful before she let me near the stove."

"Did it take long?"

"Only a few lessons. Then I got to start helping with basic chores and cooking."

"Could you teach me?" Ellen's face was free of the shadows the storm had brought. She glowed in the light of the hurricane lamp on the table. "I could cook for Uncle Edward when you have to work late."

Lily had struck a chord with Ellen she hadn't known was there. This little girl's desire to care for her uncle mirrored her own at that age. "If it's okay with your uncle. If you promise you'll still do little-girl things, too." She rested a hand on Ellen's shoulder. "Sometimes we get in such a big hurry to grow up that we forget to be a kid." She chucked the tip of Ellen's chin with her finger. "You have to promise."

"I will! I promise!" Ellen jumped from her chair and flung herself around Edward's midsection. "Please, Uncle Edward, can I? Can I?"

He dropped his spatula and pushed Ellen's hair away from the stove. He picked her up and set her farther from the hot surface. "Not until I see you're ready to be cautious. You very nearly set your hair on fire." Lily knew the harshness in his voice was born of fear from having to protect Ellen from the hot stove.

Ellen slumped in his arms, and her bottom lip slid out. "I'm sorry. I didn't mean to." She looked up at his face. "Don't be mad. I'll be careful." The pleading broke the tension that surrounded him in the instant of danger.

"I know you didn't mean to get too close, Ellen, but that's how accidents happen." He was eye level with her now. "You're not mature enough to learn to cook yet."

"But Aunt Lily said . . ."

"The matter is not open for discussion. You finish putting everything on the table now." Edward went back to the stove. Ellen put plates on the table, moping and murmuring under her breath.

"Mind your manners, Ellen." Edward kept his back to the room.

Did he think Lily would argue with him in front of his niece? Was he ashamed of his harsh reaction when Ellen got too close to the stove? Why did Edward marry her if he

221

wasn't going to let her help with decisions like this for Ellen? Had he changed his mind?

Thunder sounded through the wind. Maybe the storm would blow over with the ferocity with which it arrived. Would they be able to navigate the changing climate of their lives? She wanted Edward to trust her with Ellen. She could make decisions that would help the little girl grow into a lovely young lady.

Would he learn to trust her to do that?

One could only hope.

"Ouch." Edward muttered under his breath when he nicked his hand for the second time. The small rabbit he was whittling would be stained with blood if he didn't slow down. He'd fussed at Ellen before supper for being careless, and now he was the one at risk.

Lily's soft voice floated across the room from behind him. She and Ellen had cleared away the dishes while he came to sit in front of the fire and whittle. Or escape. Lily's presence warmed the small cabin. The way she'd flittered across the space when they'd come home, helped get Ellen into dry clothes then scolded him for wetting the floor had made him smile.

If Ellen hadn't almost been hurt near the stove, he might still be in a pleasant mood. There was so much responsibility with the child. That's why he'd asked for Lily's help. And this evening, when she'd offered it, he'd turned her down. He couldn't explain why, even to himself.

Ellen's giggle joined Lily's airy laughter. He wouldn't look back again. The last time he dared to peek over his shoulder, Lily had caught him. Her smile told him she knew he wanted to be in the midst of the activity, but his pride prohibited it. The smell of burnt onions still hung in the damp air. He'd all but ruined their meal when he added onions to the frying potatoes and forgot to turn them in the skillet. He wouldn't stand around and risk the teasing he was sure he deserved.

Another stroke of his knife and the wooden rabbit's ear came off and landed in the pile of shavings at his feet. He threw the mangled animal into the fire and reached for a fresh piece of wood. Mr. Croft had asked him to create a variety of animals. The rabbit was his first attempt.

"Want some company?" Lily moved close to the fire and held her hands out to its warmth. He didn't look up at her. The tone in her voice warned him her cheeks would be rounded with a soft smile.

"Tired of being cooped up in here with the smell of burnt onions?" He chipped away large chunks of the wood to form the beginnings of a new rabbit.

"That could have happened to anyone. I daresay you wouldn't have done it if Ellen hadn't startled you so. Children can take away your focus quicker than anything else I know." She walked to the window near the front corner of the cabin and studied the sky. "The storm seems to have lost its fury. At least the sleeting has stopped."

Fresh shavings piled at his feet. He was being more deliberate. Cutting his hand again would only embarrass him further.

Edward turned the wood in his hand. "I expect the snow to end within the hour."

"Ellen is tired. I sent her to prepare for bed." Lily stood near the window with her back to him.

"I'll go in and say her prayers with her when she's done."

"I best be getting ready to turn in, too." Lily pushed away from the window and stepped close to the hearth. It was her habit to go into her room when Ellen went to bed. It had prevented them from being alone together. They were both adjusting to the lack of privacy their hasty marriage had imposed on them.

Maybe he could soothe over his mistakes earlier by encouraging her friendship now. "Why don't you sit up awhile?" He sliced away a large corner of the wood he held and turned it in his hand.

"Are you sure?" At his nod, she continued. "I think I will. I want to mend a couple of Ellen's dresses. I could do that while you work." Lily spoke softly. "I'll just go and tell her good-night first." Lily knocked on Ellen's door and entered at the girl's quiet invitation.

Edward lowered his head and saw the sad beginnings of a bunny. He couldn't concentrate on it. He stood and moved to lean against the mantel and stare into the flames. Rushing back to town this afternoon, he'd thought only of their safety as he'd tucked Lily close and covered her with his bulk. The effect she had on him had set him reeling. The memory of the scent of her damp hair filled him. Sweet and fresh.

He hadn't been close to a woman like that since he'd danced with Eunice Hampton at the winter social just before Jane and Wesley left town. She'd been full of laughter and fun, but no emotion she stirred in him compared to the way he'd wanted to protect Lily today.

The door opened behind him. He didn't have to look to know it was Lily.

"Ellen said she's ready for you to come hear her prayers." Her heels clicked across the boards as she headed for his room.

He shook his head. He had to start thinking of it as *her* room.

When he came back into the front room, Lily sat snuggled in the corner of the settee she'd brought with her to Pine Haven. It was nicer than any furniture he had. It wasn't very big, so they'd been able to fit it into the room. There hadn't been room for everything she had, but they'd brought what they could to the cabin.

A small sewing basket stood open at her feet. She leaned into the corner of the settee so the light from the lamp on the table at her elbow spilled onto the dress she was mending.

He rocked his weight from one foot to the other. Never in his life had he entertained a lady in his home. He didn't count his sister. She'd entertained herself.

"Can I get you a cup of coffee?" He walked to the stove and poured a cup for himself.

"No, thank you." She tied a knot in the thread and used a small pair of scissors to cut it off close to the dress. "I don't want to risk spilling anything on Ellen's Sunday dress."

He set the pot back on the stove with a clink and sat in his chair by the fire. "Who taught you to sew?"

Lily must not have heard him. She looked up at him and said, "Hmm?"

He took a long drink of his coffee and set the cup on the hearth. "You told me your mother passed when you were a young girl. I was wondering who taught you to sew." He picked up the beginnings of the rabbit and started to whittle again. It would be easier to talk to her if he stayed busy. Maybe he wouldn't sound so nervous.

A smile crossed her face. "Mrs. Beverly, my father's housekeeper. She stepped in and did what she could with me and my sisters." She pulled a new length of thread through her needle and picked up another of Ellen's dresses. "I was the most interested in sewing and cooking. My oldest sister has been working the ranch for years, and Daisy moved here so long ago that I guess Mrs. Beverly had the most time to help me."

"I am indebted to her. As you can see from my attempts tonight, your cooking skills far surpass anything I could do."

She smiled at him. "Ellen told me your specialty is pancakes. Perhaps we should have them the next time you take over the cooking."

"The two of you seem to have come to some kind of agreement. How did you get her to stop being so defensive around you?" Ellen's animosity toward Lily had troubled him, but he didn't know what to do about it. He was relieved to see the drastic change in his niece's behavior. He picked up his cooling coffee and took a drink.

"She was worried I would steal your affections away from her."

He felt heat spill into his face as he sputtered and choked on the tepid liquid. "She thought that?"

"Yes, but you don't have to worry about Ellen imagining things that aren't happening. We talked about it, and she knows I'm not interested."

Not interested. What man wanted to hear his wife say she wasn't interested in his affections? In fairness, their marriage wasn't an affectionate arrangement, but her words stung nonetheless. He remembered her mentioning someone she'd planned to marry in East River.

"So, this Luther fellow still has your interest?"

Her mouth dropped open for just a moment. Then her face closed as all the progress they'd made in learning about each other disappeared. She rolled up the dress she was working on and stuffed it into the basket. She stood with an icy calm that was more powerful than the storm they'd endured on their way home.

"Wait, Lily." Edward stood. "I wasn't trying to imply anything."

"I heard no implication. I heard an accusation." She plucked up the basket and headed for her room. Now he could think of it as her room. She was using it to shut him out. He didn't know what else to think by her saying she wasn't interested in him.

Did he want her to be interested in him? He wanted her to be interested in Ellen. She'd done that. She'd built a bridge to his niece even after all the anger the child had aimed at her.

He slid between her and the bedroom door. "I didn't mean that." He put his hands on her arms. "Please forgive me."

She blew out a breath and squared her shoulders. "I am not interested in Luther Aarens. I haven't been since the moment I heard him tell his mother he only proposed to me so I could become a companion for her. That I was not someone he could ever love." No emotion accompanied her words. "I had been under the impression his attentions toward me were of a more personal nature. I was unaware he only wanted me for the service I could provide for his mother."

Edward didn't know what bothered him more — that her words were completely devoid of feeling, or the irony that after refusing to marry a man who wanted her to care for his mother, she'd married him to care for Ellen.

"I'm sorry." He didn't know what else to say.

"You've no need to be."

He didn't want to misunderstand her. "But you married me to care for Ellen." If she didn't want to care for Ellen, he needed to know now — before too much time passed. Ellen was beginning to show an attachment to Lily.

"You made no secret of the reasons for our marriage." She lifted her brows and let them fall again, her face a sad yet beautiful picture of resolve. "We can't always determine where we end up, can we, Edward? Or you wouldn't be a guardian to that precious girl, because you'd have kept her mother here. I would still be in East River happily married, but not to Luther Aarens. I might even have a child or two." She dropped her gaze to her hands. "Life isn't predictable. We have to stand up to whatever circumstances we're dealt and move forward."

"So you held no hope of romance or happiness when you came to Pine Haven?"

"I did not. I came here for independence and to start a life for myself."

"And I ruined that dream for you."

"I have a new life now. Just not the one I dreamed." Her words stung long after she stepped into the bedroom and closed the door.

CHAPTER TWELVE

Ellen sneezed again. "Uncle Edward, I don't feel so good."

He pulled the skillet off the heat and bent down to look into her eyes. Glassy orbs in the depths of dark circles stared back at him. "Uh-oh." He put a hand to her forehead. The heat confirmed the suspicion of fever he got from her pink cheeks. "You go climb into bed. I'll bring some water before I go for the doc."

"I don't want Dr. Willis!" Panic struck her face.

He picked her up like a rag doll and carried her to her room. "You're going to be fine, pumpkin. I just want the doc to make sure you don't get any sicker." He pulled the quilt up to her chin and tucked it close around her. "I'll be right back with a cool drink of water."

When he returned, she sat up on top of the quilt he'd wrapped her in.

"Here you are." Edward held the cup for her.

Ellen drank deeply and lay back against the pillow. Her hair clung to the sides of her face in wet tendrils.

"You've got to stay covered up." He tucked the quilt around her again.

"It's too hot." She thrashed her head from one side to the other. "I don't want it."

"Leave the cover on. I'll be right back with the doc." He turned to peek at her before he closed her door. There was no way he'd wait to get help for her. Fever was a dangerous thing.

He grabbed his jacket from the peg by the door and tromped off the porch in the direction of the doctor's office. Lily came out of her shop as he rounded the corner. With a full head of steam, he couldn't stop.

Lily trotted to catch up to him. "What's wrong?"

"I need to get to the doc's office." He tried to sound calm, but the urgency of his mission came through in spite of his effort.

"Ellen?" Lily's face was serious in an instant.

"Yes. Fever. Sneezing. Achy." He picked up his pace.

"I'll stay with her until you get the doctor."

He pivoted on one heel. "I'll be there as fast as I can."

Lily stepped inside the cabin. When she'd left this morning, it had barely been light. Now the curtains were pulled back, and sunshine filled the room.

"Ellen?"

The sound of faint sobs came from the child's room. Lily tapped on the door and pushed it open a bit.

"I hear you're not feeling well." Lily smiled at the sliver of a girl hidden beneath the mound of a giant quilt.

"I'm so hot, Aunt Lily." Ellen didn't lift her head from the pillow, and her eyes barely opened.

"Let me help you." Lily pulled the cover back. She went to the small window and pushed it open slightly. A soft, cool breeze floated into the room.

"Uncle Edward said I had to stay under the quilt."

"My pa used to think that, too. Then we had a doctor who told us to cool him off when he had a fever." Lily picked up the cup by her bed. "I'll be right back with some water."

She dashed into the kitchen and poured water from the pitcher for the poor child.

"Drink this. Slowly." Lily slid her arm beneath Ellen's shoulders and lifted her enough to sip the cool liquid. Then Lily lowered Ellen to rest against the pillow.

Lily retrieved the washbowl from behind the screen in the main room and brought it with a cloth to Ellen's bedside. She wet the cloth and wrung it out gently over the bowl.

Rolling up the sleeves to Ellen's gown, Lily spoke soothing words to her while she wiped the girl's limbs, face and neck with the cool cloth. She dipped it into the water again and folded it to lie across Ellen's forehead.

"How's that? Better?" Lily stepped to the bedroom door at the sound of boots on the porch. "That'll be your uncle with the doctor."

"Ellen? Are you okay?" Edward came into the room.

An urgency raced across his features. He pulled the quilt over Ellen and banged the window shut. "I told you to stay under the quilt." He sat on the bedside and touched Ellen's face.

"Aunt Lily said it would help." Ellen spoke in a ragged whisper.

Edward turned to Lily. "I don't want her to catch a chill. That's how she got sick in the first place." He clutched Ellen's small

235

hand in his.

Lily recognized the fear in his eyes. "We've got to get her fever down. When you bundle her up, it climbs."

"She made me feel better." Ellen coughed, her shoulders lifting from the pillow with the pain of exertion.

He pressed her gently onto the bed. "Try to take it easy. The doc said he'd be here as soon as he gets his bag."

Lily backed herself into a corner of Ellen's room. Her attempts to help the child had been seen as dangerous to her protective guardian. She hoped he wasn't right.

A knock sounded on the door, and Edward stood.

Lily held up a hand. "I'll let the doctor in. You can stay with Ellen."

She stepped out of the room and opened the front door for the doctor. "She's in the bedroom."

Dr. Willis wore a brown suit and carried a small black bag. "Thank you, Mrs. Stone." He moved at a brisk pace toward Ellen's room, never stopping as he spoke.

Lily put on some water to boil for broth. She went across the street and closed up her shop before coming back to help take care of Ellen.

Lord, please help this child. For all Edward's

determination to be strong, he can't make her well. Let the fever break soon. Please.

Edward stepped out of the way so Dr. Willis could see Ellen.

"She got wet yesterday, Doc. We got caught in the storm on our way back to town. I got her home quick as I could. Warmed her up good by the fireplace and made her drink hot tea." He tried to keep the worry out of his tone.

"Did you go and get yourself sick, child?" The doctor laid a hand on her cheek. Then he lifted the cloth and touched her forehead.

"It was a good idea to put a cool cloth on her face." He dipped the cloth into the water and wrung it out again. "Does it make you feel better?" He folded the cloth and draped it across her forehead again.

Ellen whispered, "Yes, Aunt Lily did it." Several deep coughs wrenched her chest. "Said it would cool the fever." The words took all her strength, and she seemed to melt into the pillow.

"Let's get you cooled off. Edward, fold the quilt back while I open this window a bit." Dr. Willis tugged the window open and backed up so the breeze would reach the bed.

A small smile touched Ellen's face.

"That's better, Uncle Edward."

Edward stood on the opposite side of the bed from the doctor. "Are you sure, Doc? Her momma always bundled her up against a chill." He took Ellen's small hand again.

"I'm sure." Dr. Willis set his bag on the side of the bed. He pulled out the pieces of his stethoscope and assembled it. "I'm going to listen to your chest now, Ellen." He put the ivory tips in his ears and listened to her breathe through the wooden bell-shaped chest piece.

He took several minutes to examine Ellen. "I'm going to give you some medicine for the cough. It tastes bitter, but most medicine does." The doctor made her swallow the first dose.

Dr. Willis handed a small bottle to Edward. "Give her a spoonful three times a day." He began to pack up his instruments. "And keep her room cool. Not damp, but cool. If the fever gets worse, wipe her down with a cool cloth." He picked up his bag. "If it starts to rain, close the window, but don't pile the cover on until the fever breaks."

"Dr. Willis?" Ellen tried to prop herself up on one elbow but fell back against the pillow.

"Yes, Ellen?"

"Am I gonna die?"

238

Edward's heart clinched. No matter how he tried to protect her, there were things in life a body couldn't foresee. They should never have gone to the Barlows' after church. He should have felt the storm coming. Like his ma used to in her bones.

"Not if I have anything to say about it." Doc Willis gave a wink and patted the side of the bed. "You'll be up running all over the place in a few days. Your aunt and uncle will probably be wishing for the quiet again. Just stay in bed. Rest and drink lots of water. It's the best way I know to put out the fire of a fever."

Relief washed over Edward at the doctor's words. A smile covered his face, and he kissed Ellen's brow. He nestled Ellen's doll in the crook of her arm. "I'm gonna see the doctor to the door. I'll be right back." He stepped into the front room and closed the bedroom door behind him.

Lily was at the stove. "How is she, Doctor?" He could hear the concern in her voice. "I'm making her some broth."

"That's just what she needs." The doctor put on his coat. "Edward will fill you in. I've got another patient coming to the office."

She thanked him and turned back to the stove. Edward could see her lips moving in silent prayer as he opened the front door.

"Doc, thank you for coming so quickly." The men stepped onto the porch so their conversation wouldn't disturb Ellen. "How much do I owe you?"

Dr. Willis rested his bag on the porch rail and buttoned his coat. "Can you put a couple of shoes on my horse?" He retrieved the bag.

"Bring her by, and I'll fix you right up." Edward clapped a hand on the doctor's shoulder. "Will she really be okay, Doc?" He had to ask, in case the doctor had put on a brave face for Ellen's sake.

"She'll be fine. Don't you worry. Good thing your wife was here to help cool her off. It's important to get the fever down quick. You were smart to snatch her up when you did. A woman like that doesn't come along every day."

"I don't rightly know how to let go and let her help me yet. I've been running my business and taking care of Ellen alone for so long."

"Just let her do what comes natural to her. She's a good woman. She proved today she's got good maternal instincts."

"I'll try."

"Remember to keep Ellen cool and make sure she takes her medicine."

Now the relief was real. "Thank you. I will. I don't care how it tastes."

The doctor chuckled. "When she starts to complain about the taste of the medicine, you'll know she's feeling better." He set a small derby on his head and left Edward on the porch. "She seems to like your wife. Maybe let her sit with the child and read, or whatever it is women do to keep young ones quiet while they heal."

When the doctor disappeared around the corner, Edward collapsed onto his chair on the porch and stared into nothing. Fear had clutched his heart when Ellen had come to him with such a high fever. He couldn't lose her. Jane would never forgive him if something happened to her daughter while she was in his care.

Lord, please help Ellen. Thank You for the doctor's help and the medicine. Please take the fever from her. And bring Jane and Wesley home.

When Edward lifted his head, regret swamped him. He remembered the tone he'd used with Lily. He'd all but accused her of endangering Ellen.

But she'd been right.

Lord, I need Your help, too. And forgiveness. From You. And from Lily.

He went back into the cabin to find Lily

241

at Ellen's bedside, feeding her broth. He sat on the opposite side of the bed holding Ellen's hand. "Does that make your throat feel better?"

Ellen nodded, and Lily gave her another spoonful of the warm liquid. "That's enough for now. You close your eyes. I promise one of us will be here when you wake up." Lily put a hand on Ellen's cheek. "Rest well."

When Ellen fell asleep, he slipped into the front room for a cup of coffee. Lily was putting on her coat. "If you'll stay with her until lunch, I'll come back for the afternoon."

"You don't have to do that. I know you want to keep your shop open as much as possible." He didn't want to hinder her from working. And he didn't know how upset she was with him about disagreeing over Ellen's care.

"It's best for Ellen if she knows we're both here for her."

"You're right. I'll take the first shift. If I have time, I'll make us some lunch while she rests."

Lily smiled a knowing smile. "Do you think that's a good idea? She might not need that much excitement today." With a wave of her hand, she was gone, laughing at his cooking skills. Or the lack of them.

She filled his thoughts while he sat by

Ellen's bed. Doc Willis was right. Lily had proved herself today. Edward might not know why things happened as they did, but he was grateful to the Lord above for Lily's help. He needed to think of a way to show her.

Lily was surprised to see Ginger and Lavinia later that morning.

"I want a couple of your finest hankies," Ginger announced.

"I want a pair of gloves. Like a lady wears to church." Lavinia toyed with the lace on a white glove with pearl buttons.

"Those gloves would be perfect, Lavinia." Lily pulled the gloves from the display so the young woman could hold them.

Ginger was searching through an assortment of embroidered hankies from France. "She's got some idea she might want to go to church. Some fellow she met at the general store started up a conversation with her. Seems he's been looking for a wife but only wants a good church girl."

"I ain't wanting to get married yet, but he did make it seem like there might be more fellas in church than we've seen since we got to town." Lavinia handed the gloves back to Lily. "I might not have enough money for these. Mr. Winston said he won't

243

pay for church gloves."

Lily smiled at Lavinia. "I'm running a special on church gloves today." She went to the glass display case and started to wrap the gloves for Lavinia. "Would you like a pair, too, Ginger?"

Ginger opened a colorful parasol and rested it on her shoulder. She tilted her head to one side while she studied her reflection in the hall tree mirror. "No, thank you, Mrs. Lily." She lowered the parasol. "My first husband was a churchgoing man. I've been in saloons too long to be accepted back in a church now."

"God never turns His back on someone returning to His house." Lily hoped the people at Pine Haven Church would welcome Ginger and Lavinia if they came.

Ginger's smile was doubtful. "You know it wouldn't be just God to face if I went back to church. His people aren't always as welcoming. From what I've heard, they aren't too happy with you for being friendly to us. I can't think they'd been any happier to see us in their church."

"You're always welcome as my guest." Lily folded the hankies Ginger had selected into a length of paper and tied it securely with string. "Never mind what people think."

"Keep telling yourself that, honey." Ginger

took her package and tucked it into the bend of her arm. "Maybe after a while it'll be true. For now, I'll be at the saloon. Everyone's welcome there."

Lavinia followed Ginger out of the shop with a wave over her shoulder. "Bye, Mrs. Lily. I might see you at church. It depends on whether the saloon opens this week."

A second visit so soon from Ginger and Lavinia was unexpected. Hopefully, they'd surprise everyone in town by coming to church.

Lord, please let me reach these ladies for You. And let others love them with Your love.

The best surprise she could wish for was that the ladies would be treated well if they did show up for services.

Lily returned in the middle of the day. They shared sandwiches, and Lily stayed with Ellen while Edward went to work.

He tried to do a full day's work in a few hours, but he couldn't concentrate. His mind swung like a pendulum between concern for Ellen and thoughts of Lily. One a helpless child in certain need of his care, the other an independent woman who fought to cover any sign of weakness or need.

He finally gave up on work and came

home. He went straight to Ellen's room to relieve Lily, who left him to watch over the sleeping child.

Edward jolted upright. He must have fallen asleep in the chair beside Ellen's bed. The afternoon had faded to evening.

He put a hand up to rub at the soreness in his neck. Ellen's breathing was raspy but even. He headed toward the front room to find Lily sitting at the table reading her Bible.

He ran a hand through his tousled hair and squinted to see her in the twilight. "I didn't mean to fall asleep."

"It's tiring to tend to the sick. I prepared supper." She stood and walked to the stove. "Is she better?"

"She's still sleeping."

Her eyes darted a glance over his shoulder to the open door to Ellen's room. "I want to make sure she has a good meal."

A moan came from Ellen's room, followed by a deep coughing spell. Edward rushed into the room and put an arm under Ellen's shoulders to help her sit up.

The child settled and sent a smile beyond him to the doorway. "Lily." The whisper cost her another coughing spasm.

"Don't try to talk. You need to rest your voice." Lily's soft tone seemed to caress Ellen as she lay back against the pillow. Lily entered the room.

Edward offered her a chair. "Will you sit with Ellen while I dish up the food?" When she didn't move to answer, he reiterated, "Please? You must be tired, too."

"Okay. It will be good to sit a spell." Lily dipped her head in agreement.

From the front room Edward could hear Lily's hushed voice, but he couldn't make out the words. Once Ellen chuckled, only to end up coughing. He picked up the tray laden with fresh bread and stew and went back into Ellen's room.

"Ladies, you must take it easy for our patient to get well. No laughing or carrying on until the fever is gone." He hoped his lighthearted tone contradicted the seriousness of his words. Lily's presence was having a healing influence on Ellen. He could see it in the girl's face.

"We're being good. Aunt Lily was just telling me about one time when her papa was sick. He coughed and coughed until he tore his nightshirt. She had to sew it up again." Merriment played in Ellen's eyes.

Edward set the tray on the bed after Lily helped Ellen to sit up. He draped a napkin across the front of Ellen's nightdress and reached for the bowl of stew. "Want me to feed you?"

"I want Aunt Lily. She can tell me more stories."

Edward turned to look at Lily, his eyebrows raised. "Would you mind?" He offered her the bowl and spoon.

"I'd be glad to entertain the patient." She nodded toward the door. "You may take a break, if you'd like. We girls will be fine on our own for a bit."

Edward released the stew to her, careful not to brush her fingers with his. The heat of the bowl wouldn't move him like the warmth of her touch. He left the door ajar and headed for the stove.

He sat in front of the fire with a bowl of hearty stew. Dipping the bread into thick gravy, he savored Lily's cooking skills. She had spoiled them with her delicious meals.

From the sounds of giggling and laughter in the bedroom, it seemed she was also adept at nurturing children, despite his earlier belief to the contrary. Did she know she possessed so many talents? Her hats were beautiful, for sure, but the food and caring were natural. Care for her fellow man came easily to her.

That caring was the reason she wanted for customers. It was one thing to reach out to people. It was another thing entirely to do it to one's own detriment. Sacrificial caring was a strong Christian principle. He hated how it had marred her reputation among the good people of Pine Haven. When they got to know her as he and Ellen did, her true heart would be evident to all.

If only they'd give her time.

Deep in thought, he didn't hear Lily enter the room.

"She wants to rest now." Her voice drew him to its warmth. "It seems she's a little better. She was able to eat most of the stew."

A final swoop of his spoon around the inside of his bowl gathered the last bits of potatoes and gravy. He retraced the spoon's path with his last bite of bread and popped it into his mouth. He stood with the bowl in one hand and wiped his chin with the wrist of his sleeve.

"Who can blame her? This is the best stew we've had in this house in . . . well, in longer than I can remember." He set his bowl on the table and took Ellen's dishes from her. "Are you going to eat?"

"Yes." Lily ladled stew into a bowl and looked over her shoulder toward the bedroom. "Maybe we can get her to eat a little more after a while. She hasn't eaten much today."

"I'm glad she's been able to sleep." Edward stacked the bowls in the basin to wash later.

Lily examined her fingers, touching the nails, then turned her hands palm up and looked at him. "I'm sorry for upsetting you earlier."

Edward saw sorrow and hope in her eyes. "I wasn't upset with you." They stood with the table separating them. "I was worried about Ellen."

"I overstepped my bounds. I do that. I do or say something without thinking it through first." A nervous laugh bubbled in her throat. "Papa says it puts people off. He's forever scolding me for it."

Edward moved around the table. "You were right, you know." He reached a hand toward her, but the right to touch her wasn't his. He dropped it to his side. "Doc says cooling the fever was helpful. Thank you."

Blond waves framed her face, and relief turned her blue eyes to violet. Such beautiful eyes. This time she reached to rest a hand on his sleeve. It was as though a bird rested on his arm. The weight of it was so light he had to look to confirm its presence, but the wonder of it paralyzed him.

The air stilled. Peace settled between the two of them.

"I'm so glad. I don't think I could have

stood it if I'd caused Ellen more suffering. I know that was your concern."

He laid his hand over hers. "Thank you for understanding. Please forgive me for my harshness."

"If you'll forgive me."

A tug beneath his hand beckoned him to release her. A rightness in the comfort of her touch told him to resist. Sparks flew from the fireplace as a log crackled and shifted. He wrapped his fingers around her hand and rubbed his thumb across her knuckles. The violet eyes widened.

"Uncle Edward?"

Coughing and whimpers dragged him back to reality.

"Coming, Ellen." He released Lily's hand. "There's fresh coffee on the stove."

The violet faded to blue, and the moment was over. Had it really happened?

Lily picked up her bowl. "I'll see to the dishes after I eat."

"Thank you for the supper."

Lily waved off his thanks. "Let me know if I can help."

"I will."

More coughing made him realize it was time for Ellen's medicine. He went into her room to tend to her. While he soothed the child back to sleep, he wondered if he could

251

soothe his heart back to its normal rhythm.

How could the touch of a callused hand bring comfort? Was it wise for him to allow himself to be comforted by her? He rubbed his sleeve at the memory of her hand under his.

The more he learned about his wife, the more he liked her. He'd have to be careful. She'd been faithful in her promise to help him with Ellen. He couldn't risk making Lily uncomfortable in their relationship by letting himself fall for her. She'd made it plain she wasn't interested in him. Ellen would suffer if he made Lily uneasy around him.

He didn't know who would suffer more. Ellen? Or him?

CHAPTER THIRTEEN

"What is that caterwauling?" Lily threw back the quilt, slid her feet into slippers and tied on her robe. "How's a body supposed to sleep with all that racket?" It had taken her hours to fall asleep. Thinking about her reaction to being so close to Edward had kept her awake. It wasn't only the closeness they'd felt, but the sudden backing away that had hindered her rest. This middle-of-the-night screeching was not a welcome sound.

She crept quietly through the front room of the cabin. Edward lay on his back, stretched out near the fire, snoring lightly.

The moon was high in the sky when she opened the front door to find a yowling kitten on the step. A tiny paw wedged between two boards was the apparent reason for its distress. She pulled the door closed behind her to keep from waking Edward or Ellen.

"You poor baby. No wonder you're crying

so." She stooped to extricate the paw and landed on her seat on the porch when the freed animal launched itself at her.

"Oh, my. You are upset, aren't you, little one?" Lily pulled the kitten from its perch on her shoulder and cradled it in her hands. Tiny claws nipped at her flesh. Then a pink tongue dragged roughly across the knuckles on her thumbs. The crying turned to mews and nuzzling.

"You're trembling." Lily pulled the kitten into the lapel of her robe. She took the orange-and-black ball of fur to her room and wrapped it in a towel.

"I'm guessing you're just old enough to be away from your mother, but not quite confident." She rubbed the tiny head with the towel and promised her help to the lost animal.

By the time the sun came up, Lily had a plan. She hoped Edward would consent.

After breakfast, Lily and Edward assessed Ellen's improvement. They decided to leave her to rest. Edward would work and check in on her frequently. Lily would open the shop and come home for lunch.

Lily bundled the cat into a basket and covered it with a towel, praying it would be silent until she got it out of the cabin. She wanted to make sure it was healthy before telling Edward about it or giving it to Ellen.

She crossed the street and stepped onto the walk in front of her shop. She set the basket on the boardwalk and unlocked the door, humming a chipper tune at the thought of Ellen's reaction to her idea.

"Mrs. Stone." Winston Ledford's voice startled her when she reached to pick up the basket.

"Mr. Ledford." Lily's breath caught. She was forced to stop when he blocked her path.

"How is business?"

"Everything is well." She leaned to look beyond his shoulder.

"Looking for your Mr. Stone, are you?" Cold eyes awaited her reaction.

Lily stretched to her full height. "Not that it's any of your business, but I'm concerned about our niece. She's been ill."

"I'm sure you'll take good care of her." Cynicism dripped from every word. "I hear you've gone out of your way to be helpful to my girls."

"I make it my practice to be helpful to all my customers."

"Just be careful not to discourage my girls. I don't mind if you sell them hats and such, but I won't tolerate you interfering with their work." A serious weight filled his tone.

Lily caught sight of Edward opening the doors to his shop. He stopped to study her for a moment. She turned her attention back to the saloon owner.

"Mr. Ledford, any conversation I have with Mrs. Jones or Miss Aiken is entirely my business. I won't let you, or anyone else for that matter, tell me what to do." She hiked the basket up higher on her arm and took a step toward him. "So don't bother trying to threaten me again. I don't threaten."

He chuckled. What on earth could cause the man to chuckle when she was giving him such a solemn speech? She turned to follow his gaze toward the bank. Mrs. Croft was coming through the doorway, towing her reluctant husband by the sleeve. Exasperated, Lily pivoted in the direction of Edward's shop. His retreating back told her he'd seen and disapproved of her. Again.

"I think you may be correct, Mrs. Stone. I don't see you as a threat at all. I don't have to worry about you affecting my business. All I had to do was stand in the middle of town and engage you in conversation. You've affected your business by associating with me. I give it two weeks, at the most three, before you won't be an issue for anyone in Pine Haven." He touched the brim of his hat. "Good day to you."

The spiteful man left her standing on the sidewalk. Behind her was her shop, empty of customers for days on end, save for the preacher's wife and Mr. Ledford's employees. Behind her stood a nosy woman who chose to believe the worst of her without giving her an opportunity to prove her true Christian character. But the most painful of all was seeing the back of the husband she'd married to protect her name as he walked into his shop.

Why did it hurt so badly to be rejected? She'd come here to escape the confines of being at someone else's beck and call. To be on her own. But she was caught in the middle of a town in transition. She'd fooled herself to believe she could bridge the gaps between the old and new. She'd wanted to be left alone. Not to be alone.

A rumbling purr and the rustle of the towel covering the kitten drew her attention. Did Edward really believe she'd be consorting with the saloon owner? Had he opened the doors of his business a moment earlier, he'd have known it was a random encounter.

Why hadn't anyone been close enough to hear her rebuff him? If only she had a witness to her resistance to the man's attentions.

Lily stepped into her shop and closed the door. The little girl in bed with a fever needed the cheer a tiny kitten could bring. The cleaning and grooming of the small animal must be done before she approached Edward. She was certain the frightened animal would scratch and resist. But putting a smile on Ellen's pale face would make it worth the effort.

Edward may be angry with her, but surely he wouldn't refuse Ellen the joy of a warm, furry friend.

Edward tied on his leather apron. He refused to look at Lily standing in the open doorway of his shop. "Ellen is resting and I'm busy."

In spite of his frustration at her continued association with Winston Ledford, it took all his focus to keep from welcoming her. He wanted her here. He'd tried to help her. Her determined refusal to control her behavior in public was an obstacle not just to her business but to their relationship, as well.

A nagging voice in his head reminded him of her honorable goals. Of her caring nature. His angry mood silenced the voice. Seeing her on the street with the saloon owner rankled him for reasons he wasn't willing to explore.

He picked up a shovel and scooped coal into the forge in preparation for the morning's work.

"I've brought her something." She held the basket out for him to see.

Edward blew out a long sigh and turned to her. He had to put as much effort into this arrangement as he expected from her. He dropped the shovel back into the hopper, causing black dust to float in the air between them.

"I think God sent us a little help for her to pass the time while she has to rest." She took a step toward him.

The towel in the basket moved. Now he was curious.

"What is it?"

"See for yourself." She held the basket closer.

A purring sound greeted him as he lifted the towel. The kitten looked to be about two months old. "Where did you get such a critter?" He dropped the towel back into the basket but left the cat uncovered. Button eyes of green watched his every move.

"He came to me in the middle of the night." The teasing chuckle in her throat chipped away at his ill humor. "He did, did he?" Edward dropped the metal shank he'd need for his first project on the edge of the forge near the growing heat of the fire. "What did you do? Sleep with your window open?"

"No." Lily smiled at him in earnest. "He woke me from a sound sleep, crying because his paw was caught in the boards of the porch steps."

"You know, if you fed him, he'll never leave."

"Oh, I know. That's why I made sure to feed him right away."

Edward eyed the tiny creature. "How did you get him without me hearing you?"

She smiled, a slight lifting of the corner of her lips. "It might be hard for you to hear over your snoring."

"Well, you may as well give him a name, then. He's yours for life."

"I think Ellen will love him." She placed the basket on his workbench and lifted the tiny pet with her gloved hands.

Edward backed away from her. "I think he'll be a great cat for your shop."

Lily moved closer, petting the speckled fur with one hand while she cradled the kitten against her coat with the other. "But isn't he cute?"

"Not to me." A hand went up, palm out, to emphasize his disagreement with any notion that the cat should stay with Ellen.

"He's adorable. I know Ellen will think so."

"Nope. Not for one minute." He shook his head back and forth while she continued to pursue him with the animal.

She leaned in close and offered the cat to him, tripping over the corner of the coal hopper. The shovel slipped to the floor with a metallic crash.

Startled, the cat launched itself from Lily's hands to the front of his shirt. Lily stumbled backward and lost her balance. Flailing in an effort to stay on her feet was useless. She landed on her seat in the mound of coal. A cloud of dust rose around her. Before he could help, she pressed both hands on the sides of the hopper and pushed herself up.

Lily clapped her gloves together. A shower of powdered coal drifted to the ground, leaving a fine layer on the front of her pale blue skirt.

It didn't escape his notice that her clothes and hats complemented the color of her hair and eyes. Even covered in soot, she was as fine a lady as he'd ever seen.

"Are you all right?" Edward hoped she wasn't hurt. He extricated the tiny claws from his shirt and dropped the kitten into the basket.

"Perfectly fine, thank you." Without looking away from him, she rubbed her skirt smooth and tugged at the hem of her coat, leaving a streak of black wherever her ruined gloves touched.

He dared not laugh at her. The flash of light in her violet eyes warned him. But the rumble of humor bubbled in his chest as he fought back a grin.

She picked her chin up, stretching her spine to reach all of the height God had given her.

Certain the top of her head would nest pleasantly under his chin, he smiled.

"Is there something you find amusing?" Lily put a hand to her hair, and he chuckled. Her eyebrows shot up.

An unsuccessful attempt to compose himself was followed by outright laughter when she brushed a knuckle across the tip of her nose, leaving another streak of coal.

"Really, Edward, I do not see why you are so amused. You may be big and strong and handsome, but your manners are sorely lacking." Lily's eyes grew wide. "What I mean is . . ."

"I heard you. You don't need to explain." She'd called him handsome. Something in her voice when she said it made him wish it could be true.

"May I offer an apology for my lack of manners? It's not every day I see someone so prim and proper in such a state." He stepped to a bench on the far side of the shop and retrieved a clean rag. "There's some water in the rain barrel outside the front door. Feel free to freshen up, if you'd like." He held the rag out like a peace offering.

Lily reached for the rag and saw her sleeve. Then she peered down at the front of her skirt. "Oh, my. Is it everywhere?" She looked to him for the confirmation she knew was coming.

"Afraid it is." A smile threatened to crease his face.

"I must be a sight."

"I'd say you are." He grinned then. "Please forgive me. I didn't mean to laugh at your misfortune."

"Really?" She touched the rag to her nose and pulled it away. His face let her know she'd only made it worse. "I discern no end to your mirth at my expense."

"It's just amazing to me how you can manage to look so pretty all covered in soot like you are."

Lily felt her cheeks flame. He probably only called her pretty because she'd foolishly said he was handsome. "Now you're just being silly. There is nothing pretty about my present state."

He stepped close and took the rag from her. With a gentle hand he dabbed at her nose and cheek. "That's better." His eyes locked on hers and dared her to breathe. "Just as I expected. Still as pretty as ever." One corner of his mouth lifted.

Lily's head reeled. He was too close . . . and tall . . . his muscular build imposing. Was she leaning toward him? Could she stop herself? Did she want to?

She'd been around strong men every day at her father's ranch, but this man was different. By not moving, without a word he asked her permission to stay near her. Was he asking to come nearer still? As her husband, did he think she should welcome his closeness?

The space of his workshop seemed to shrink. The heat from the fire in the forge seemed to grow hotter even though the bellows was still. She fought the urge to step back.

Dredging up new strength, she spoke. "Edward, I . . ." The whisper died in her throat.

"Uncle Edward?" Ellen's voice called from behind her. "How come I don't hear any hammerin'?" A disheveled head poked around the corner of the forge. She must have entered through a back door.

Lily took a step back. Edward pushed the end of the metal piece into the fire and pumped the bellows.

"Lily! I thought you were going to stay at your shop all morning." Ellen stepped toward Lily with outstretched arms.

Lily caught the child's arms before the anticipated hug. "I'm all dirty. Don't let it get on you."

"Why did you come here instead of to the house?" Curious eyes lifted to quiz her.

"I needed to see your uncle first."

"Why?" Ellen flung a glance over her shoulder at Edward. "He ain't sick."

"Speaking of sick, why are you out of bed?" Edward's face bore disapproval and compassion at the same time.

"I'm tired of being in bed. And my fever is better. You said so."

"You still have to stay in bed until you're completely recovered. Doc's orders."

Lily sought Edward's permission with her eyes to share the kitten. Surely he was too kind to deny the child this small comfort.

265

The kitten meowed in his basket on the bench.

Ellen's brows climbed her tiny forehead. "Uncle Edward?" She tucked her handkerchief doll into the pocket of her pinafore and reached for the cat.

"No, Ellen." Edward picked up his bellows and frowned at Lily.

"Oh, please." Ellen's voice was muffled as her nose nuzzled the fur of the tiny kitten. She lifted her pale face. "Has he got a name? Is he yours? Where did you get him?"

Lily chuckled at the string of questions. "He showed up on the porch steps last night. He doesn't have a name, and we were just discussing who will keep him." She gave a nod to Edward. "You'll have to ask him."

"Can I keep him, Uncle Edward?"

"No." Edward set the bellows aside and turned the metal in the fire.

"Please, Edward." She added her pleas to the little girl's.

"Can we call him Speckles? He's got so many speckles." The calico kitten licked at Ellen's hands.

"That's a wonderful name, Ellen." Lily was triumphant.

His shaking head marked the end of Edward's argument against the cat. "It appears I am outnumbered. But there will be conditions."

Lily laughed at his expression of mock defeat.

Ellen gave a weak laugh. "Can he take a nap with me? I'm supposed to stay in bed, but I get lonely."

"I think Speckles would like that very much." Lily touched the small animal's head.

"Aunt Lily, you're all speckled, too. Maybe I should call you Sparkles instead of Aunt Lily. You're all covered in shiny coal dust."

It was Edward's turn to laugh. "It sounds fitting to me."

"Very funny." She smiled at the two of them laughing and happy. It was a relief after the stress of Ellen's fever. "Ellen, I've got just enough time to tuck you back in bed before I have to go back to the shop."

"Thank you, Uncle Edward." Ellen snuggled the kitten close, and Lily retrieved the basket.

"Don't thank me. It was Aunt Lily's idea." He crouched in front of her. "It's only for while you're sick. Speckles goes back to her shop when you're well again."

The little girl put on a brave face and turned to Lily. "Can I come visit him there?"

"You certainly may."

"Back to bed with you, young lady."

Edward dropped a kiss on Ellen's head as he stood. "I'll be over in a few minutes to give you your medicine."

"You go on ahead. I'll be right along in a minute." Lily watched Ellen snuggle the kitten high into the curve of her neck. The little girl whispered to Speckles as she walked back the way she'd come.

"Edward?" A new idea formed in her active mind. Why hadn't she thought of this in the first place?

Edward pulled on thick gloves and picked up his hammer. "What is it now, Lily? I can see your mind churning away behind your eyes. I am certain this can't bode well for me." He checked the tip of the metal and pushed it back into the glowing coals.

"Actually . . ." She drew out the word, trying to decide the best way to broach this new subject.

"See. There it is. The plotting and planning I suspected." A smile pulled his lips into a thin line and dimples creased his cheeks.

"This idea would make it easier for you while Ellen is recovering. And it would keep her from being lonely."

"I thought Speckles was going to take care of that problem."

"He will, for the most part." Lily shifted

268

from one foot to the other on her tiny heels. The hem of her skirt stirred the dust at her feet.

"I'm waiting." Edward's smile turned to a suspicious grin.

"What if Ellen stays with me through the day? I can make her a place in the workroom to rest. You can work without interruption, and she can keep me company."

The grin faded. "That's very kind of you, Lily, but she'll be fine at home."

"I know you're busy. You've got to shoe a horse for Dr. Willis, and you've still got to finish the other hat stands for me. And the sign."

"What about your work? Ellen needs her medicine, and she'll have to eat. Not to mention the cat will have needs, too." He stood between the forge and the anvil shaking his head.

"I don't know why I didn't think of it before." Lily took a tentative step and placed a hand on his arm. The strength she drew from the touch was more for herself than to assure his attention. "I'm offering. And if we're being honest here, we both know I probably won't be very busy today." She tried to keep the disappointment from her voice.

Was it just a couple of weeks ago she

hoped to be busy with customers, making new friends and living a life independent of the responsibility of tending the needs of others? How quickly Ellen had made her way into Lily's heart. The thought of the child alone in bed for the day was sad.

"Please let me do this. For Ellen. It's why you married me."

"I married you so she would have a motherly influence in her life."

"If she was my own flesh and blood, I'd want her close by while she is sick." She saw his resolve waver. "It's what we agreed to."

CHAPTER FOURTEEN

The January sun was setting, and a cool breeze had threatened from the west as he'd walked across the street to Lily's place. Without having to worry about Ellen, he'd been able to shoe Doc's horse and make good progress on the remaining stands for Lily. The drawing for the sign was complete, too.

The bell rang as he entered the shop. Lily must have seen him coming across the street. "We're in the workroom."

Ellen was perched in the middle of the makeshift cot Lily had made for her in the corner of the workroom, the kitten nestled asleep in her lap. "Uncle Edward, I was good today. I took a nap this morning and again after lunch." She rubbed the kitten's ears. "Two, if you count that short one before you came."

Lily stood near the cot. "I'd say she'll recover quicker than we first thought. Dr.

271

Willis stopped in and was pleased with her progress. He thinks if we keep her quiet and restful for a few more days, she'll be as good as new."

"When he brought his horse by this morning, I told him she was here."

Edward had noticed the pristine shop when he arrived. The floors shone, and every hat was displayed with care. Lily must have worked while Ellen slept. Not one trace of a customer could be found.

"Are you ladies ready to go home?"

"I am." Ellen climbed off the cot and put the kitten in its basket.

"You two go ahead. I'll close up shop and be there in a few minutes." Lily bolted the back door and straightened the cot before following them into the front of the shop.

Edward lifted Ellen, and she wrapped her legs around his middle, the cat and basket hanging from her arm. "Don't be too long." He adjusted the child while Lily tucked a quilt around her small frame to keep her warm for the short trip across the street.

"Just a few minutes." She closed the door behind them.

By the time he had Ellen tucked into her bed with the kitten on the blanket, he heard Lily come into the cabin. He sat with Ellen, half listening to her ramble on about her day, never losing track of Lily's movements in the cabin. First she'd gone to her room and hung her coat in the wardrobe. Then she washed her hands in the bowl in her room. He strained to hear her light steps as she went to the stove to start their supper.

"I had fun with Speckles. He likes me. You really do need to let him stay with me all the time. He'll be lonely at night at Aunt Lily's shop." Ellen stopped petting the animal and looked up. "Are you listening to me, Uncle Edward?"

"Hmm?" He sat up in the chair and leaned his elbows on his knees. "Sure. You don't want the cat to be lonely."

"Yay!" She jumped from the bed and flung herself at him, kissing his cheek. "Thank you, Uncle Edward! Thank you!"

Lily came up behind him. How he heard her over the noise Ellen was making, he wasn't sure.

"What has happened in here?" Lily smiled and waited to hear what the commotion was all about.

"Uncle Edward said Speckles can stay here with me. Even after I'm well."

He didn't. "What?" He looked from Ellen to Lily. "I didn't say that."

"Yes, you did. You said 'sure.' "

Oh, no. He'd have to pay more attention,

or these two would have his life turned upside down.

"I said, 'sure, I heard you,' not 'sure, you can have a cat.' "

"I'll leave you two to sort this out." Lily laughed. "I need to get the corn bread into the oven."

Upside down? It was too late. In the past few months, he'd gone from being a contented bachelor to full-time uncle, and now to guardian and husband. His world was more than upside down. It was topsy-turvy. Strangely, it wasn't as unsettling as he'd thought it might be.

When he tucked Ellen into bed later that night, she insisted on recounting her day to him, saying he wasn't paying attention before supper, so she'd tell it all again. She loved the hats Lily made. Did he think she could make pretty things when she grew up? On and on, she rattled about things Lily said and did. When she finally settled against the pillows after another dose of the dreaded medicine, she sighed and pulled the kitten into the circle of her arms.

"Uncle Edward?" Her words were whisper soft, weak with fatigue and the remains of the illness.

"Yes, sweetheart?" He touched her forehead and was glad to note her fever wasn't as high as it had been the previous day.

"Do you like Aunt Lily?"

Her eyes were closed. Could he save his answer in hopes she'd fall asleep?

Ellen turned onto her side and snuggled into the pillow. "Do you?" she asked again.

"Yes, I do." He straightened the blanket and extinguished the wick in the lamp on the bedside table. The shadows in her room danced in the glow of the moonbeams shimmering through the barren trees outside her window.

"Good. Me, too." Eyes closed, a yawn settled Ellen deeper into the night. "I know she's pretty. But I think she's strong, too."

"I think you're right, little one." He kissed her forehead.

"Thank you for letting me keep Speckles." Her words were barely a whisper as slumber pulled at her.

"You rest now. I love you." He turned in the doorway and took one last look at her sleeping form. She was right. Lily was pretty and strong. Unlike any woman he'd ever known. She was grounded in her faith, even when putting it into practice put her reputation at risk. She was beautiful. There was no denying that. In fact, Lily was disproving a lot of his long-held beliefs about women. And life in general.

If only he could shake the image of her engaged in conversation with the saloon owner. Why did she continue to jeopardize her standing in the community by associating with Winston Ledford?

He closed the door to Ellen's room and turned to see Lily on the settee, one of Ellen's dresses in her lap and her sewing basket at her feet.

"Is she all settled in?" Lily concentrated on the needle she was threading.

Edward looked over his shoulder. "Yes. She was asleep before I left the room." He went to the stove and poured himself a cup of coffee. "Can I get you a cup?"

Lily looked up from her mending with a small smile and a shake of her head. "No, thank you."

She was the picture of solace. How had this woman never married before she came to Pine Haven? Were the men in her hometown daft? Lily should be sitting in a home full of love and children of her own, not in front of his fire, mending Ellen's clothes after having cooked them a meal. She deserved to be loved. Just like Ellen deserved her mother and father.

Then Winston Ledford's face came back to him, smiling at Lily in the street. Had Lily allowed her charitable heart to cast her

276

in a negative light in her home community, too? People could be persnickety creatures when it came to what they considered appropriate behavior of a young lady.

He drank a large gulp of his coffee and strangled on its heat. He sputtered and lowered himself into his chair near the fire.

"Are you okay?" Lily looked up again.

"Fine. Just drank it too fast."

"You better be careful." She spoke absentmindedly, but it was just the opening he needed.

"Speaking of being careful." He paused and considered his next words. "There's something I need to say."

"You sound serious." Her hands stilled. "What is it?"

"I saw you this morning." He cleared his throat. "Talking to Winston Ledford again."

The slow intake of breath and slight rise in her head warned of her dismay. "Again?" Her even tone was taut with tension and the effort to control it.

"Well, you have talked to him before."

"I have." She wasn't making this easy.

"It's just that I married you to protect your reputation, and . . ."

The calm left her. "And what? Do you honestly think I'd risk my reputation after paying so dearly to restore it? You aren't the only one who gave up something for this marriage."

She was right. He was benefiting from her relationship with Ellen. Her world had turned upside down in a much shorter time than his. She was probably reeling from the spin of it.

He started over. "What I mean to say is, I think it would be easier to protect yourself in the future if you avoid the likes of Winston Ledford. He can only hurt you."

"He came up to me on the street. What was I to do? Short of being rude, I had to at least speak to the man." She tilted her neck back and looked at the ceiling. "And the irony of it all is that he's as upset by my kindness to Mrs. Jones and Miss Aiken as everyone else in town."

"He's upset? Was he unkind to you?" He was out of his chair before he realized it. It was one thing for him to caution Lily, but another thing entirely for that snake of a man to treat his wife in a manner unbecoming of a gentleman.

"He warned me not to upset his girls, as he calls them."

"Did he threaten you?" He sat on the settee beside her and reached for her hand. It trembled in his. "What did he say?" If he harmed Lily in any way . . . He forced

278

himself to listen to her answer rather than marching out the front door and into the saloon to confront the man.

"Not exactly. He just told me not to discourage them. He doesn't want them to be tempted away from the life he's offered them." She sighed. "In the end he said he didn't have to do anything to me. He said I'd destroy myself just by being kind to them." She looked up into Edward's eyes. "And to him." She shook her head. "But I wasn't kind to him. I told him not to threaten me. I told him he couldn't tell me who to talk to and not talk to."

Edward put his other hand over hers and held it snug until the trembling stopped. "I'm sorry."

She squinted her pretty blue eyes at him. "You're sorry? You didn't do anything."

"I did exactly what Winston Ledford did. I tried to tell you what to do and who to associate yourself with."

"But you're trying to protect me." Her eyes softened when she said the words. "And he was trying to protect himself."

"I'm not that good with explaining myself, but I really do want to protect you."

Lily laid her other hand on top of his. Its warmth and gentleness were welcome.

"You know, Edward, we want the same

279

things. I want my business to succeed for me, but also for Ellen and for you. I don't want to do anything to put that at risk."

"I realize that. I knew it before, but Winston Ledford has a knack for infuriating me."

"Are you jealous?" She started to smirk. Then, as if she heard the words after she said them, she pulled her hands away. Her voice lost all its mirth. "There's no need to be."

He tugged her hands back into his. "I know." He gave her hands a light squeeze and released them before going to stoke the fire.

They had reached a new understanding of one another tonight. He knew it would help them as they cared for Ellen. But he was beginning to wonder how much they could help each other.

Before they turned in for the night, Lily convinced him to let Ellen spend the day with her again tomorrow and every day until Doc said she could return to school.

Morning would bring a new day. Filled with what, he did not know. But he was eager to find out.

"You need to stay on the cot. I promised your uncle Edward."

"I just want to go outside for a minute." Ellen juggled the kitten and her doll in her small hands.

"It's time to rest. You've been up a bit more today. I don't want you to overdo it and relapse."

"What's relasp?" Ellen squinted at Lily and dropped her doll. Speckles wriggled free and swatted at the edges of the doll's hem.

"Relapse." Lily picked up the doll. "It means to go backward. The time you've spent resting has made you stronger. If you try to do too much too soon, you'll get worse instead of better." The doll was worn and dirty. She unfurled the wrinkled edges of its dress.

"I don't want to get sicker." Ellen harrumphed and leaned back against the pillows. She pulled at the kitten's ears. "But I'm tired of resting. I thought all this resting was gonna make me not be tired."

Lily laughed. "It will. It just takes time. Remember, Dr. Willis said the hard part would be resting when you started to feel better."

"Well, this must be the hard part then. 'Cause I'm ready to get up."

"I think I know something we can do that won't tire you."

Hope stirred in Ellen's eyes. The fever had left her sockets sunken and dull. The color had started to come back into her cheeks, but fatigue washed it away again in a matter of minutes if she exerted herself.

"What can we do?"

"I can get a basin of warm water and some soap. You can give your doll a bath."

"It won't hurt her?"

"No, of course not, silly girl. No more than it hurts when you take a bath." Lily chucked Ellen under the chin and gave her the doll.

"Sometimes, Momma had to scrub mighty hard behind my ears and under my finger-nails." Ellen giggled.

Lily set the basin on her workbench and helped the child onto her stool.

Together they worked to clean the doll. Endless play had soiled the handkerchief but not beyond repair. When they set the doll on the bench to dry, Ellen went back to her cot without argument.

"Do you think my momma misses me as much as I miss her?" Ellen lay back and pulled Speckles close.

Lily didn't want to give Ellen false hope about the return of her parents, but she didn't think Edward wanted her to make the child think they were never coming back. She answered the only way she knew how. "I'm sure she does." Lily pulled a quilt over the child. "Didn't she tell you so in her letters?"

"The letters stopped coming." A tear slid down one cheek, and Lily sat down to draw Ellen into her arms.

"Oh, honey, they were too sick to write." They rocked back and forth, Ellen sobbing and Lily crying in silence. Lily remembered the pain of realizing her mother was gone.

"I wish they'd come back." Ellen lifted her head and gulped in air, then collapsed against Lily and wailed.

"Hush, baby. It's okay." There were no words to ease the pain in Ellen's heart. Lily knew she wasn't qualified to help her, but Edward wouldn't be back for hours. "Don't wear yourself out with crying."

"I can't stop. My heart hurts. And I want my momma!" Her voice climbed in hopeless desperation with each word.

Lily tried her best to comfort Ellen. What did one say to a child who didn't know if her parents were coming back for her? The weeping spell and Lily's rocking motion lulled the sad girl to sleep. She was gently snoring when Lily went into the front of the shop.

One look out the window confirmed that

hers was the only shop void of business again today. How long could she stay open without regular customers? If it weren't for the trickle of lady passengers who stopped in while the train took on water, she wouldn't have sold more than two hats this week. Thankfully, those ladies were generally pleasant and happy to spend their money.

Maybe she should write a letter to her father and let him know what was happening in Pine Haven. She didn't want him to be taken by surprise by her lack of steady business when he came to town.

The train whistle blew, announcing the arrival of new passengers.

She could write tomorrow. If no one came today. Or maybe next week. Maybe this lull would blow over and she'd never have to share her struggles with him. It would be enough to convince him she was content in her marriage — failing as a shop owner was something she hoped to avoid.

"How was your afternoon?" Edward ruffled Ellen's hair and scratched the cat behind the ears. He'd had a long day's work and was looking forward to a good meal. Lily keeping Ellen with her for the day had allowed him to catch up on several small projects.

"Better than the morning," Lily said. "The trade from the train was better than yesterday afternoon."

"What have you two been up to?" He took off his jacket and hung it on a peg by the door.

"I helped with the corn bread." Ellen was excited. She was still a bit pale, but he was glad to see her feeling better.

"She worked hard." Lily put plates on the table. "As hard as someone can when they're resting."

Again Lily had helped Ellen and made her feel special. He was tired from having lost sleep while Ellen was so ill. Tonight nothing would make him happier than sitting around the table with this beautiful woman who gave so freely of herself without expectation of reward.

"It smells delicious." Edward looked at Ellen. "You better make sure there's plenty of butter on the table for me."

"Yes, sir!" A happy girl put the butter on the table and went to her room.

"Thank you for all you've done for her." He caught Lily's hand in his when she turned back to the stove. It was delicate and warm. Soft and strong at the same time. "You've really made her life better."

"She wanted to learn." Lily didn't look at him.

"She's wanted a lot of things I couldn't give her." He hoped he wasn't making her uncomfortable, but he couldn't resist reaching out to her. "You're the first person who's taken the time with her."

"Ellen is a delightful child. Anyone would be blessed by spending time with her."

A chuckle escaped his chest. "We both know she did her best to run you off in the beginning."

"Only because she was afraid." Her quick response was serious. He had to lean in to hear Lily's whispered words. "Afraid I'd take you away from her."

He gave her hand a slight squeeze. Lily tugged to pull her hand away.

Edward didn't release her. "Instead, she brought us together." He didn't blink for fear he'd miss her reaction to his words.

She slid her hand from beneath his. "She knows she'll never have to worry about you leaving her."

Ellen's voice interrupted them. "Are you coming? It'll all be cold if you don't come now." She slid into her chair at the table and put her doll on the seat by her.

Lily untied her apron and hung it by the back door. She smoothed the front of her dress and came to the table. He watched her every move from his seat opposite her. She unfolded her napkin and laid it in her lap before reaching for Ellen's hand and bowing her head so he could say grace. Everything about this woman was refined and beautiful.

As he thanked God for the meal, he wondered what she must think of him. Or if she thought of him at all.

In true Texas fashion, Sunday morning the wind howled outside his window. Last Sunday's snowstorm had blown in with a fury and was gone in hours. Most of the week had been sunny with mild weather. Today promised to be another blast of winter.

Edward was grateful he didn't live where the weather stayed cold and brutal for months on end. Enduring the scattered days of cold was enough for him.

"I'm ready." Ellen came from her room.

"The wind is a mite rough. We could stay home today." He touched the glass on the window with the back of his hand to gauge the outside temperature.

"Uncle Edward, I'm well. Doc Willis said so when he came by yesterday." She pulled her new hat to adjust the angle.

287

"He said your fever is gone. He didn't say for you to go out in the wind." Why must everything be an argument with this child?

Lily came out of her room wearing her blue coat and pulling on her gloves. "Why, Ellen, you look fetching today."

Lily was fetching, too. The blue of her coat matched her eyes. Her golden hair glimmered in the morning light spilling through the windows.

"Thank you, Aunt Lily." Ellen tugged at the ribbon. "I did the bow like you showed me." Lily had given Ellen the hat on Friday after supper. It was stouter than anything she owned, but very pretty at the same time. The new hat seemed to make Ellen glow. He fought back his sadness at the thought of what her parents were missing by not being part of her life.

Edward forced his attention back to deciding whether or not Ellen should go out today. "She wants to go to church, but I'm not sure about the weather."

"I promise to bundle up and stay warm. I won't even ask to play outside."

Lily asked Ellen, "Are you certain you'll be able to sit still while everyone else is playing?"

A solemn expression accompanied the child's response. "I will." She turned to

Edward. "Please, can I go? Aunt Lily said she made my new hat so even bad, cold weather couldn't hurt me." She swiveled back and forth without moving her feet. The bottom edges of her coat caught on the motion and swished like the church bell he heard ringing in the distance.

"I don't know." He opened the door to gauge the wind.

"Please, Uncle Edward. I miss my friends. You already made me miss Bible class."

Lily added, "I think she'll be okay."

"Well, if you promise no argument about dawdling outside in the weather, I guess we can risk it."

"Oh, boy!" Ellen skipped to the front door.

"Whoa, there. No running and getting all excited. I don't want you to overdo it."

"I won't. I don't want to relasp." Ellen grabbed his hand and tugged him out the door. Lily followed them down the steps. "Let's hurry so I don't get cold."

Edward laughed and caught her up to put her on the wagon seat. "Cover up with that blanket."

Lily took his hand, and he helped her into the wagon.

"Thank you, Edward." Her voice was quiet as she tucked the blanket close around her legs. He climbed aboard, and they made their way to the church.

"I'm afraid we might be in for some more cold weather, the way the wind's blowing."

"As long as it doesn't snow and storm like it did last week, I'll be fine." Lily put her arm around Ellen and pulled the child close.

"I just hope it holds off till after the service. The thought of being caught out like that again doesn't appeal to me." Edward pulled up close to the church door and set the brake. He swung his weight off the side of the wagon, boots stirring up the dirt as he landed.

"Ellen." He took his niece by the waist and set her down. He turned back to the wagon. "Lily."

"Thank you." Lily held out her hand to him.

Instead of taking her hand, he encircled Lily's waist with his hands and lowered her to the ground. Heat spilled into her cheeks as he released her.

"Hold a seat for me." He gave her a wink and climbed back into the wagon. "I'll be right in." He didn't know why he had the sudden urge to flirt with his wife like a schoolboy, but he did.

Lily stood frozen on the spot where he had set her down. Had he winked at her? Her

290

eyes saw it, but her mind wasn't sure.

Ellen called from the church doorway. "Come on, Aunt Lily."

Just inside the front door, Lavinia Aiken stood wringing her hands and making a valiant effort to blend into the wall. Mrs. Croft entered and gave a small snort as she made her way to her customary seat.

"Lavinia, you came." Relief at Lavinia's presence pushed all thoughts for herself from Lily's mind. "Do you see the gentleman who invited you?"

"No. Mr. Ledford was right. I don't belong here." She probably would have backed away, but Lily took her by the hand.

"You do, too. Church is for everyone." Lily smiled. "I see you wore the gloves."

A smile turned to a smirk. "Ginger told me it wouldn't matter. Said I could dress like a lady, but I wouldn't be welcome here."

Lily faced the front of the church and tucked Lavinia's hand inside her elbow. "Yes, you are. Come sit with me." The drag against her progress as she headed toward an open bench made her wonder if she'd be able to convince Lavinia to stay.

A small gust of cool air stirred the hair at the nape of Lily's neck as the door opened and closed behind her. In an instant Edward was at Lavinia's other side. "Good morning. Welcome to Pine Haven Church."

Lily could have kissed him for his kindness. She released Lavinia and introduced them. "Edward, this is Lavinia Aiken. Miss Aiken, Edward Stone, my husband." She didn't know how long before she'd grow accustomed to referring to him in such a way.

Edward said, "Pleased to meet you, Miss Aiken." A slight smile lifted Lavinia's face.

"Uncle Edward, sit here." Ellen pulled Edward's hand, and he slid onto the bench beside her. "Is she your friend, Aunt Lily?"

"Yes, Ellen. This is Miss Aiken. Miss Aiken, this is Ellen Sanford, my niece."

"I like your gloves. Did you get 'em at Aunt Lily's shop? That's where I got my hat." Ellen tugged at the bow.

"Yes, thank you." The quiver in Lavinia's voice diminished with each passing minute. "Your hat is quite lovely."

Reverend Dismuke stepped up to the lectern, drawing everyone's attention to the front of the church.

"Please sit with us." Lily indicated the seat beside Edward and Ellen. She stepped in next to Edward. Lavinia sat on the end of the bench.

Joy at having Lavinia in church beside her filled Lily's heart. She could forget all the empty days in her shop and the gossip she'd

292

endured. She'd shared the love God had for her, and Lavinia had responded to it. Nothing else mattered.

The deep voice that sang beside her during the opening hymn held a higher place of esteem to her. Edward had shown kindness, not just to her but to Lavinia, as well. He was a respected member of the community and the church. His acceptance of someone new in their midst would carry a lot of weight.

Lily treasured his acceptance of her as his friend and not just someone to help with Ellen. All the more so, as she learned his character. Living in the same home with Edward and Ellen had given her the opportunity to see how genuine his goodness was. This close to him in church, where every time he shifted in the seat he bumped her shoulder, was proving to be a serious distraction. She might have to spend extra time in Bible study this week to make up for missing most of the sermon.

Somehow they were making this arrangement work. The only time she'd seen him upset or angry was when there was danger, like the night of the fire, or a potential problem, like trying to protect her reputation.

She had grown to love Ellen. And now she

was beginning to enjoy Edward's company. If his actions and demeanor today were an indication of his feelings, he wasn't unhappy, either.

Did she dare to hope they were building a lasting relationship?

Chapter Fifteen

Immediately after the closing prayer, Lily found herself pulled into a hug by Daisy. "Good morning, little sister."

"Hello, Daisy. This is my friend, Lavinia Aiken."

"I'm Daisy Barlow. It's so nice to meet you."

Certain Daisy knew who Lavinia was and why she'd come to Pine Haven, Lily appreciated the enthusiastic greeting.

"Won't you join us for lunch?" Daisy asked.

"Oh, I couldn't possibly." Lavinia was shying away.

"I'm concerned about the weather." Lily turned to Lavinia. "Why don't you come to lunch at our home? I prepared a stew this morning. The cold creeping through the walls last night made me want something hearty today." She leaned in close and lowered her voice. "I even made a cake. Just because it's Sunday, of course."

Edward buttoned his coat. "You ladies make your plans. I'm going to get Ellen wrapped up in the wagon. I'm ready for some of that stew. I hope you'll join us, Miss Aiken."

Daisy patted Lily on the arm. "Well, maybe next week the weather won't be so chilly. I hope you will make plans to attend the Winter Social. It's only a couple of weeks away."

Lily nodded her agreement. "I'm looking forward to the opportunity to get to know more of the ladies in town."

"Harold and Minnie Willis have offered their barn for the event. It's one of the biggest in the county and close to town. You should come, too, Miss Aiken. It'll be great fun." Daisy smiled and said her goodbyes.

When lunch was over, Ellen was sent to bed for a nap. Edward excused himself to work in his shop. Lily knew he was going to whittle and only left the house to give her time to visit with Lavinia. His thoughtfulness pleased her, but it was no longer a surprise. If she stopped to think on it, he was always doing something for someone else.

Lily pulled her fork across the plate, gathering the last of the crumbs and icing.

"Thank you for staying for dessert, Lavinia. A cake always makes it feel more like Sunday to me."

"I haven't had a meal like this since I came to Pine Haven." Lavinia took a sip of hot tea.

"Did you enjoy the church service this morning?" Lily had waited to broach the subject, not sure Lavinia would want to talk about it.

"To be honest, I was a little surprised."

"How so?" She hoped it was a good surprise.

"Everyone was so nice." Lavinia stared into the fire. "Well, almost everyone."

Lily knew she was referring to Mrs. Croft. "The church is a haven for everyone in a community. A place where you can be loved and helped. Most everyone tries to live up to that purpose."

Lavinia turned to her. "Do you think they would accept me every week?" Wariness caused her voice to wobble.

"I'm sure of it."

Lavinia looked back into the flames. "The part where the preacher man talked about all things being new . . ." Her voice trailed into silence.

"That's one of my favorite verses in the Bible. I love knowing God will help me start

297

over." Lily spoke softly. She was hoping to encourage Lavinia, but the words were true for her, too. The new start God had given her in Pine Haven came at a time when she needed hope.

Please give me the right words, Lord. Help Lavinia to see how much You love her.

"Is that for anybody, or just people in the church?" Lavinia's questions were sincere.

"It's for anyone. God gives us all the opportunity to start our lives over with His care and direction. He removes the effect our past has on our future. He gives us new direction and purpose."

"I'd like that." Moisture filled Lavinia's eyes as she looked back at Lily. "Ever since I got to Pine Haven I've felt I was disappointing my family. None of them ever worked in a saloon. They were all honest, God-fearing folks." She hung her head. "I think they'd be ashamed of me."

Lily chose her words with care. "Sometimes in life we find ourselves in difficult circumstances. We don't always see the choices God has put before us. We can choose what looks like the only path and discover later our true purpose is in a much different direction." Lily paused.

That's what she'd done when she agreed to marry Luther. How grateful she was that

God revealed a new choice by allowing her to come to Pine Haven. She couldn't imagine going back to a life where she didn't count. Where all that mattered was what she did for someone else, and no one saw her for who she was and the value she had as a person.

Finding herself married to Edward, a virtual stranger when they'd pledged themselves to each other, had changed her life. In her heart she realized God had given her a better future with Edward and Ellen than she'd have had with Luther. She was beginning to think it was better than her plan to be alone, too.

"Is it too late for me to change paths?" Lavinia's breath caught on a sigh. "The more I think about spending every night of the week dancing with strange men, the more scared I get. I don't want to be someone men only see as a way to forget their troubles and have a good time."

"It's never too late." Lily leaned back in her chair. "I'm proof of that."

"You?"

"Yes, me." It was her turn to stare into the fire. "I spent years caring for my sick father, while all my friends married and started families of their own. After a while, people stopped seeing me as Lily, and I became Mr. Warren's daughter. I was the girl who served the punch at social events, never the one who got asked to dance."

"But you're so pretty. How could anyone overlook you?"

"My duties to my father kept me busy. Over time, I grew comfortable. Then I withdrew from any opportunity. The withdrawal threatened to become bitterness. I began to feel trapped, but I knew a good daughter wouldn't abandon her father in his time of need."

The memories of Luther's first attempts to woo her flooded her mind. In hindsight she saw his unabashed efforts to pawn her off on his mother. She remembered the evenings she talked with the older lady over coffee while Luther begged off to work in his office. How had she been so blind?

"It was so bad that when my father regained his health, I jumped at the first — and only — suitor who presented himself. I came to my senses the night I heard him telling his mother he'd never really love me, but I would be a good companion. For both of them."

"No wonder you wanted to come here. I'd rather work on my own than have a heartless man take care of me." Lavinia gasped. Her eyes widened as the weight of her words sank in.

"We aren't so different after all. In my situation, it was a suitor. In your case, it's Winston Ledford." Lily smiled at her. "At least you've realized it before you're as old as I am."

"But you had your faith in God. What can I do? I've come all this way because I didn't have anyone or anything left at home."

"God has given us all a measure of faith. All we have to do is believe."

Lavinia thought for a few moments. "I'd like to change paths like the preacher said today. I don't want the old things in my life to continue. I want a new life, but I don't know how."

"It's simple. Like Reverend Dismuke said, just pray and ask God to guide you. He will."

"Will you pray with me?"

"Gladly." Lily took Lavinia's hand and prayed for her new friend. She thanked God for their friendship and prayed for God to show Lavinia the path He had for her life — and for Lavinia to have the strength and determination to follow it.

"Thank you." A new light of hope shone in her eyes when Lavinia spoke again. "I know I don't want to be a part of the saloon. But I don't know what kind of work

I can get in Pine Haven. The saloon was my only means of support. Mr. Ledford won't take kindly to me deciding I don't want to work for him."

"We'll think of something." Lily was so pleased Lavinia wouldn't be working at the saloon when it opened in a few weeks — so glad she spoke without thinking. "In the meantime, you can stay in the rooms above my shop."

Shock covered Lavinia's face. "I can? Won't the landlord mind if you take in a boarder?"

It was more important for her friend to be away from the saloon than for Edward to give his permission first. "I'll settle everything with my husband." Another thought came to Lily. "And I'll write a letter to my father to see if he can make a place for you at the hotel."

"Oh, Lily, I don't have money to stay in the hotel." Worry drew her brows together.

"Not as a patron. To work there. My father is buying the hotel in town. He and my sister and his housekeeper are moving to Pine Haven soon."

"Really? A respectable job?" Surprise lit Lavinia's features. "I'll do anything. Scrub floors, wash clothes, cook. Whatever they need."

Lily laughed at her giddiness. "It's settled, then. You can stay over the shop until we hear from my father or you find another job and a place of your own."

Edward came in the front door, a cold wind blowing behind him.

Lily rose from her place on the settee. "I need to step over to the shop with Lavinia. We may be a while." She decided it would be best to talk to Edward about Lavinia's plans when the two of them were alone.

He stood in front of the fire warming his hands. "That's fine. If you're late, I'll give Ellen a light supper and turn in. I've got a busy week ahead."

Lily and Lavinia worked in the rooms above the shop to prepare it for Lavinia. With no extra room in the cabin, Lily had left her bed when she moved into Edward's home.

By the time Lily got home, Edward was stretched out before the fire asleep. Watching the moonlight as the wind howled outside her window that night, she pondered the best way to approach Edward. Would he care that Lavinia was staying over the shop? Surely not, if it was just a short stay.

She smiled at the peace that had flooded Lavinia after they prayed. Lily's Millinery and Finery might not be doing as well as she hoped, but it was worth every penny she'd lost in business to see a young woman choose a better life.

Lord, keep her safe and help her find a job.

It was easier to pray for Lavinia than it was to deal with her own situation. Would her business continue to suffer? How would people view her now that Lavinia was staying in her rooms?

Tomorrow they would set the place in proper order for Lavinia's stay. Rearranging her former home was the easy part.

A cloud danced across the face of the moon. She'd have to talk to Edward in the morning.

Edward awoke with a start. He had a busy day and would need to drive Ellen to school to keep her out of the cold. He could hear Lily moving around in her room.

He rapped on her door.

Lily called softly. "Just a minute."

He spoke through the door. "I just wanted to let you know I'm going to get the wagon. I've got deliveries to make today and want to drive Ellen to school."

Her muffled voice came to him. "Okay, but I need to talk to you."

"Can it wait? I need to load the wagon, too."

"Sure. I'll wake Ellen and make some breakfast."

Loading the orders took longer than he anticipated. When he came back inside, Lily was on her way out the door. "I've got to run. Can you come by the shop today to talk?"

"I'll try, but I can't promise today."

"I left breakfast on the table for you."

"Thank you." He closed the door against the brisk morning.

He turned to see Ellen almost ready. "Let's get going so you're not late."

He dropped Ellen at school and headed to make his first delivery. As he crossed the intersection in the middle of town, he looked to see if the road was clear. He was dumbfounded to see Lily follow Miss Aiken into the saloon.

What was she thinking? Had she given up on ever having a successful business? She had promised him that she understood why he wanted her to avoid Winston Ledford.

"Whoa!" Edward pulled the reins and made a hard left turn. He set the brake and jumped from the wagon in front of the saloon. Disbelief that he was about to push open the swinging doors of a saloon caused him to shudder. He'd vowed never to darken the door of this establishment. Why did this woman have the power to draw him into situations? Could he save her from herself? Did she want to be saved?

"We're not open." Winston Ledford stood at the end of a magnificent hand-carved bar. A crate of whiskey being unpacked by a man behind the counter evidenced the future ugliness that would, no doubt, take place in the room.

"I'm not here for business. I've come for my wife." Come to get her. And to leave. All as quickly as possible.

A smirk stretched across Winston's face. "The ladies in the saloon are not available for gentlemen until we open next month."

Edward clenched his fists at his side, willing himself to stay calm. This man was as slick as any snake he'd ever seen. "My wife is not one of your ladies."

"You saw her come in here, didn't you?" The smirk became a grin.

A door opened near the top of the stairs running along the wall opposite the bar. Both men turned at the sound.

"Edward, what are you doing here?" Lily started down the steps, a valise in one hand. Lavinia followed her, carrying another bag.

"We'll talk about that outside." He met her at the foot of the steps. "Let me take that." He took both valises and followed the ladies to the front door.

"Come back anytime." Winston leaned against the bar, arms folded across his chest. His suit was pressed and clean, the tailoring exact, the very picture of arrogance. "You're always welcome."

The ladies left without acknowledging his words.

Edward leveled a glare at the man. "You'll be doing yourself a favor if you stay away from my wife."

"I'll do as I please, Stone. I always do."

"Don't say I didn't warn you." The saloon doors swung wildly behind him.

He dropped the valises into the back of the wagon.

"Would you care to tell me what's going on here?" He struggled to control the grit in his tone. He looked from Miss Aiken to Lily.

Lily smiled and laid a gloved hand on his sleeve. "It's awfully cold. Can we tell you after we get back to the shop?"

Edward extended a hand to help them into the wagon. It took all his restraint to remain quiet as he climbed aboard and turned the wagon around for the short drive to Lily's shop.

Once the ladies were inside and he'd unloaded the valises, Edward closed the door against the wind.

"Now, if you don't mind, I'd like to know exactly what you were thinking going into a saloon. Especially after all that has happened since you've been in Pine Haven." Try as he did to prevent it, his words rang with acidity. Miss Aiken was in the background when he directed his indignation at Lily.

"You were asleep last night when I got home. I tried to talk to you this morning, but you didn't have time. That's why I asked you to come by the shop today." She had the audacity to look hurt. "Surely you know me well enough by now not to question my actions or motives." Pain filled her voice.

He'd hurt her again. Would he ever get it right with this woman?

Lord, You know she gets the better of me. Give me wisdom.

"Please don't be angry with Lily. It was my fault." Lavinia took a step toward him. "She was helping me get my things." She pointed to the valises at his feet.

He'd carried the bags for them. Blinded by his anger, he'd gone through the motions of helping them without considering the implications of the heavy bags. And how quickly they must have packed them.

Edward turned to Lily.

She finished Miss Aiken's explanation. "Lavinia has decided she doesn't want to work or live in the saloon." Her eyes begged him to understand.

Miss Aiken spoke again. "Lily offered to help me. I didn't think about how it would look for her to go with me, or I'd have gone alone."

Lily broke in, "I didn't want to risk Winston Ledford trying to manipulate her or force her to stay."

"I see." He pulled his hat off and spun it in his hands. The anger was replaced with regret. "Will you forgive me, Lily?" Once again he'd misjudged her. She was always helping someone. And it seemed all she got for it was grief. From him and everyone else.

"I shouldn't." One side of her mouth pulled up. "You've got to learn to trust me."

"You're right. Again." Lost in the blue depths of her eyes, he found himself swimming in emotions unfamiliar to him. A sensation of falling caught him off balance. So much so, he had to adjust his footing.

"I'm so sorry for causing this misunderstanding." Miss Aiken's voice came to him.

He cleared his throat. "It's not your fault."

"Since you're here, I have some business I'd like to discuss with you." Lily's straightforward manner effectively closed the subject.

"If you'll both excuse me, I'll head upstairs." Miss Aiken eyed her valises before disappearing into the workroom.

The stairs creaked with her ascent before Lily spoke again.

"There's more to tell you about Lavinia."

"What?" The hair on his arms and neck bristled. If Winston Ledford had harmed that poor girl, he'd be paying another visit to the saloon. Twice in one day, after a pledge to never go, would be unavoidable.

"Oh, Edward, it's the most wonderful news." She reached her gloved hand to his sleeve. It was a habit of hers that gave him pleasure.

Lily lowered her voice and leaned close to him. The scent of honeysuckle filled his next breath. "After lunch yesterday, Lavinia talked to me about the sermon. She's prayed and asked God to redirect her life according to His plan." Beautiful blue eyes turned to violet as he watched joy overwhelm her.

"That is wonderful news."

"It complicates matters to a certain degree."

"How do you mean?"

"Now she doesn't have a job or anywhere

to stay. If it's not a problem for you, I've offered for her to stay here in the rooms over the shop."

Edward saw her big heart expanding to include another person in need. Since he'd met her, she'd married him for Ellen's sake, offered friendship to ladies who were shunned by everyone else in town and now she was willing to take in someone with nowhere to go. Was there no end to her generosity? Did she see the potential for continued harm to her business if she followed through with this plan? "Are you sure this is a good idea?"

Hopeful eyes pleaded with him. "As the landlord, you have final say."

"Have you considered what people will think?" He hated the words, but they had to be said.

Lily smiled. "Edward, don't you see? Now people will see how important it is to reach out in love to others."

"Some may, but others will gossip. What if Miss Aiken changes her mind and wants to return to the saloon?"

"Without a safe place to start a new life, that's exactly what could happen. I know with friends and time, she can make a go of it."

"I wish everyone had your optimism." He

311

huffed out a sigh. "If you really want to do this, I have no objection as the landlord."

"Thank you, Edward!" Lily stepped up on her toes and brushed her lips across his cheek.

The air stilled, and she froze in place, pink staining her face. Their eyes locked as she lowered herself onto her heels, hand still resting on his arm. Surprise at her kiss turned to pleasure. He put a hand over hers. "You're most welcome, Lily. I'm glad I can do something to make you happy." The gravel in his voice was beyond his control. "Very happy."

Her other hand went up to cover her mouth. He took a step back and set his hat low over his brow. With a smile he said, "Let me know if you need my help arranging the furniture upstairs."

He sat on the seat of his wagon, knowing he had a full day's work ahead of him. No amount of work would take his mind off the wife he'd left rescuing a friend.

God, help me to understand her motives and see her heart before I jump to protect her. I want to be a good husband.

He lifted the reins and let them fall to signal his team it was time to go. What would it be like to be Lily's true husband? Not just her protector and friend, but the person she turned to for comfort and support — because she loved him. He left town behind and headed to a nearby ranch to make his first delivery, the memory of her kiss fresh on his mind. Could they build a true marriage on a foundation of convenience?

"What have you done?" Lily spoke to herself.

Lavinia appeared in the doorway to the workroom. "Do I need to find somewhere else to go?"

Watching Edward leave without a backward glance, Lily soaked in the stupidity of her actions. How could she kiss him? Their marriage wasn't one of love or affection. They'd both agreed to that before the ceremony.

But his eyes — the surprise she'd seen in them. Was it filled with pleasure? Or was she completely out of her mind? How could she face him tonight?

She turned to answer Lavinia, but her mind was on the blacksmith. Tonight couldn't come soon enough. Nor could she dread its coming more.

That evening, when Lily walked into the cabin, Ellen met her at the door wearing her Sunday best.

"Uncle Edward is taking us to the hotel for supper. He says it's time we had a treat." Her young face glowed with anticipation.

"He did, did he?" Lily removed her hat.

"Yep, and I can eat dessert, too."

Edward came out of her bedroom. "I'm guessing Ellen has shared the news." He was also wearing clothes he usually reserved for church services. They'd agreed to keep his things in her room for Ellen's sake. Careful scheduling allowed them to change clothes without raising suspicions in the child's mind about their marriage. Ellen was always in bed before them, and Edward rose in the mornings before she awoke.

"Yes, she seems to be excited about a special dinner."

"I hope you don't mind. I thought you'd enjoy a rest from cooking." He paused before adding, "You work so hard all day, and then in the evenings, too."

She smiled, pleased at the kind gesture. "I look forward to it."

At the restaurant, Lily sat in the chair Edward held for her. "This is lovely. No wonder Papa is so happy with his purchase." She put the linen napkin in her lap and took in the beauty of her surroundings. They sat at a table near the fireplace. Sconces glowed against the floral wallpaper.

"My momma picked the colors." Ellen wiggled in her chair. "She said eating in a pretty room makes the food taste better."

"Did she now?" Edward winked at his niece. "Did she also tell you that little girls in pretty rooms must be still?"

Ellen drew in a fanciful breath, inhaling the atmosphere. "I know. It's just been such a long time since we came here." She stilled and dropped both hands into her lap. "It kinda makes me miss Momma and Pa."

"I think being in this lovely room your mother decorated should make you feel close to her." Lily put a hand under Ellen's chin. "It's okay to be happy and remember happy times."

A strong sniff preceded agreement. "I'll try."

Edward used the leather-bound menu to hide much of his face, but she knew he was fighting the same memories Ellen fought.

"We don't have to eat here. I have plenty of ham for sandwiches at home. I can bake a batch of cookies while we eat them." She reached for her reticule.

The menu lowered slowly, and Edward caught Ellen's eye. "Do you wish to leave?"

"No, Uncle Edward. I'm starting to like it. We just didn't come for such a long time. I forgot how it makes me think of Momma."

"It's settled, then." He turned to Lily and gave her a dimpled smile. "You've cooked for us every night. Tonight we would like to treat you. This is the best place we know to do that."

"If you're certain." Lily placed her reticule back on the corner of the table and picked up a menu. "The smell of fresh bread has given me an appetite."

"If I'd tried to cook for you at home, the only smell would be bacon frying to go with flapjacks." Edward chuckled. "Or maybe some burning onions."

"I love the smell of bacon." She laughed with him.

"Me, too," Ellen chimed in and laughed with them. "But I want fried chicken tonight." She looked at Lily. "Uncle Edward can't fry chicken. He tried one time. There was a fire!"

Edward's face turned red. "It was a small grease fire. Contained in the skillet. No one was hurt." The volume of his voice lowered with each defensive word as though he recognized their futility.

Lily smiled at his protest and thought of the fire that brought them together. The smile faded. That fire hadn't been contained. Only the future would tell if anyone would be hurt by the consequences of that night.

They ordered their food and sat talking while they waited for it to come.

"Miss Aiken seems to be happier." Edward took a long drink from his water glass.

Was he as nervous as she was? The way he tugged at the collar of his best shirt made her think so. Was he remembering how she had kissed him?

Thinking it best to keep the conversation on safe topics, she answered, "She is. It's as if the weight of the world has lifted from her shoulders. I've written to my father inquiring about the possibility of her working for him."

"You've been a true friend to her."

"We all need friends." She couldn't stop the smile from covering her face. "I'm grateful for you and Ellen."

He raised his glass. "We are the ones who are grateful for you."

The food arrived. Ellen's hearty appetite overrode her manners, and Edward cautioned her to eat slowly.

The meal was delicious, and Lily found herself relaxing in Edward's company. Ellen's childish banter made them both laugh. Could they settle into being a friendly family that shared in special occasions and enjoyed being together?

Edward took a roll from the bowl in the center of the table and buttered it. "You've certainly had a hand in spoiling her to good food."

"Aunt Lily, could you teach Uncle Edward to make biscuits like yours?" Ellen spoke around a mouthful of potatoes. "That way, when you have to work late, he can make supper."

Edward raised an eyebrow and waited for her answer. Could she work in close proximity to a man who set her on edge? Would she make a complete fool of herself by falling at his feet or spilling flour all over the kitchen?

"I'm not much of a teacher, Ellen."

"You taught me stuff." The child reached for her glass of milk and drank deeply.

"Children are easier." No, she didn't think she could teach Edward. The way his eyes penetrated hers. Searching. What would he find there?

A few weeks ago it would have been a lonely woman no longer seeking companionship, someone convinced she'd rather be alone than used or taken for granted again.

Tonight he would find someone who surprised even her. The days and weeks in Pine Haven had brought a myriad of changes to her life. For the first time she had lived alone. That hadn't gone as she'd anticipated. The rejection she faced and the likelihood her shop would fail before her father arrived had surprised her. The confidence that dared her to try this adventure had shifted. Her marriage to Edward, finding herself as a wife and substitute mother, had shifted her heart.

Living in Pine Haven was not about being her own person anymore. It was about finding peace. Knowing she was living her life in a way that pleased God. Knowing Lavinia was waiting for her at the shop was more important than a hat sale or a shipment of parasols.

In seeking a place to belong, Lily had found a new person inside herself. Someone who was willing to risk everything if it meant another human being would be better for the effort.

Sitting in this hotel, having supper with two people she'd grown very fond of, Lily realized the seeking was over. She'd found what was missing from her life. Acceptance.

CHAPTER SIXTEEN

Edward put his silverware on his empty plate. He watched Lily savor the food and thought about the night he'd brought her here after their wedding.

He put up a hand and pulled at his collar. The strangling sensation was something he remembered from being a lad trying to work up the nerve to speak to a girl at school. "Have you decided if you want to go to the church social?"

"That would be such fun!" Ellen pushed the last of her roll into her already full mouth.

"Ellen, remember your manners."

"Yes, sir." The little girl speared green beans and waited.

The interruption had kept Lily from answering him. "I'd like to take you."

"I think we should all go." Lily smiled at Ellen but didn't look at him.

Edward leaned forward. "Ellen will be there."

Lily turned to him.

"I'm asking if you'd consider letting me take you to the Winter Social like a social call." There, he'd said it. Now he could breathe.

Well, maybe after she answered.

Pink lit Lily's cheeks, and she worried her bottom lip with her teeth. Then he saw it. A glimmer of light. Replaced in an instant by caution. Had her sudden kiss given him false hope? Part of him wanted a real marriage. Would Lily be willing to try to build that with him? Was courting her after they were married the right way to approach her?

"I'd be honored to accompany you."

"But . . ." He waited for the withdrawal of her reluctant consent.

"What about Lavinia? I can't leave her on her own so soon. It's important for her to feel she's part of the church family."

Swoosh. Air filled his eager lungs. "She may come along with us."

"Are you sure?"

"As long as you are saying yes, I'm sure." An excitement bubbled inside his chest. For a minute he imagined himself not unlike Ellen. So happy he couldn't be still.

"That's settled, then." Lily's smile was

demure. And beautiful. Her voice soft. "Now, Ellen, tell me. How is Speckles doing today?"

Lily's blue eyes lingered on his face while she listened to the latest adventures of the mischievous kitten.

This would be the best Winter Social in years. He was certain of it.

Edward flipped the last pancake onto a plate and set it on the table just as Lily opened the bedroom door. "Good morning."

"Good morning to you, Edward. What has you up and about so early?" She came to the stove and poured a cup of coffee. The skirt of her dress brushed against his leg. It was a dress he hadn't seen. The ruffles on the cuffs were white against the pale green of the sleeves. Everything she wore was feminine and beautiful. Just like her.

But this morning he had a different young lady on his mind. "I wanted to talk to you for a few minutes before Ellen wakes." He indicated the table, and they both sat down. Ellen's reaction to the hotel dining room had him concerned about how the child was handling her parents' absence.

"This looks wonderful. Two meals in a row where I didn't have to cook?" Lily thanked him for cooking and said grace over the food. "What do you want to talk to me about?"

"What did you think about Ellen's mood last night at the hotel?" He speared a piece of ham and added it to the pancakes on his plate. "I think she's trying very hard to be patient about Jane and Wesley not being here, but I don't know if it's time we started planting the seed in her mind that they may not return."

Lily put her fork down. "Do you think that's necessary? Is there no hope?"

"I wish I knew. I've contacted the town doctor again and the sheriff. Neither of them has heard anything more than they were able to tell me before we married." He looked toward Ellen's room. "I just don't want her to have false hope and be crushed later."

"That's one way to look at it." Lily focused on some unseen place. "What would you tell her?"

"At this point, just that we can't find them." He shook his head, hating that he was in the position of breaking his niece's heart. "She might take it better if we tell her what we know in stages."

Lily dropped her voice to almost a whisper. "I remember when my mother passed, how I felt. I don't know how hard it would have been to not know what happened. It was tragic to know my mother was gone from this life, but to wonder if she was sick and couldn't get to me . . . I don't know how I'd have felt about that. Especially at Ellen's age. She's too young to have so much put on her."

"That's what I'm afraid of. If we don't tell her anything, will she go on talking of Jane and Wesley as if they'll be home in a few weeks? If we start to hint at the possibility that they might not return, it may help ease the blow."

"I'd like to give her hope." Lily's blue eyes darkened with sorrow.

"She's going to have to adjust to the idea that we may be her parents from this time forward."

"I think having an uncle and aunt who love her is keeping her from feeling abandoned."

"I do, too, but I won't give her false hope. I can't pretend, when the sheriff and the doctor have all but said they're gone."

"But they haven't said it." She reached across the table and put her hand on his. "If you won't give it more time, at least give her hope."

A thump from Ellen's room let them know she was awake. "I'll give it two weeks. I'll contact the sheriff again." He lowered his voice. "Then we'll have to tell her."

"I pray you hear good news." Lily pulled her hand back as Ellen opened her door.

Edward couldn't help but notice the extra care Lily showered on Ellen during breakfast, coaxing a smile more than once with her antics. Ellen's doll was transformed by their imagination into a lovely princess dining in a palace by the time he got up from the table. He stood behind Ellen's chair and mouthed *Thank you* to Lily.

Lily had been good for Ellen. No matter what happened, he knew he'd done the right thing by marrying her.

Only God knew who would benefit more from having her in their lives — Ellen or Edward.

"You haven't been here two weeks, and you've learned more about making hats than I did in three months under the milliner at home in East River." Lily put one of Lavinia's creations on a stand in the front window.

"Do you really think it's good enough to put in the window?"

Lavinia's timidity was surprising. How did this sweet young girl ever imagine herself as a saloon girl? And why did Winston Ledford think she was up for the job? Once again, Lily offered a silent prayer of thanks that Lavinia had responded to God's love for her.

"I do." Lily tied the ribbon and turned the angle just so. "It's a good thing Edward finished these extra stands and brought them. We've been busier in the last week than I was the first week I opened."

Lavinia dropped her head. "I feel so badly for causing you all that trouble."

Lily dismissed her concern with a heartfelt smile. "The trouble was all but forgotten when you walked away from the saloon. I told you the church folks and people in town would see the change in your life."

"I'm glad people have realized your kindness and friendship to me was the reason I was brave enough to turn to God for a new life." She dabbed at a tear threatening to fall from her lashes. "I can't imagine if I had to be at the saloon when they open tomorrow evening."

"Thankfully, you'll never have to worry about that again." Lily handed her a feather duster. "If you'll dust in here, I'll bring out the other hats we made last night."

"Yes, ma'am." Lavinia gave a playful bow and took the duster. She became serious when she straightened. "Thank you again for letting me help you here until your father arrives. I know my room and board are costing you."

"The sales of the hats you've made are more than covering the costs. I think Ginger must be telling people to come here, too." Lily reached into the cash box and pulled out an envelope. "As a matter of fact, I've got something for you. Here is your commission on the things you've sold."

"Lily, you can't pay me. We agreed I would help out."

"That was before you revealed your God-given talents." She pressed the envelope into Lavinia's hand. "After you finish the dusting, why don't you see if Mrs. Croft has a ready-made dress you can purchase to wear to the Winter Social on Sunday?"

The clothes Mr. Ledford had purchased for Lavinia had been left at the saloon. She wore the few things she'd brought with her when she'd moved to Pine Haven. Lily knew she needed more.

"Are you sure she wants to see the likes of me in her store?"

"Yes. She spoke to me after Bible study on Wednesday evening." Lily put her hands on Lavinia's shoulders. "Nothing too flowery, mind you, but kindly just the same. Something about noticing what a good worker you are."

They both laughed.

"I guess seeing me sweep the sidewalk every morning when she goes to the bank and post office has made us friends of a sort." Lavinia tucked the envelope in her skirt pocket. "Thank you. I'll go as long as we aren't busy."

Lily went to look out the front window. The Winter Social was in two days. Since their supper at the hotel, Edward had been kind and attentive. They'd even shared a cooking lesson. She noticed he laughed more readily. She made it a habit to sit in front of the fire after Ellen went to bed at night. They'd talked about everything from their childhood to their favorite Bible verses.

He made one excuse after another to come to her shop. He'd made two trips with her orders — first the additional stands, then the sign. Yesterday he'd come back to mount the sign on its hinges in the window sill. She pulled at the loose tendrils hanging at the base of her neck and looked through the glass, wondering if he'd come again today. A smile betrayed her hopes to anyone who might see.

Lost in thought, she didn't notice Winston Ledford until he stood facing her on the opposite side of the glass. She started and backed away. He opened the door and entered.

"Ladies." He removed his hat.

"Mr. Ledford." Lily noticed Lavinia backing into the workroom and stepped to block his line of sight. "What can I do for you?"

"You've done more than enough, Mrs. Stone." He peered over her shoulder.

"If you're not interested in making a purchase, I'm rather busy." She refused to be frightened of this man or his threats.

"I warned you not to interfere in my business."

"I have not." God had successfully drawn Lavinia away from his business. She trusted the Lord to protect her from Winston's anger.

"Lovey's presence here speaks to the fact that you have, indeed."

"Miss Aiken is not your business."

"She is the reason I am short on workers for my new establishment. I've come to speak with her."

"She does not wish to speak with you." Lily had known he wouldn't settle so easily when Lavinia left. They'd discussed how they would handle any attempts he might make to contact her.

Ignoring Lily, he called out, "Lovey, come here."

Lily heard the rustling of Lavinia's skirts. "There's no need, Miss Aiken. I'll take care of this." She opened the door and gestured for him to leave.

Taking advantage of her leaving a clear path, Winston stepped toward the workroom.

"I believe my wife has asked you to vacate the premises, Ledford." Edward's voice resonated from behind her. With her back to the door she hadn't seen him approach, but she'd never been more glad to see him. "As her landlord — and husband — I'm going to insist you comply with her wishes at once."

Lily could see the wheels of the saloon owner's mind turning, deciding how likely it would be for him to come out ahead in a confrontation with Edward. Wisely, he opted to leave.

"This is not over, Lovey. You can't hide in this hat shop forever." Winston turned to Lily. "You leave me little choice today, but whether you like it or not, I am a merchant in this town now. I will make a success of it. And I will not allow you, or anyone else, to get in my way."

"Careful, Ledford. I'm restraining myself. If anything were to happen to these little ladies, or if they became concerned something might happen to them, I'd be forced to protect them. You don't want to be the cause for that concern," Edward said.

"You misunderstand, Stone. My purpose is to offer viable employment to ladies in this town. Making more money in a month than this hat shop will see in six." He was tall enough to look down on Edward as he passed him to leave.

Unintimidated, Edward turned to fill the doorway. "Your presence isn't welcome here. Remember that."

He closed the door and turned to Lily. "Are you all right?"

"We're fine. Thank you for showing up when you did."

Lavinia came from the workroom. "I'm so sorry. I can find another place to stay. Do you think there's a possibility I could start working at the hotel before your father arrives?"

"It's not your fault, Miss Aiken." Edward watched out the window as Mr. Ledford walked toward the center of town.

Lily gave her a brief hug. "You're not going anywhere. I've grown accustomed to having you here."

"I can't believe he came here looking for me. I told him when I left that I wouldn't be back." Lavinia began to dust the shop.

"Try to stay out of his way as much as you can. He'll get the point soon enough." Edward turned to Lily. "I'll be watching him. If either of you feels threatened at any time, let me know."

She was determined not to be intimidated. "Thank you, Edward. I pray it doesn't come to that."

Lavinia moved to the other side of the shop with the duster, and Edward leaned closer to Lily.

"Are we still on for the Winter Social?"

She smiled at him. "Yes. Ellen asked when she brought Speckles to visit this morning. She said he would be lonely while she was in school." She indicated the basket in the corner. "Poor little thing had been crying before she got here. It might have something to do with an incident she said involved an ash bin at the edge of the hearth." Lily giggled at the thought of Edward cleaning up after a kitten he hadn't wanted in the first place.

"That cat should be grateful to be inside." A mock snarl crossed his face. "I've spent more time cleaning up after the little rascal than I can spare. Be warned. He's not as cute as he looks."

"Like you?" She giggled until she heard Lavinia excuse herself from the room.

"Looks like you've gone and said it now." Edward gave her a wink.

"Oh, my. I'll have to be more careful. You might go getting the wrong idea." Enjoyment in his presence filled her with satisfaction. Taunting him was one of her new favorite things to do. That strong masculine face turning pink pleased her to no end.

"I best be going." Edward opened the door, ducked his head a bit and walked onto the sidewalk.

"I'm glad you came." She wiggled her fingers at him and held her breath until the door closed.

The Winter Social couldn't come soon enough. For the first time in her adult life, she was excited about attending a social event. No one would expect her to serve the punch or wash up when everything was over. She would go as Edward's wife and enjoy the afternoon and evening.

Yes, this new life suited her just fine. New friends, a successful business — now that everyone realized the positive results of her association with Lavinia and Ginger — and a husband who winked at her when he came to her rescue.

Rescue? Did she really need Edward to rescue her from Winston?

No.

Was it nice to know he was there if she did?

Absolutely.

Edward laughed and picked his hat up off the ground. He beat it against his leg to remove the layer of dust it had collected when it was knocked off the table by his worthy opponent in the final arm-wrestling match. It was the one event at the Winter Social all the men enjoyed.

Doc Willis clapped him on the back. "Wouldn'a thought I could beat a man who swings a hammer all day long."

"To be honest, that's probably how you won. I didn't think you could, either." Edward laughed and turned to look for Ellen. He found her among the children eating cookies in the corner. The barn had been set up with sections for each activity. A smaller place than the Willis ranch couldn't hold a crowd this size. The food was along one wall, the games for kids were in one corner, and the men were testing one another's strength in the opposite corner. The ladies were gathered at the tables visiting, the meal long since passed.

"If I can have everyone's attention . . ." Reverend Dismuke stepped onto a makeshift platform fashioned of hay bales with planks of wood across the top. "It's time for the pie auction."

The men cheered and gathered around the preacher. Someone off to one side held up the first pie.

"Remember, you'll be sharing the pie with the baker, so bid carefully. This pie was made by my wife. I thought we best auction it first, so there's no fighting over it at the end." Several people chuckled, and Reverend Dismuke smiled at Peggy. Not wanting to miss out on the excitement, the ladies had come to stand behind the men. "You all know the money we raise tonight goes to help fund the school for the rest of the year, so bid like the providers you are."

A sporting round of bids followed as several pies were sold to the husbands of the women who baked them. Laughter and teasing filled the atmosphere as the bids went higher and higher.

"This next pie is from a newcomer." Lavinia's pie was held in the air. "It smells mighty fine. You can't see it from where you're standing, but these look like some of the finest pecans of the crop. Miss Aiken, where are you?"

Lavinia tried to hide her face, but Lily pointed her out.

"Who'll start the bidding for this pie?"

For a few seconds Lily was afraid no one would bid. She watched Lavinia withdraw into herself. Her arms folded across her chest, and her head hung as she clinched her jaw.

Then a quiet voice came from the opposite side of the barn with a substantial bid. Lily tried to see the bidder, but she was too short. Lavinia peeked up at her.

"Do you know the bidder?" Lily could see her friend's face brighten with relief.

"It's the young man from the general store who invited me to church." Lavinia spoke in hushed tones. "I've seen him in service a couple of times since I started attending, but he hasn't spoken to me."

The reverend called for more bids. After a short round of back and forth, Lavinia's pie sold for a good sum. She put her hand over her mouth to catch a bubbling giggle that threatened to draw attention to her.

Lily smiled and hugged her friend. "You've done it, Lavinia. You've made a place for yourself among the good people of Pine Haven."

"Thank you, Lily. I couldn't have dreamed it without your friendship and encouragement."

A shy cowhand approached holding his newly purchased pie. "Miss Aiken, would you please join me for some pie?"

The two walked toward the tables where everyone had eaten the meal earlier.

"You should be very pleased with yourself." Edward's voice came from behind Lily. "That young lady's life is forever changed for the better because of you."

"God made the difference for her." Lily dashed a happy tear from her lashes. "I just got to be a witness to the transformation."

Edward threw one hand into the air and called out a price. Lily turned to see her pie was up for bids.

An ominous bid came from a spot near the back of the barn. Unnoticed until this moment, Winston Ledford had entered the barn. Lily's mouth dropped open. Several ladies gasped. A low rumble from some of the men signaled their agreement with the ladies.

Lily heard Mrs. Croft's voice above the others. "The nerve of that man! What is he doing here?"

Edward looked at Winston. He held his hand up and topped Winston's bid.

Winston doubled Edward's bid.

The crowd no longer masked their curiosity.

Edward did not look away from Winston.

He raised his price again.

Winston countered with another doubling of the offer.

Lily knew it was more than anyone had paid for a pie that night. Not even the wealthiest of ranchers had offered so much money. She leaned in close to Edward and whispered. "It's too much money. He's trying to provoke you."

Edward turned to Reverend Dismuke. "I will pay three times his offer."

"Going, going, gone! Sold to Edward Stone. Thank you for your contribution to the school fund." The crowd applauded. Lily knew it wasn't just for the amount of money raised, but the show of wills they'd witnessed between the two men.

Without hesitation, the preacher asked for the next pie, and everyone's attention moved to the bidding.

"Edward, you didn't have to do that. It's so much money." Lily put her hand on his arm.

He covered it with one of his own and lowered his head so their eyes were level. "There was no way I would let that man buy your pie. You are not for sale." He gave her hand a squeeze. "Would you care to join me for dessert?"

A smile of relief and gratitude crossed her

face. "I'd like that. May I ask Ellen to share it with us?"

"You may." Edward released her and went to collect his pie. "I'll be right with you."

Lily saw him head in the direction of Winston Ledford. Somehow she imagined the saloon owner wasn't accustomed to anyone getting the better of him. To see her husband win their contest of wills pleased her immensely. Pleased and excited her. For the first time in her life she hadn't been at the punch bowl. She'd been at the center of attention.

The attention hadn't been fun for her. But the victory Edward claimed meant she was no longer a wallflower. And the sweetness of the pie wouldn't be the only memory her mind would savor when the night ended.

After he confirmed that some of the men were watching Winston Ledford leave the property, Edward started to relax. He paid his bid and collected his pie. Lily and Ellen sat with punch cups when he came to the table.

"Aunt Lily's pie is the best one ever!" Ellen picked up her fork while he cut wedges for everyone.

"Looks like it to me. I've never seen such a fancy crust." He winked at his niece and gave her the first piece.

The three of them laughed and ate their treat in relative privacy, nestled as they were in the corner of a barn filled with people.

Edward had reached for a second slice when Ellen's demeanor started to change.

"Did you eat too fast, Ellen?" Lily must have noticed it, too.

"No." Ellen sniffed, and her eyes swam in fresh tears.

In an instant Edward was beside her, squatting to be level with his niece as she sat on the bench. He touched her forehead with the back of his hand. No fever. "Do you hurt somewhere?"

"Here." She pulled her doll from her pocket and held it to her chest. She sniffled, and the tears fell onto her cheeks.

"Does your tummy hurt? Or has someone hurt your feelings?" Lily asked softly.

"I miss Momma and Papa." She sobbed in earnest now. "Momma loves the socials." Ellen buried her head in his shoulder. "And Papa always buys her pie."

He folded her into his arms and rocked her. Tears soaked his shirt. "Honey, I know. I miss them, too."

Lily reached a hand to rub Ellen's back while he held the child close.

He put his hands on Ellen's shoulders and

pushed her back just enough to see her reddened face. "Let's get you home." He'd been afraid this was coming. The child couldn't continue to wonder and wait on her parents. He had to tell her what he knew.

The background noise of others eating pie and laughing had faded away when Ellen started to cry. Now it crashed into his mind like a maddening wave of chaos. He had to get Ellen home. To console her. To protect her. To tell her the truth.

Edward stood, bringing Ellen into his arms like a babe cradled against its mother. "Please see to a ride for Miss Aiken while I get Ellen to the wagon."

He carried Ellen into the night and wrapped her in a blanket on the front seat of the wagon.

Lily joined them, and he leaned to speak softly in her ear. "We need to tell her."

Lily exhaled and her soft, warm breath teased his neck above the collar of his shirt. Her whisper was more faint than his. "Must we? Now?"

He took her hand and gave it a reassuring squeeze. "She'll only get more distraught later if we don't face this."

He felt the answering pressure of her gloved hand in his as she said, "May God give us the words." He turned to Ellen, where she sat on the edge of the seat.

"Ellen, we need to talk about your momma and papa." He held the child's hands in his and looked up into her tearstained face.

"I don't want to, Uncle Edward." She sniffed big and stuck out her bottom lip. "You don't look happy. I don't want to hear anything about them that's not happy."

Lily moved in close beside him and put a hand over his on Ellen's. "Uncle Edward wants to help you understand."

Ellen swallowed a gulp of air. "I'm afraid you're gonna tell me Momma won't come back. Her or Papa."

Edward cleared his throat. "They've been gone a long time, Ellen. Sometimes things happen that can't be helped. If your momma and papa could be here, you know they would."

"They're coming back for me!" Ellen's voice rose in desperation.

Suddenly, Edward couldn't believe his ears.

"I'm here, baby girl."

Ellen squealed and threw her arms wide. Edward caught her as she lunged from the wagon. He set her down, and she ran into her mother's open arms.

Edward was speechless. Jane was crying

and kissing Ellen's face. He put an arm around Jane, thrilled at the sight of his sister. And worried by Wesley's absence.

"How? When?" Surprise at her sudden appearance left him befuddled.

Jane laughed through her tears and spoke to him over the top of Ellen's head. The child had become lodged in her embrace. "I just arrived. I came by wagon with friends. I'll explain it all to you."

He leaned close and asked quietly, hoping Ellen wouldn't hear, "Where's Wesley?"

Ellen leaned back and looked up into her mother's face. "Where's Papa?"

Jane squatted in front of Ellen and put a hand on each of the girl's shoulders. "Honey, Papa wanted so much to come home to you."

"Where is he?" Ellen looked around, searching the shadows of the moonlit night.

Edward's heart broke at the pain he saw on his sister's face. He could only imagine what she'd been through. He put a hand on her shoulder to reassure her.

Jane looked up at Edward and then back to Ellen. "I got very sick. That's why my letters stopped. I was too sick to write, but Papa took good care of me."

"He's a good papa." Ellen's lips trembled. Edward knew her mind was trying to prepare her for what her heart didn't want to hear.

Jane continued, "Yes, he was. No one could have loved you or me more than he did." She took a deep breath. "That's why he never left me while I was sick. But then he got sick, too."

A tear slid down his sister's face. He'd do anything to take from her the sorrow he saw in her eyes.

"Your papa was sicker than I was. He helped me get better, but . . ." Her words halted. Finally she was able to finish. "Papa couldn't get better. He was just too sick. I'm so sorry, Ellen, but he passed. Last week."

Ellen cried, "No, Momma!" The little girl fell against her mother's shoulder and wailed.

Edward went down on one knee and wrapped the two of them in a hug. He held them while they wept. He sensed Lily behind him and knew she was praying for them. Had it only been minutes before that he'd tried to find the words to prepare Ellen for this possibility?

When Jane was able to calm Ellen to a point that he felt it was best to go home, Edward helped his sister and niece into the back of the wagon. Jane's friends had their wagon nearby, and he arranged for them to bring Jane's things by his home the next day.

He covered Jane and Ellen with a blanket and helped Lily onto the seat beside him. Ellen, worn-out from her tears, fell asleep with her head in her mother's lap.

Lily hadn't said a word since Jane had come upon them while they talked to Ellen. He knew she'd worried over Ellen's reaction, should anything have happened to her parents. Now, they were facing it.

CHAPTER SEVENTEEN

Edward carried Ellen into the cabin and laid her on her bed. When he came back into the front room, Jane and Lily were introducing themselves.

"His wife?" Jane turned when he came into the room. "I thought you were never getting married."

He looked from his sister to his wife. "A lot happened while you were gone."

"I can see that," Jane said. "It's lovely to meet you, Lily. I wish I'd been here for your wedding."

Lily began, "If you'd been here —"

"I wish you could have been here, too," Edward interrupted. He'd come to stand by Jane and tried to shake his head without Jane noticing. "It was a simple church ceremony. Just after the first of the year." He didn't want Lily to tell Jane the circumstances of their marriage. He didn't want Lily to seem less than a real wife to his sister. Where the need to protect her came from, he couldn't say. Over the time they'd been together, it had just become part of who he was.

Jane looked to Lily. "I'm glad to have a sister."

Lily acknowledged her words with a forced smile. Edward didn't know what was going on in Lily's mind, but he could see the storm brewing in her violet eyes.

Their whole world had changed tonight. Again.

Having Jane home was a blessing he'd begun to think would never happen. Losing Wesley was a burden he hated for his sister and niece to bear.

Lily finally spoke. "Have you eaten?"

Jane tugged her gloves off. "Not since breakfast, but you don't have to bother. I can grab some bread and a slice of cheese."

"It's no bother. You must be famished from traveling so far." Lily tied on her apron. Edward watched her now-familiar movements as she broke eggs into a bowl.

He took Jane's coat and hung it by the door. "Come sit at the table. I'll get you a cup of coffee, and you can tell me everything."

Sadness filled Jane's face. She sat in Ellen's chair at the table and told them all that had happened since she and Wesley had left Pine Haven. They'd established their business and had hopes of doing well. They made preparation to come for Ellen just before they took ill.

"But the sickness . . . that was the worst of all." She hung her head. "So many people. Most of our neighbors. It struck our area of the city, and in a matter of days people were sick and dying. The doctor was overwhelmed, though I guess it wasn't as bad as it could have been. They were able to keep people from coming into our part of town. In a matter of weeks, it had died away. It hit the young and old worst. The doctor said because Wesley tended me so long, he was weaker when he got sick." A tear dropped from her lashes. "He died because he was taking care of me."

Edward's heart broke for her. As displeased as he'd been by their decision to leave Ellen behind, he now realized that to take her would have put her at risk of death. He thanked the Lord for letting her be safe with him.

"I'm so sorry for the loss of your husband." Lily put a plate of scrambled eggs and toast in front of Jane. "He must have loved you dearly."

Jane smiled up at Lily. "He did. The doctor tried to get him to send me to the hospital, but he didn't want me to get worse. He thought being around others would make me sicker. The hospital in our area filled up with patients. In the end, we had to be taken to another hospital."

"How did you have the strength to come after all of that? Why didn't you wire? I would have come for you." Edward hated the thought of her suffering alone.

"I know. That's why I didn't send a telegram." She asked Lily, "Isn't that just like our Edward? He'd drop everything and dash off to help someone else."

Lily turned to him. Her eyes were solemn. "That's one of the first things I learned about him."

Jane continued, "By the time Wesley passed, we'd spent all our money on hospital bills. Wesley had borrowed against the business. I sold it to have the money to pay the undertaker and settle the mortgage."

"Jane, I'm so sorry about Wesley, but don't you worry about you and Ellen." He didn't know what else to say. His sister had gone away dreaming of a better life only to find herself back in the same place, but without her husband and practically without funds.

"We'll get through this." He put a hand on her shoulder. "We always do."

Lily listened to Jane's heart-wrenching story. Watching Edward's compassion for her grief, Lily remembered how kind he'd been to her the night of the fire. He'd rushed into a burning building to save her. And after risking his life for her, he'd pledged himself to her to protect her reputation — and for the sake of his niece. She'd never known anyone more selfless.

He sat at the table listening to his sister's plight, and Lily knew he'd never leave Jane or Ellen without his support and care. Without Wesley to provide for Jane and Ellen, he would take responsibility for them.

Would Jane want to open the bakery now? If she did, what was to become of Lily's Millinery and Finery? There were a couple of vacant buildings in town, but until her father arrived, Lily had no way of securing another location.

Jane and Ellen could sleep in Ellen's room tonight, but that would never do for a permanent arrangement. And Edward couldn't continue to sleep on the floor in front of the fire. He deserved a bed and the privacy of a bedroom in a cabin filled with women.

There were so many questions. And no answers.

Lily's mind swirled with it all. "If you don't mind, I'm going to turn in for the night."

"Thank you for cooking for me, Lily. You'll have to let me return the favor." Jane was a picture of kindness, a woman anyone would love for a sister-in-law.

"She's an amazing cook, Jane. You're in for a real treat." Edward beamed as if he was proud of her. Was he?

"Jane, if you'd like, I think I have something you could use to sleep in for the night." Lily stepped into her room. She pulled a nightgown and robe from her wardrobe. Jane was a bit taller than her, but it would do for a night. When she turned around, Jane was at the bedroom door.

"This is so thoughtful." She accepted the clothes. "I'm sorry for barging into your home like this."

Edward came to stand behind Jane. "You're always welcome in my home."

My home. Did he not consider it to be her home, too? Lily watched them and wondered what her role in his life would be after tonight. Nothing was happening like either of them expected.

Edward asked, "Jane, why don't you sleep

with Ellen? We'll figure out something more permanent over the next few days."

"Thank you, Edward. I knew I could count on you." Jane turned and slipped into Ellen's bedroom, closing the door quietly behind her.

"I think I'll say good-night." Lily moved to close the door.

Edward put a hand on the door. "Would you mind sitting up a bit? There's a lot to talk about." He grinned at her. "Please."

This was the playful expression he'd begun to wear over the past few days. He seemed to be inviting her out of her shell and into his life. But all that had changed now.

"For a little while." She went to the stove and poured them each a cup of coffee. They sat at the table, and she cut him another piece of the pie he'd won at the auction. She cringed when she thought of the price he'd paid. "Was it only a few hours ago that we were at a pie auction?"

He used the side of his fork to cut a large bite. "It seems like days instead of hours."

Lily ate a bite of her pie while he polished off most of his piece.

She put her fork on the plate. "What will you do about caring for Jane and Ellen?"

"I guess it depends on what Jane wants to

do." He took a drink of coffee. "I'll talk to her about that in the morning."

"It's all so sudden for her. Losing her husband and having a child to raise without a father. It's a lot for any woman."

"I'll be there to help her. She won't be alone like a lot of widows." He pushed his plate toward the center of the table.

"You're very reliable. That must be why she trusted you to care for Ellen while they were gone." She couldn't bring herself to look at him but stared into her coffee. "I'm so heartbroken for that dear child over the loss of her father, but so relieved that her mother is home to care for her."

"Because we thought they were both gone, it is a blessing for Jane to be back."

"I'll help you do whatever you decide is best." He no longer needed her. With Jane home, Ellen had her mother. And with her husband dead, Edward had the added burden of Jane on him. It wasn't fair for him to have to care for her, as well.

"Thank you. You've been a tremendous help with Ellen." He went to put his plate and cup in the basin. "She'll need us all now to help her adjust to her pa being gone."

"I'll pray for her. God knew what He was doing by establishing such a strong relationship between you and Ellen. She'll turn to you more now than ever before." She put her dishes in the basin. "If you don't mind, I'd like to turn in."

He reached for her hand. Had he reached for her this afternoon, she'd have expected a warmth and tenderness at his touch. Tonight, her heart was cold with confusion. Her future once again lay before her, clouded by situations beyond her control.

"The pie was delicious. Worth every penny." He touched her cheek with the back of his other hand, the knuckles rough from hard work. Work he'd have to increase to keep up with his new responsibilities.

Lily had forgotten all about Winston Ledford and his challenge. The music in the barn and the sounds of laughter had faded from her mind. Tonight she heard the echo of her heart as it cried out to be loved by a man who had only married her to care for a child who no longer needed her.

She loved him. More than anyone or anything she'd ever loved in her life. In a way she'd never loved before. Why did her heart spill this truth to her now? When the one she needed didn't need her anymore.

Tomorrow might hold unwelcome changes in her life. She wouldn't let her heart lead her this time. Luther had tempted her with the idea of love. A love he never had for her. Edward had never offered her love. Only his name in exchange for nurturing Ellen.

She stepped out of his reach. "I'm glad you liked the pie. It was for a good cause. The school is important to the community."

Edward put his hand in his pocket. "I see. So you think I bought the pie for the school?"

"No." She twisted her hands together in front of her. She didn't want to hurt him, but if she opened herself to him, only to be rejected later, she didn't think she'd have the courage to move beyond it. "I know you bought the pie to protect me. The same way you married me to protect me."

The grin he'd used to entice her into sharing pie with him moments before was gone.

She finished her thought before she lost her courage. "It's the same way you'll protect Jane and Ellen." She fought back tears. "You're a good man, Edward Stone."

"Lily, are you upset with me? Have I done something wrong?"

"No. You've done everything right." She couldn't bear it if she broke down in front of him. Realizing she loved him had tilted her world on its axis. She needed time to sort it all out. Before she said or did any-

355

thing to make herself look foolish or needy. The last thing she wanted was for him to take care of her because he had to.

Why didn't she see it before?

All that time when she'd resisted helping others because she faded into the background of life, she'd wanted to be appreciated for who she was — not what she did for others.

She'd done the same thing to Edward. Unknowingly. She couldn't use him. It would make her no different than Luther. Was that how he saw her? Did she look to him like someone who had only accepted his offer of marriage for what she would benefit from it?

Her love for him poured over every thought she had. Nothing was the same anymore. Not the way she felt about him. Not even the way he looked to her was the same. He'd always been handsome. Through the filter of love she saw him for who he really was. Inside. A loving champion. A brave protector.

Used by everyone who could benefit from him.

She wouldn't do that to him. Not anymore. She needed time alone to pray and think.

"I need to go to bed. Please forgive me.

I'll do the dishes in the morning." She opened the door and looked back at him. "Good night, Edward."

He stood silent, perplexed by her retreat.

Inside her room, she leaned against the closed door, eyes lifted in prayer.

Lord, help me. I never thought to love him, but I do. What do I do? If he still needed me, we might be able to make something of our marriage. As it is, I can't risk destroying our friendship by letting him know how I feel.

If Jane and Ellen moved out, their marriage would change. Hiding her newly discovered feelings without Ellen acting as a buffer between them would make their marriage more challenging. She could move into Ellen's room and treat him like the friend he had become. Could her heart bear it?

Lily was up early the next morning. Spending the night in anxious prayer had yielded no answers. The only positive thought was Ellen in the arms of her mother. In the end that was the thing that mattered most.

Hoping to avoid questions from Jane, Lily dressed quickly and went to wake Edward. His reaction to Jane's questions about their sudden marriage let her know he didn't want his sister to know the details of their relationship.

She knelt to lean over his sleeping form and wished he loved her. He lay on his back. The steady rise and fall of his chest, coupled with the peaceful expression, made her want to let him rest. Unable to help herself, she reached to move a wisp of hair that fell across his forehead. He stirred, and she snatched her hand away.

"Good morning, Edward," she whispered and put a hand on his shoulder to nudge him a bit. "I thought you'd want to be up before Jane wakes."

He drew in a deep breath and opened his eyes. The cloud of sleep in them cleared to a smile like none he'd ever given her. Light shone in their depths. Without the guard of wakefulness, did he harbor feelings for her, too? "Lily." He lifted his hand and caressed her cheek.

The door to Ellen's room opened, and Jane came into the room. Lily jerked to her feet. Edward leaned up on one elbow.

Jane spoke first. "I'm sorry, I didn't mean to interrupt . . ." She left the rest of her thought to hang in the tense air.

"You've no need to apologize." Lily tried to think of something else to say. What would her sister-in-law think of her? Edward sleeping on the floor, and his wife sneaking around in the early morning to wake him didn't portray an image of a happy newly-wed couple.

Edward lumbered to his feet. "You're not interrupting, Jane." He folded the quilt and tossed it onto the settee. "Lily was just . . ."

He looked to her for help, but she didn't know what to say. "I was just deciding what to make for breakfast." She hurried to the stove. "How about oatmeal? It's a chilly morning."

The three of them set about their morning routine. No one mentioned the awkwardness of Jane discovering Edward in the front room. Ellen woke while Lily cooked. She came to the table without brushing her hair. Her doll hung over from the crook in her elbow.

Lily tousled her hair. "You need to brush your hair."

"Momma does it for me." Ellen backed away from her touch.

Jane turned from stoking the fire. "Ellen, did Aunt Lily teach you to brush your hair?"

Ellen shot a glance from Lily to her mother. "She did, but you always did it before. I like it when you do it."

Lily turned back to the stove and ladled oatmeal into bowls. Edward didn't need her help with Ellen now that Jane was back. It appeared Ellen didn't need her, either.

Jane spoke to Ellen. "I'll brush your hair tonight before bed as a treat. This morning you will do as your aunt Lily said." Ellen tromped into the bedroom and closed the door. Jane smiled at Lily. "She has always been a mite stubborn. Thank you for teaching her. She has such thick hair, I always found it quicker to do it myself. You've saved me much work in the future."

"Ellen is a sweet child. She likes to have her own way, but she is a dear."

"What a gracious description of my little one." Jane chuckled and came to pour milk for Ellen and coffee for the adults.

Lily liked Jane. She admired the way she spoke to Ellen. She appreciated that Jane hadn't belabored the situation this morning by insisting on knowing why Edward wasn't in the bedroom with his new wife. Jane was considerate, someone Lily would choose for a friend. She hoped Jane wouldn't think less of her if she found out that Edward hadn't wanted to marry her.

Edward came in the front door carrying an armload of firewood. He put the wood on the hearth. "I hope you two are getting to know one another." He brushed his gloves together and pulled them off.

"We are, brother dear." Jane set the platter of ham Lily had cooked on the table. "You've married quite a nice person. Ellen told me Lily has even taught her to brush her own hair."

He came to the table. "Lily has taught us all a lot. Even taught me and Ellen a bit about cooking." He caught Lily's attention and winked at her again. If he didn't stop this open flirtation, how was she to rein in her heart?

Ellen came out of her room dressed for school with her hair neatly brushed. Jane pulled her into a hug.

"Momma, do I gotta go to school today?" Ellen's eyes were filled with hope for a day at home. She dropped into her seat at the table.

"Not today, moppet. I want to spend every minute of today with you." Jane sat beside her daughter.

Edward prayed and the food was passed around the table. "Jane, we need to make some arrangements for your future."

A pall settled over the table. "I've been thinking about that all the way home from Santa Fe." Jane put her fork down and looked at Ellen. "How would you like to help me open the bakery and run it? We're going to need to earn money, and I could use a good helper."

Ellen swallowed big. "Do you mean it? I can help?" Her eyes filled with tears as her young heart tried again to digest the loss of her father. "But how will we do it without Papa?" She dashed the back of her hand across her eyes. "And Lily has her shop in the bakery now."

Jane looked at Edward and then back to Ellen. "You let the adults work out the details. You just be ready to become a baker." Jane put a hand on Ellen's on the table. "Without Papa here, we'll have to take care of ourselves." Sadness washed over Ellen at the words.

Edward cleared his throat. "I'm going to make certain you're both taken care of."

Lily listened like a stranger in the place she'd come to think of as home. She'd allowed herself to become the mistress of this house, and now she sat listening to Edward pledge himself as provider to his sister and her daughter. Where would she fit in the scheme of things? Did she?

As soon as she could, Lily excused herself and headed to the shop, leaving Edward and his family to plan a future that might not include her. She couldn't sit and listen. Edward would have to tell her later. If Jane was going to take over the building, Lily didn't know what would happen to her business.

With a deep love for Edward filling her heart and mind, she knew the shop wasn't important. Not when her marriage was on the brink. Would he want her out of his life, the same way his sister was about to say she wanted Lily out of her building?

Edward and Jane walked into Lily's shop to the sound of the clanging bell. He rubbed his hands together in the warmth of the room.

Jane looked everywhere at once and spoke softly to herself, "Oh, my. This is lovely."

Lily came through the doorway that led to the workroom. "Good after . . . noon . . ." The words died on her lips when she saw him and Jane. Her face was pale, and her eyes were the lightest blue he'd ever seen them.

"We wanted to come by and let you know what we've worked out." He hoped Lily would be as pleased with their decision as he and Jane were.

Lily stopped beside the glass display case that held her most valuable merchandise and put a steadying hand on the heavy piece of furniture. "I'm ready." She looked as if she was braced for bad news.

Jane burst out with their plans. "I'm going to open my bakery!" She looked around the shop with a smile as big as Texas. He'd wanted Jane to do this before. Watching her excitement confirmed his belief that her own bakery would go a long way toward making her happy again.

Lily balled the hand that held the side of the display case into a fist. Her knuckles grew white. "I'm very happy for you. You deserve a fresh start after all you've been through."

Edward grinned at Lily. "I knew you'd agree. That's what I think, too. It will be something positive that she and Ellen can do together. It's not the life we all hoped they'd have." He put a hand on Jane's shoulder. She smiled in acknowledgment of his sympathy. "But I think it's the best way to move on with their lives."

Lily wrung her hands in front of her skirt. "When do you plan to open?"

Jane had moved to the front window. "Almost immediately. Ellen and I will move in this afternoon."

"That soon?" Lily looked surprised.

"I don't want to put you and Edward out any more than I already have. You've been so gracious to care for Ellen, but I think the sooner she and I get settled into our new life, the sooner she'll accept her father's passing and begin to heal."

Lily paled. "Do you think she's ready for such a big adjustment so soon?"

Edward answered her. "I think it will give her something to keep her mind on. Give her hope." He added, "Plus, she's been telling her mother about the things you've taught her."

"Where is she?" Lily looked through the front glass as if expecting to see Ellen outside the shop window.

"She's packing her things. She promised to have everything together before Edward and I return, so she can scurry on over," Jane answered. "Edward was kind enough to come along so I could satisfy my curiosity about what you've done with this place. Everything is lovely. Much nicer than I'd imagined it could be."

"I did my best." Lily's voice wavered. "It's a lovely building."

Jane nodded. "The windows were what caught my eye. Beautiful displays are so important for drawing the customers in."

The door opened with a flourish, and the bell announced Ellen's arrival. She flung her arms around her mother. "I'm all finished." She gave Lily a giant smile. "Isn't it wonderful, Aunt Lily? Me and Momma are going to open the bakery at last. She's even gonna let me help name it." She took a deep breath and asked her mother, "Can I start bringing my stuff across the street? It's not too heavy."

Edward laughed. "I'll carry everything over this afternoon." Seeing these three ladies safe and happy was more than he'd dared to dream. His heart still contracted a bit when he looked at Jane with Ellen. He was so grateful God had seen fit to spare Jane. Ellen wouldn't grow up without her loving mother in her life. Edward would do everything he could as her uncle to make up for the void left by her father's passing.

"I'm very happy for you, Ellen." Lily's love for his niece was apparent. "You'll have to let me know which name you decide on. I want to be one of your first customers." Lily looked at him then. He saw the brewing storm in her eyes as they darkened.

He wanted to speak to Lily alone. "Now that you've shared your news, Ellen, why don't you and your mother have lunch at the hotel? I imagine she might even let you have dessert today."

"Can we, Momma? Just the two of us?" Ellen tugged on Jane's hand.

Jane laughed at her daughter's excitement. "If you promise to be on your best manners." She put a hand on Edward's sleeve. "Thank you for all your help. I don't know what I'd have done without you at the bank today. And thank you, Lily, for being so kind. I know my arrival has unsettled your world. I'm grateful for all you've done for Ellen and Edward."

"It has been my joy to spend time with Ellen."

Ellen left her mother's side and went to hug Lily. "I had fun with you, too, Aunt Lily." She released her and went with Jane out of the shop.

Edward watched them go and turned to see Lily wipe a finger under one eye. "Are you crying?" He went to her side.

"I'm fine." She took a step back. "If you'll excuse me, I've quite a lot to think about." She pivoted to go into the workroom. He put a hand on her elbow.

"Lily, tell me what's wrong. I know the news about Wesley isn't what we'd hoped for, but it's almost like a miracle that Jane is home with Ellen."

She kept her back to him. "God was merciful. I know that my father was a rock to me and my sisters after our mother passed. Jane and Ellen will help each other heal. It's good they have the bakery to give them something to look forward to." Her voice caught, and he tugged her elbow until she turned to him.

"What's wrong then?"

"Don't you know?" Lily spread her hands out and spun to the left and right. "All of this. How am I supposed to close my shop in one afternoon? Where will I store everything until I can figure out what to do? And there's the question of Lavinia. Where will she go?" She almost didn't breathe for talking so fast. "I guess she could sleep in Ellen's room tonight, but she can't stay there. I'm sure you'll want me to move my things in there." She stopped and looked at him, despair in her eyes. "Or do you want me to do that this afternoon?" She gasped and choked back a sob. "Or do you want me there at all?"

Her words spun in his ears like a twister. Where had the torrent come from? "Why would you close your shop? And why can't Lavinia stay here?"

"There isn't room upstairs for three people. It's just big enough for Jane and Ellen. And if she wants to open the bakery immediately, I'll have to have my merchandise out of the way." She sighed and looked over his shoulder. "And the sign." Tears filled her eyes, but she didn't let them fall. "It fits so perfectly in this window. I don't know if I can find somewhere new and use it. It's exactly what I wanted. You captured the heart of my designs when you made it." She turned to him. "Do you think you could alter it?" She sniffled on the last words.

"Alter it?" He reached for her hands. "It's fine right where it is."

"But it's going to be a bakery now." Her frown was full of sorrow, not anger.

"Oh, Lily, did you think Jane was going to come in here and run you out?"

"She said she wanted to move in this afternoon. She talked about the display windows and Ellen said she could carry her things across the street."

"All of that is true. Jane loved those windows from the first time we looked at this building. And she is moving this afternoon."

"That's why I've got to figure out what I'm going to do with everything." She stopped crying and stared at him. The strength she'd shown in every situation came to the fore again. "Lavinia will help me." She pulled her hands, but he didn't let her go. He would never let her go.

"Lily, Jane is buying the building between the post office and the bank. I went with her to the bank to arrange a loan to help her until your father arrives and buys the hotel."

A cloud crossed her face. "Two doors down from here?" Her voice was very soft, wary even.

"Yes. It was actually built by the same man who built this place." He leaned close to her. "It has the same display windows."

"It does?" Confusion still filled her face.

"It does." He put a hand on her cheek. "So you don't need to close your shop. Jane is going to start fresh in a new location. She'll still be across the street from me, so I can keep an eye on her and Ellen."

"But what about us?" There was a plea in her words that gave his heart hope. Hope he never thought he'd experience. After a lifetime of working and doing good for others, he'd given up hope of having something wonderful for himself. Somewhere along the way, he'd become content to muddle through life without thinking about all he was missing by being alone.

Since he'd married Lily for the sake of Ellen, he thought this was just a new chapter in the story of his life — with the same ending. He'd solve someone else's problem with little to no thought or benefit for himself.

But his life had changed forever the day he'd married her. When he'd brushed that

370

kiss across her gentle cheek after Reverend Dismuke had spoken the ceremonial words over them, his heart had awakened. Like a new morning with just a twinge of light breaking through the darkness of a long night, the changes had been gradual. The darkness gave way to shadows that were banished in the full light of a new day. Today. The day he knew he loved Lily with every part of who he was.

God, please don't let her dash my hope. I never dreamed You'd bring someone as amazing as Lily into my life. Please let her love me as much as I love her. If not, please let her stay long enough for me to show her how I feel.

Lily didn't know what to think. Or how to feel. She'd gone from contentment with Edward and Ellen the day before to realizing she loved him. Then his sister, a woman who truly needed him, had come into their lives and turned everything upside down.

That wasn't fair. Lily's life had turned upside down when Edward swept her into his arms the night of the fire. No matter how she'd dismissed his kindnesses and attention, he'd won her heart. But did he want it?

Edward squeezed her hands in his. "What about us?" His handsome face crinkled into a smile. "You and me?" The smile grew.

She couldn't hide her biggest fear. "You don't need me anymore."

He pulled her hands together and pressed his lips to her knuckles. "You don't think I need you?"

Her head spun. She couldn't think straight if he kissed her. And those eyes. They drew her into the brown depths. She could see her reflection in the dark center. "You married me for Ellen."

He grew serious. "I did."

Lily didn't realize she was holding her breath. "You didn't lie to me about why you wanted us to marry, but I've grown to believe you would be a part of my life forever. And now you don't need me anymore."

A twinkle danced in his eyes. "What do you intend to do?" He released her hands.

"I guess I could move into Ellen's room, unless you want me to move here with Lavinia." She hadn't had time to think.

"I don't want you to do that."

"But with Jane here, you don't need me." She braced herself for his response. How could she survive without him? He'd gotten inside her thoughts. Her prayers. Her dreams.

Edward leaned back a bit. "Do I need you? Will I be able to take my next breath without you?"

Lily stumbled a step away from him. Catching one hand in his, he righted her. She didn't speak.

"I will. But I can guarantee you, that breath won't be as sweet. I'll get hungry tomorrow, and I'll eat. But I won't be satisfied."

He tugged on her hand. "I can still see, but without you, nothing is as beautiful."

Lily's mind reeled with a dance she never thought she'd dance when she'd watched life pass her by from behind a punch bowl in East River. She seemed to melt in front of him. An aching, slow dissolving of the fear of his rejection.

He took advantage of this rare moment of her silence. "When you offered friendship to Miss Aiken and Mrs. Jones, I thought you were taking too much of a risk." His smile was so distracting. The words tumbled from his lips. She must concentrate. In the space of just a few minutes, her world spun around. The nuances still unclear, she forced her focus on his words.

"You proved me wrong." He smiled and

373

dropped his hand to her waist. "When you didn't want to tell Ellen that her parents were probably not coming back, I thought you were refusing to face reality and trying to protect Ellen from the inevitable truth. To be honest, I'd given up hope of Jane coming home again. The letters had stopped. Then the telegraph came saying they'd been gravely ill and couldn't be found."

She wanted to stanch the flow. His heart had been evident from the first day they met, from the minute she felt it beating in his chest when he carried her out of the fire. Only a selfless man would care like he did. For Ellen. For the church. Even for Mrs. Croft in all her orneriness.

"Edward."

He shook his head to silence her. "I didn't think they were coming back. Over and again you've shown hope and faith." He released her and stepped back.

She tried to breathe. To take in every word. To embrace the hope he was talking about. Hope she'd relinquished in the dark of last night.

He took her hand and stared into her eyes. "You taught me by example. So much so, I'm going to take a big step for me." He reached to tuck a strand of hair behind her ear, the touch gentle and full of caring. "I'm going to have faith you'll be willing to risk your happiness with someone who's settled with contentment for too long. I don't just need you. I love you." He pulled her hand back to his lips and brushed the knuckles with a promise.

She found her voice. "I was so weary of helping others all the time. That's why I made the needlework of the verse in the workroom. I had to remember to care for others more than I care for myself. I got lost taking care of others before." She put her other hand in his and pulled them together between the two of them as she leaned closer. "But I've learned that when I help others, I'm becoming a better person. You've shown me the joy of helping others. You sacrificed your life to take care of Ellen — and then to marry me and save my reputation in this town. When I took care of my father, I was happy to do it, but I got tired. Taking care of Ellen was a joy. Taking care of you will be my life's delight. I love you."

She leaned away from him and warned, "I'm never going to be able to avoid controversy. If I see someone in need, it doesn't matter to me what people will think if I help them."

Edward gathered her into his arms. He kissed her temple. "That's one of my favorite things about you."

All the breath swooshed from her when he dropped to one knee, taking both her hands in his. "Will you stay married to me, so we can spend our days loving and caring for each other?"

His eyebrows wrinkled his forehead as he waited.

"On one condition." Lily couldn't believe this was happening. How did the loneliest woman in East River become the happiest woman in Pine Haven?

"What would that condition be?" Dimples came into view, teasing her for an answer.

"Only if you promise to catch me when I fall."

"I promise." And he proved his word by pulling her off balance into his waiting arms.

EPILOGUE

March 1881

The day was finally here. The morning train would arrive soon.

Edward reached to help Lily from the wagon. The feel of her waist in his hands as he set her to the ground never grew old. How had he managed to snare such a lovely woman?

"You can let go now." Lily tapped him on the shoulder.

"I don't want to." He winked and grinned.

Ellen ran up the sidewalk with Speckles in his basket. The kitten dug his claws into the wicker, seemingly accustomed to her boisterous ways. Ellen had convinced her mother that Speckles should live with them.

"I can't wait to meet your papa." The child gave Lily a hug. "Uncle Edward says he's real nice."

Laughter bubbled in Lily's throat. "He is. I think your uncle Edward might be just a bit nervous to meet him again today."

"He might be nervous, but Uncle Edward ain't never scared." Ellen skipped over to a nearby bench and sat playing with Speckles.

Edward covered the hand Lily tucked into his elbow with one of his own. "I know God brought you here. The letters your father and I have exchanged since our marriage have been pleasant. I see no reason to be nervous." Funny how tight his collar felt as he said the words. Mr. Warren had agreed for them to marry, but it was the first time he'd meet the man as his son-in-law.

Winston Ledford stepped through the door of the depot onto the platform.

"Ledford." Edward greeted the man, trying to follow Lily's example of being hopeful that people could change.

Edward felt Lily's reassuring squeeze on his arm. "Hello, Mr. Ledford."

"Stone, Mrs. Stone." Winston touched the brim of his hat with two fingers.

"I hear you two are the guests of honor at a big shindig today."

"We are," Lily answered for them. "My father is hosting a celebration of our marriage. You're welcome to come. We want to share how God has blessed us with all our friends and neighbors."

"No, thank you, Mrs. Stone. You may have

won Lovey over to your Bible ways, but not me."

"You'll be in our prayers," Lily countered in her true Christian fashion, loving people who didn't know they needed to be loved.

"Don't know as I can stop you from praying, but don't expect to see me in your church." Winston Ledford made his way to the edge of the building and disappeared around the corner.

"Some people take longer than others to realize God loves them." Edward pulled her close. "Don't give up. You won me over."

"You didn't need winning over." She smiled at him. "You just needed to remember how big God's love is."

Jane joined them on the platform. "Ellen insisted we be here for your reunion with your family." His sister embraced Lily. "I think reunions are wonderful." She smiled at Ellen as she bounded up to them.

"I'm especially pleased to meet the man who made it possible for me to stay in Pine Haven. Because of his purchase of the hotel, I had the funds to open the bakery." She kissed Ellen on the top of her head.

"Momma lets me work in the bakery, too. Momma's Bakery will be mine when I grow up."

Lily smiled at Ellen. "Tell me again how

you chose the name for the bakery." She knew her niece loved to share the story.

"I always called it Momma's Bakery. She makes the best bread and cakes I ever ate, and everybody loves her cooking. Your store has your name on it, so Momma should have her name on the bakery."

Edward rubbed Speckles behind the ears. "I'm relieved to have you back in town, Jane, and to know you're staying. Don't know what I'd do without Ellen to make me smile."

Lily added, "I'm glad you found a good location. My shop is doing so well, with Lavinia's promise to stay on and help, I'm able to keep up. I wasn't sure how I'd handle having to move."

A whistle blew in the distance. The train would arrive in minutes.

Edward pulled Lily aside.

"I love you." He whispered the words to her. "Are you ready?"

The violet of her eyes told him she was. "Yes." She lifted a gloved hand to touch the side of his face. "Lavinia is closing the shop now. Daisy and her family will meet us at the hotel. They thought Papa would want a moment to greet his new son-in-law before the celebration. Daisy can hardly wait to tell him and Jasmine about their coming addition. She didn't want to take away from our moment. So much joy for Papa in one day."

He put an arm around her shoulders. The sweet scent of her hair filled his senses. "I've been thinking about something."

She turned to look at him, their faces almost touching. "What would that be?"

"With Jane and Ellen moving into their new home over the bakery, it's been awfully quiet at our house."

"It has been." She leaned against his shoulder, and he put his other arm around her.

"Maybe we need to give Ellen a cousin or two." She jerked her face to his. Pink flooded her cheeks.

"I'd like that very much." She stepped up to kiss his cheek.

"Is that so?" He grinned at her. "Before I met you, I thought I'd spend the rest of my days alone or with Ellen."

Lily took a step back and stumbled. He caught her by the elbows and settled her onto her feet.

"God always puts someone in your life to love you." The softness of her answer pulled him in. "And someone for you to love."

Dear Reader,

I hope you enjoyed *The Marriage Bargain*. Lily's need to be valued for more than what she could do for others, and Edward's determination to protect his young niece, are both reasonable objectives. Motivation is important for any goal to be valuable.

Corrupt motives can tempt anyone. We see Mrs. Croft's motivation as, at best, a curious soul, at worst, a nosy and interfering neighbor. Jane and Wesley were driven to succeed. Lily was motivated to take Winston Ledford's money in response to the way he treated her.

God often reminds me to question my personal motives for things. Even when they are pure, my methods can be faulty. Lily learned this when she determined to start a new life and wanted to protect herself from becoming lost in another person's needs.

I pray the characters in *The Marriage Bargain* will remind you to love even when it costs you, to reserve judgment on situations you only see from the outside, to pursue the dreams God has given you and to recognize the people God has put in your life to love you — and to be loved by you.

Visit angelmoorebooks.com for the latest

news and to connect with me on social media.

God bless you.

Angel Moore

ABOUT THE AUTHOR

Angel Moore fell in love with romance in elementary school when she read the story of Robin Hood and Maid Marian. Who doesn't want to escape to a happily-ever-after world? When not writing, you can find her reading or spending time with her family. Married to her best friend, she has two wonderful sons, a lovely daughter-in-law and three grands. She loves sharing her faith and the hope she knows is real because of God's goodness to her. Find her at angelmoorebooks.com.

The employees of Thorndike Press hope you have enjoyed this Large Print book. All our Thorndike, Wheeler, and Kennebec Large Print titles are designed for easy reading, and all our books are made to last. Other Thorndike Press Large Print books are available at your library, through selected bookstores, or directly from us.

For information about titles, please call:
(800) 223-1244

or visit our Web site at:
http://gale.cengage.com/thorndike

To share your comments, please write:
Publisher
Thorndike Press
10 Water St., Suite 310
Waterville, ME 04901